"A fast-paced story highlighted by the differences in temperament and style between the local law enforcement officer and the federal agents, [with] a final, satisfying conclusion." —*Mystery Scene Magazine*

"A haunting depiction of heartbreaking crime. Skalka does a wonderful job of showing how people can both torment and help each other."
—Sara Paretsky, author of *Fallout*

Praise for DEATH RIDES THE FERRY, the fourth Dave Cubiak Door County Mystery

"A smooth yet page-turning read. . . . [Skalka] brings the region alive for readers with a you-are-there verisimilitude." —*New York Journal of Books*

"Another deftly crafted gem of a mystery novel by Patricia Skalka. . . . A simply riveting read from cover to cover." —*Midwest Book Review*

"Skalka is equally skilled at evoking the beloved Door County landscape and revealing the complexities of the human heart, as Sheriff Cubiak's latest case evokes personal demons. This thought-provoking mystery, set in a beautiful but treacherous environment, is sure to please."
—Kathleen Ernst, author of *The Light Keeper's Legacy*

Praise for DEATH BY THE BAY, the fifth Dave Cubiak Door County Mystery

"Reveals a remarkable ability to create atmosphere. . . . Clearly, Skalka knows how to chill her readers' blood, and she leaves them with haunting questions."
—*Peninsula Pulse*

"Rife with memorable scenes in such unexpected places. . . . *Death by the Bay* wouldn't be a traditional Skalka mystery, though, if it didn't include an unexpected twist or two." —*Isthmus*

"A touching and original story. Sheriff Cubiak is the kind of man you would always want to handle such personal and painful matters."
—Maureen Jennings, author of the Murdoch Mysteries

DEATH CASTS A SHADOW

DEATH CASTS A SHADOW

A DAVE CUBIAK DOOR COUNTY MYSTERY

PATRICIA SKALKA

THE UNIVERSITY OF WISCONSIN PRESS

The University of Wisconsin Press
728 State Street, Suite 443
Madison, Wisconsin 53706
uwpress.wisc.edu

Gray's Inn House, 127 Clerkenwell Road
London EC1R 5DB, United Kingdom
eurospanbookstore.com

Printed in the United States of America

This book may be available in a digital edition.

Library of Congress Cataloging-in-Publication Data

Names: Skalka, Patricia, author. | Skalka, Patricia. Dave Cubiak Door County mystery.
Title: Death casts a shadow / Patricia Skalka.
Description: Madison, Wisconsin : The University of Wisconsin Press, [2022] |
Series: Dave Cubiak Door County mystery
Identifiers: LCCN 2021049362 | ISBN 9780299338701 (cloth)
Subjects: LCSH: Sheriffs—Wisconsin—Door County—Fiction. | Murder—Investigation—
Fiction. | Door County (Wis.)—Fiction. | LCGFT: Detective and mystery fiction.
Classification: LCC PS3619.K34 D384 2022 | DDC 813/.6—dc23/eng/20211117
LC record available at https://lccn.loc.gov/2021049362

Map by Julia Padvoiskis; illustration by Carla Marie Walkis

Door County is real. While I used the peninsula as the framework for the book, I also altered some
details and added others to fit the story. The spirit of this majestic place remains unchanged.

For
Samuel and Townes,
With much love and hope for the future

There are only two families in the world,
the Haves and the Have-Nots.

—Miguel de Cervantes, *Don Quixote de la Mancha*

DEATH CASTS A SHADOW

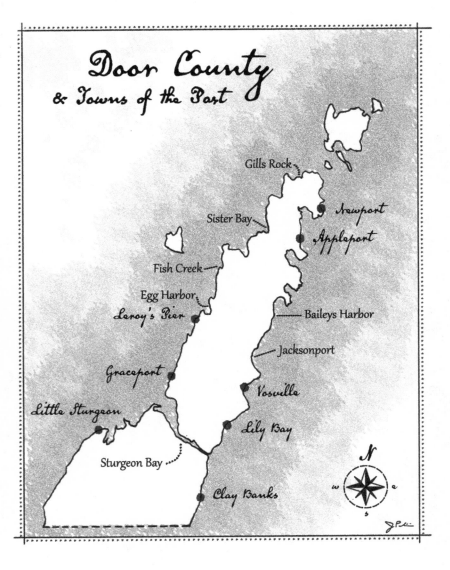

Door County

& Towns of the Past

Gills Rock

Sister Bay

Newport

Appleport

Fish Creek

Egg Harbor

Leroy's Pier

Baileys Harbor

Jacksonport

Graceport

Vosville

Little Sturgeon

Lily Bay

Sturgeon Bay

Clay Banks

N

W   E

S

THE FLYING LADY

1

Dave Cubiak tore the cellophane wrapper off his new calendar and laid the pages across the desk. Starting with January there were twelve sheets, one for each month. He liked the way the year opened up before him, the days unsullied and full of promise. Before long the squares would oveflow with reminders about the meetings, conferences, and appointments that went with the job of being the sheriff of Door County, Wisconsin. The calendar was a gag Christmas gift, a present intended to elicit a laugh. No one on the staff expected the sheriff to actually use it. But Cubiak had a penchant for doing things the old-fashioned way. He wore a wristwatch and sent letters by snail mail. He read print books because he liked turning the pages and scribbling notes in the margins.

That morning Cubiak made his first entry in the calendar. Looking down at January, he ran a hand to the last Saturday of the month. Then he circled the date in red, and in neat, small letters, he printed *Joey* in the square. His son had won tickets to a basketball game between the Milwaukee Bucks and the Chicago Bulls slated to be played on that day in Cubiak's hometown. This would be his first time in Chicago with the boy, walking the familiar streets of the city where he had been born and raised, where he had been a cop and the father to a different child until she and her mother were killed and he had fled north to a new life. Was he up to it? Cubiak capped the pen and looked out the window. Memories and doubts swirled through his mind like the flakes riding the wind in the thick maelstrom of snow falling outside.

Door County was buried in snow. On the day after Thanksgiving, a fierce storm rolled in and dropped fourteen inches on the peninsula. An anomaly, folks said, but since then a half-dozen record-breaking snowfalls had slammed the area. Drifts piled to the eaves, and towering ridges of frozen muck blocked visibility along the roads and intersections. Stop, enough already, said the locals. Cubiak kept his thoughts to himself. Secretly he hoped for another blizzard, one that would make the highway impassable on the day he had marked in red.

At two, he sent half the staff home. At three, he dismissed everyone but the emergency dispatcher. Winter was the department's slowest season. During that stretch of long nights and short days, the sheriff and the deputies could ease up and take time for themselves, for the appointments and personal business they ignored during the high seasons when tourists and part-time residents migrated back and pumped the economic lifeblood back into the peninsula.

At half past the hour, he left as well. The drive was uneventful until he reached Jacksonport. Just as he turned into his driveway, a white Rolls-Royce crested the dune behind his house. Like a great bleached whale, the vintage vehicle rose over the snow-capped hillock and rolled forward through the falling snow. When the car stopped, the flying lady on the hood was inches from the sheriff's jeep. Cubiak stared at the gold ornament and blinked. The middle-aged man behind the wheel smiled. He was tall and erect. A tweed newsboy cap sat low on his forehead and shadowed his face. The cap wasn't quite a chauffeur's hat, but close enough.

The lane left no room for the boxy Rolls to slide past the jeep, and for an absurd moment the two men played a stationary game of chicken. Finally, the Door County sheriff gave in and shifted into reverse.

As the Rolls floated by, the other driver nodded and tipped his cap in a formal greeting. Cubiak raised a hand in return, but his attention was on the woman who sat behind the driver. She was swathed in fur. Between the billowy white hat that came to her brows and the coat with the upturned collar that caressed her elegant cheekbones, it was impossible to determine her age. She could have been young or old or somewhere in between. But the fur could not disguise her posture. It was the kind that came with money and breeding. The woman kept her eyes straight ahead. If she noticed his polite nod, she did not respond.

Cubiak watched the car disappear behind a veil of snow before continuing down the lane toward the lake. Against the backdrop of the icy shore, the tiny white lights glistening in the kitchen windows looked warm and welcoming. The sheriff stomped the snow off his boots and opened the side door. Cate was at the sink, humming the tune to a carol he didn't quite recognize and washing a saucer from their rarely used bone china, a relic from her former life.

"It looks like you were having high tea with the queen," he said, shrugging off his jacket.

Cate laughed. "You saw the car?"

"Hard to miss," he said. He paused to inhale the sweet aroma of cinnamon and cloves that filled the room. "Who was it?"

"Not the queen. Not exactly anyway," Cate said over her shoulder. She rested the cup in the drainer and shut off the water. Wiping her hands on her apron, she turned toward him. "But you're not far off. Her name is Regina Malcaster, and for as long as I can remember she's been the grande dame of Northern Door. Her father was friends with my grandfather, and she was friends with my aunt Ruby, that sort of thing."

"Why was she here?"

"She came to ask for a favor."

"A woman in a chauffeur-driven Rolls came here asking for a favor?"

"Not from me, from you."

"Me? The car went right past and she didn't even acknowledge me."

Cate sighed. "I think she was embarrassed. Certainly, she wouldn't want her driver to think that the visit was anything more than a social call."

Cubiak pulled out a chair and sat down. "All right, what gives?"

"Regina is worried about her niece, Lydia Malcaster. Well, Lydia is actually a niece by marriage. Her late husband was Regina's husband's nephew. Apparently, she has been acting strangely."

"Meaning what exactly?"

"Secretive. Not herself."

"Considering the winter we've had so far, I'd think half the people in the county are feeling a bit off."

Cate sat down next to her husband. "Regina hinted rather strongly that she would appreciate having you look in on Lydia."

Cubiak groaned and rested his elbows on his knees. "I'm the sheriff, not the county social worker."

"Regina didn't say so specifically, but she implied that Lydia may be in some kind of trouble." Cate hesitated. "She's really worried about her."

"Why doesn't she just call me?"

"I suggested as much, but she's trying to be discreet. It's the old money in her talking. Problems are never faced head on. They are handled obliquely."

"Preferably by someone else." Cubiak reached over and took Cate's hand. "All right, I'll see what I can do. I have a staff meeting in the morning, and if nothing else comes up, I'll head north afterward. But I'm doing this for you, not for her."

That evening they were halfway through dinner when Joey looked up. "Dad, you haven't forgotten about the game, have you?"

"Nope. I marked the date on my calendar this morning."

"All my friends are jealous."

"You won the tickets fair and square. You were the lucky one this time. Next year, some other kid will get to go."

"I know." Joey sopped up the dregs of the spaghetti sauce on his plate with a piece of bread. "Did you go to the games with your dad when you were a kid?"

What Cubiak wanted to say: My dad was always too drunk to go to a basketball game with me. What he said: "No, he wasn't interested in sports, and anyway we couldn't afford the tickets."

"You mean you never saw the Bulls play?"

"I went with friends a few times later on, when I was older. They were still playing at the old stadium then. Of course, we ended up in the rafters and could barely see anything."

"Coach said these are good seats." Joey looked over his plate and surveyed the table. "What's for dessert, Mom?"

When they finished eating, Joey went to his room to practice his lines for *Our Town*, the upcoming school play. He had the role of Stage Manager.

"What do you think he's going to be, a basketball player or an actor?" Cubiak asked as he cleared the dishes.

Cate shrugged. "That's anyone's guess. He's tall enough for the game and good enough for the stage, but probably neither." She took a plate from him. "Are you sure you're okay with this?"

"With what? Doing the queen's bidding?"

"Taking Joey to Chicago for the game. You haven't been back in twenty years."

"I went to Malcolm's retirement party."

"That hardly counts. You drove straight to the ceremony, stayed for a couple of hours, and then came back. This time you'll be there for the weekend. It's not going to be easy."

"Yeah, well, life's not easy, and maybe it's time." He looked at Cate. "Maybe it's past time."

"I'll come along, if you want."

Cubiak squeezed her hand. "I know, and I appreciate it, but I think this needs to be a guys' weekend."

A GENTLEMAN FRIEND

2

By ten the next morning, Cubiak finished with the weekly staff meeting. He was back at his desk trying to think of an excuse to forgo the visit to Regina Malcaster's niece, Lydia, when the phone rang. It was Cate, calling to remind him about his promise.

"What if I make the drive up there and she's not home?"

"She's there. Regina spoke with Lydia a few minutes ago and confirmed that she is in for the day."

"This sounds like a conspiracy of women," the sheriff said.

"Isn't that the best kind?"

He grunted.

"You're a dear," Cate said, and hung up.

Lydia Malcaster lived at the north end of the peninsula, nearly forty miles from the justice center. Stepping from the warm building into a blast of frigid air did nothing to alter the sheriff's mood, but once the jeep was warm and he was on his way, his attitude improved. The snow had stopped and the roads were dry. In winter Door County was like a sleeping bear, quiet and tucked in, preparing for the onslaught of the twelve-hour-long workdays that marked much of the rest of the year.

Farther north, there was more snow, few cars, and even fewer people out and about. Despite enjoying the drive, Cubiak grew increasingly convinced that he was on a fool's errand. His baffled host would serve him a cup of tea and a casserole of local gossip. He hoped for a flat tire or an urgent message summoning him back to the station, but the jeep didn't falter and the radio remained mute. He checked his phone. No signal.

The Malcaster home was tucked deep in the woods at the tip of the peninsula. As he slowed to make the turn into the entrance, a faded green pickup roared out onto the narrow road. Snow caked the front plow attachment and covered the sign on the driver's door. The sun's glare hid the driver's face. The sheriff waved a hand in greeting but the gesture was lost in the snow cloud left in the truck's wake.

The stately house at the end of the drive matched Lydia Malcaster's pedigree. Unlike new construction that gaped raw and out of place, the fieldstone mansion conveyed a settled, permanent sense of belonging, as if it had emerged from the ground along with the surrounding forest and its slate roof and leaded windows had as much claim to the land as the roots and branches of the native flora.

A brightly lit Christmas tree in a corner window and a red-berried wreath on the front door projected a cheery holiday greeting. The setting was picture perfect, from the snow-covered ruffle of bushes that hugged the house to the scarlet cardinal that trilled from a high pine bough as Cubiak made his way up the stone walk.

The sheriff rang the bell and listened as a muffled chorus of chimes echoed through the house. He waited until the sound faded to silence and pressed the bell a second time. Again there was no hint of movement inside. He was turning to leave when he heard the click of a lock being released.

The door opened several inches. A petite woman with a bob of silver hair surveyed him with cool green eyes.

"You're not Bobby," she said.

"No, I'm not." The sheriff introduced himself.

"Cate Wagner's husband." The woman broke into a warm smile, but her wariness showed in the way she kept one hand on the knob and clutched the door frame with the other.

"That's me." Cubiak returned the smile. Early in his marriage to Cate, he had bristled at the honorific, but by now he had grown accustomed to it. Cate's history in Door County stretched back nearly fifty years, more than twice his time on the peninsula. Taking into account her family's presence, her heritage could be traced more than a century to the day when her grandfather bought ten acres of forest outside Gills Rock, holdings that would eventually expand to include a large swath of land.

"And you are Lydia Malcaster?" he said.

"I am." She blushed and her cheeks colored to a shade of pink that nearly matched her angora sweater. "Sorry, Sheriff, I should have recognized you from Cate's last exhibition. I'm sure I saw you there." She released her grip on the door frame and tucked a strand of her short hair behind her ear.

"This is a surprise," she went on, slipping her free hand into the pocket of her white wool trousers. The outfit was casual wear for a woman of her age and station, but to him she was dressed up. Whiffs of snow blew in, settling on her hair and the carpet. "Please, come in," she said, as if suddenly remembering her manners.

She stepped back to let him pass, and then she closed the door and threw the lock. "Habit," she said. "I know most people don't bother locking their doors, but being alone up here . . ." She stopped and laughed. "But I guess I don't need to worry with you in the house."

Once Cubiak was inside, Lydia seemed unsure what to do. Still smiling, she stared at him a moment, her face a question mark. "What exactly can I do for you, Sheriff?" she said, and then continued before he could reply. "I don't imagine that you're here soliciting funds for the Crime Prevention Foundation. Besides, I already gave."

"To be honest, I stopped in to make sure everything's okay. You do live way up here alone."

Lydia frowned. "Who sent you? One of my *friends*?" She flung the word at him like a barb.

Cubiak hesitated, and then he dropped the pretense.

"Your aunt Regina is concerned about your well-being and asked me to check in with you."

"The queen bee. I should have known," Lydia said, rolling her eyes. Then she softened her tone. "I shouldn't be so hard on her. Regina means well—it's just that sometimes she can be overbearing. At any rate, I appreciate your candor, and since you came all the way up here, I may as well put your mind at ease."

With that she turned and headed across the foyer, trailing perfume into the living room, where it mingled with the rich pine aroma wafting from the elaborately decorated tree. The result was not unpleasant.

Lydia arranged herself in a gold brocade wing chair that gave her command of the room. Tucking her slippered feet under a matching ottoman, she motioned the sheriff to the facing chair. He sat, his back to the tree. She hadn't bothered to take his coat or invite him to remove it, an indication that she intended for this to be a short visit. He felt pellets of sweat rise along his chest and spine.

"I have a gentleman friend, newly acquired," Lydia said, jumping right in. "I made the mistake of mentioning him to Regina, and she immediately expressed her disapproval. I assume that you know that I was married to her nephew, Zachary Malcaster?"

Cubiak nodded.

"Regina loved Zack like a son, and I think she felt that I was being disloyal to his memory. I told her that no man would ever replace Zack in my heart but that at the same time there might be room for someone else, a companion at the very least. I know she's trying to accept that idea, but she's also raised the alarm about my well-being. Rightfully so, I might add."

"And that would be because . . ."

Lydia cleared her throat and folded her hands in her lap.

"I'm a widow and I have money. I can't hide either fact, but taken together, the circumstances make me a target for unscrupulous men. They are hustlers of one sort or another, and they are legion. *Fortune hunters* is the term used, I believe. I'm quite aware of the horror stories, but this situation is different." She blushed. "I sound ridiculous, don't I? That's what Regina said, not in so many words but the implication was obvious. Everyone thinks their situation is different, special. It's true love, they say. If only you understood, they insist."

She locked eyes with Cubiak. "Do you understand?"

"I know what it's like to be lonely, if that's what you mean."

11

Lydia stiffened and looked away. "Lonely doesn't even begin to describe what it's like to be alone after you lose the person you love," she said.

For a moment they sat in unspoken agreement.

"Why don't you tell me about him, your gentleman friend," Cubiak said gently.

Her soft smile returned. "His name is James Dura. He was an old friend of my late husband's. He and Zack were together in school in Madison. They were roommates for a couple of semesters and teammates for all four years."

"Your husband played football, didn't he?"

"They both did."

"You knew Dura back then?"

"I didn't know any of Zack's friends from his university days. I met my husband when he was at Marquette working on his MBA."

"In Milwaukee?"

"Yes, that's where I'm from originally. By then James had returned to his hometown, somewhere out east, Pittsburgh, I believe. There was no reason for him to come back."

"Not even for your wedding?"

Lydia shook her head. "We didn't have much of an actual wedding. My mother was very ill at the time, and out of deference to her we opted for a small, private ceremony. I wore a white suit, not even a wedding dress. Zack's cousin was his best man. My sister was my maid of honor, and besides them, we invited family members and a few local friends. But Zack talked about James often enough; he talked about the whole team those first few years. Then after a while, one gets busy with work and life. You lose touch with the old friends and make new ones."

A whistling noise came from the rear of the house.

"Oh, dear, I forgot that I had the kettle on." Lydia hopped up from the chair. "A cup of tea, Sheriff?" she called as she hurried out.

While Lydia was gone, Cubiak slipped off his jacket and looked around the room. Her touch was evident in the warm, soft colors of the walls and furnishings. Her wealth and good taste showed in the dazzling array of art on display. Four large oils depicted a large oak tree in the different seasons. The rest were flowers: a watercolor of a rose garden and a half-dozen botanical prints that looked very old.

He was studying a vibrant abstract of something that he guessed was a blue vining plant when Lydia reappeared. She had pinked her lips and exchanged the slippers for white ballet flats.

"Like it?" she said, setting down a silver tray. "It's a Chihuly."

"Interesting, but a little rich for my blood," he said.

Once he was reseated, Lydia poured the tea and held up the platter of cookies. "I made them myself, but I have to warn you that baking isn't my forte. They won't win any prizes but they're edible," she said.

The sheriff broke off a piece and set the rest down alongside his cup. "How long were you and your husband married?"

"Thirty-eight years. Zack had been retired for four years when he died. We were preparing for a river cruise in Europe when he had a fatal heart attack. There was no family history of cardiac disease, and he'd passed his physical just a few months before. The doctors couldn't explain how or why it happened. It was all very sudden and unexpected."

"I'm sorry."

She nodded. "Thank you. Everyone says that, but to most people the words don't mean much. They have no idea what it's like to wake up one day and find your life in shreds. I felt so cheated. *He'd* been cheated. We both had. All the plans, gone. Everything, gone. We had no children, so it was only the two of us. And then I had no one."

"No other family?"

"Besides Regina, not really. My father and sister are both deceased. My nearest relative is a distant cousin whom I'd seen a couple of times, but she lives on the West Coast."

"Your friends?"

Lydia stiffened and flashed her eyes at him. "Many of them were our friends, and after Zachary died, they disappeared as well. Dropped me like the proverbial hot potato. It sounds harsh, but it's exactly what happened. I was persona non grata, the woman alone."

She hooked her hands together at her waist and gave a sharp, bitter laugh. "How ironic that when you're at your absolute lowest, when you can barely hold yourself together, you're seen as a threat. Men whom I'd known for years, who'd been forthcoming with hugs before, hardly dared to touch me. A pat on the shoulder perhaps. And the wives, old friends as well, became the protectors of the castle. In the world of couples, a single woman is the odd one. Oh, I'm sure they found ways to rationalize their behavior. Where do we put her at the table? That sort of thing. She wouldn't be comfortable, they'd tell themselves. The truth is that I would have been painfully uncomfortable, but I was more miserable being at home alone." She pinned her gaze on her visitor. "How many evenings was I supposed to sit here by myself, waiting for the phone to ring?"

There was no answer, so he gave none.

"I had my book club, of course, and my church group, and if it hadn't been for those activities, I don't know what I would have done. But only women belonged to them. Intelligent women certainly, and while I enjoyed their company and still do, I find that women tend to be of a like mind. Even when they don't agree, there always seems to be something missing in the ensuing discussions. Maybe I'm old-fashioned but it seems to me that men think differently, and I missed that male perspective."

"How did you connect with him then, this James?"

Lydia gave him a hard stare. "It's James. Not *this* James. About six months ago, I received an email from him. I wasn't going to read it but the name sounded familiar, and then I remembered that my late husband had a friend with that name, so I did. He said he'd seen Zack's obituary in an old alumni magazine and wanted to extend his condolences. He said he'd hesitated because it was already years since Zack had died but that he'd only found out."

"Do you have any idea how he got your email address?"

She sighed and brushed a crumb from her lap. "Oh, you are such a cop, aren't you? But maybe I had suspicions, too, because I asked him the same question. He said that he'd had to guess at it and that after several attempts he got it right. It's not so hard, when you think about it. I use my full name and Gmail. I think that's fairly common now."

"Is he still in Pittsburgh?"

"Not anymore. Several years ago, he took a job with the government and moved to Washington."

"James and your husband were contemporaries, which would put him in his late sixties. Why isn't he retired?"

"He was for a couple of years. Retired and divorced and bored. He started a consulting business just to have something to do. He planned to work part time, but then this other opportunity came up and he said he couldn't resist. His contract runs out in spring. And before you ask, he couldn't give me any details about the work, other than that it involved international travel. Currently he's on site somewhere in the Middle East."

She looked at Cubiak. "I can see the wheels spinning, but we both know the world's a mess, and that there are people working behind the scenes doing only Lord knows what to keep a lid on any number of precarious situations and protect our country's interests. James is a petroleum engineer; my guess is that whatever he's involved with has to do with his expertise."

"You haven't actually met him yet?"

"That's correct."

Lydia picked up her cup and saucer and then set them back down. "I'm not a fool, Sheriff. I know that taking advantage of lonely mature women seems to be a popular pastime. I have a folder full of stories about the kind of con jobs perpetrated on women of means. James doesn't fit the pattern. He's different."

Cubiak rubbed his jaw. "If you say so."

"You're a born cynic, aren't you?" Lydia said.

The sheriff shrugged. "I'm not sure if I was born to it, but cynicism comes with the job."

"And it's probably a good thing in your line of work, but beyond that . . ." She left the statement hanging. Then she gave him a taut smile and stood.

"Come with me. There's something you need to see."

Lydia led him back through the foyer and down a set of carpeted stairs. "The house is built on a slope," she explained as she pointed to the tall stained-glass windows on the lower level.

She had started down the passage to the right when a car roared up and stopped outside.

"Somebody needs a muffler," Cubiak said.

"It's just Tracey, Tracey Fells, my housekeeper. She told me she's saving for one." Lydia shrugged. "Kids."

"How old is she?"

"Twenty-three."

"Hardly a kid, then."

"From where I stand, Sheriff, nearly everyone is a kid." As she spoke, the front door opened.

"Tracey has a key?"

"Of course, she has a key. Do you think I want to arrange my life around her schedule?"

At the end of the hall, Lydia stopped in front of the door on the left. "Zack's office, his man cave, I guess you could call it. After he died, I redid the rest of the house, but I didn't touch anything in here. This was always his personal room. I guess it still is," she said, opening the door to a dim room full of heavy, oversize furniture, the opposite of everything he had seen upstairs.

"My husband was a very tall guy. I always felt like a Lilliputian in here," Lydia said as she circled around the massive bespoke desk to the windows. "We planted those when we built the house, thirty-five years ago." She indicated the stand of birch trees in the yard. Then she turned and flipped a switch, and a bank of lights lit a wall filled with black-and-white photos of Zack's glory days on the University of Wisconsin football team. Zack as "Athlete of the Year." Zack as "Most Valuable Player." Zack with the team the year they swept the season. The players had confident smiles and the steady eyes of youthful, fresh-scrubbed, all-American football heroes who stared into the camera and into the bright future each of them anticipated.

"Zack was the quarterback. He's front row, center." Lydia touched a fingertip to a rugged, young man with hooded eyes and a soft smile.

"And James?"

Lydia gave a quick laugh. "I had to ask him. Remember, we'd never met."

She slid her finger over the glass and stopped at a figure who stood near the end of the second row. James had light hair. He was tall, like the others, and square jawed. His stance was relaxed and easy but couldn't disguise the underlying arrogance in his manner.

Lydia flipped another switch.

"Look here," she said, walking across the room toward a recessed alcove where four metal statues stood on a rough plank shelf.

"This is Zack's collection of Frederic Remington bronzes: *The Bronco Buster, The Rattlesnake, Coming through the Rye*, and *The Outlaw*." She tapped each one as she named it. "His grandfather won the first statue in a poker game, if you can believe it, and after that he was so enthralled by Remington's work that he bought several more. Regina's husband kept one, but the others eventually came to Zack. He was given *The Bronco Buster* as a high school graduation gift and took it with him to Madison.

"The point is that James asked me if Zack still had the statue. Only someone who knew my husband back then would have been able to do that. In fact, James joked about the times they didn't have enough money for pizza on Friday nights and talked about pawning the bronze for something to eat. I'd heard the same story from Zack several times. It's crazy to think that they would even consider doing something that absurd, but then, I guess boys will be boys. At any rate, the story proves that they were school chums."

"The statues must be very valuable."

"I'm sure they are." Lydia turned and went on in a mocking tone. "And let's not forget that I have jewelry as well, and this house, and a stock portfolio that Zack assembled, plus an inheritance from my parents, which by itself is sufficient to keep me in tea and cookies for the rest of my life. I know what you're getting at, Sheriff." Her words cut razor sharp.

"Then you won't be surprised when I ask if James ever approached you for money."

Lydia sniffed. "Touché. But no, he hasn't. James has never asked for anything. Quite the opposite, in fact. For the past two months, he's been lavishing me with gifts. Which means that I have something else to show you."

To the sound of the vacuum running somewhere in the house, Lydia marched Cubiak down the hall, up the stairs, and along a rear passage to a room off the kitchen.

"This is my little hideaway," she said as they entered. The view of the yard implied that they were at the other end of the house from Zack's office. The white rug and walls and the pastel watercolors were all in keeping with Lydia's style. She led him to a laptop that sat open on a slim, glass-topped desk.

"See this," she said, indicating the image of white roses on the screen. "James has sent me virtual bouquets every day for the past four weeks and always my favorites. Blue dahlias, white roses, iris . . . everything I like. It's very sweet but so extravagant. I've told him he doesn't have to, but he says it gives him too much pleasure, especially since it's winter here and I must be missing my garden."

"How does James"—Cubiak stopped himself from saying *this* James—"know which are your favorite flowers?"

Lydia fluttered a bejeweled hand at him. "Intuition? Magic? I have no idea, really. Maybe I said something. But the flowers are the least of it."

She picked up a pale-green folder from the corner of the desk. "Do you want more proof of what I've told you? It's all here. When James's contract is finished, we're going on a trip. The Indian Ocean to see the blue whales. Katmandu for the temple monkeys. A canoe expedition through the Amazon basin. Machu Picchu. A cruise to Easter Island. James made all the arrangements. He not only took care of the reservations, he also bought all the tickets. Everything first class. No skimping, he said, not at this stage of our lives. It'll be the trip I've always dreamed of. Take a look and see for yourself."

She thrust the folder at Cubiak. "I made copies of the itinerary and the receipts. They're all here."

He skimmed the top sheet that detailed the complex logistics. Then he flipped through pages of scanned material, adding up the fees. Around the world in $90,000.

"That's quite an outlay of money," he said as he handed the file back to Lydia.

She blushed. "Too much. And that's not including meals! I know that James meant well, but it didn't seem fair for him to pay for everything. We went back and forth about that for several days, but I insisted on contributing my share."

"You gave him forty-five thousand dollars?"

Lydia stiffened. "I paid my way."

"Did you talk to anyone else before you did this?"

"No, not really. I hadn't discussed the trip with anyone, except Tracey, I guess. She was in here dusting when I was printing out the receipts, so I showed them to her. I was just so thrilled I thought I'd explode. She was flabbergasted. She'd never heard of half the places we'd be going to, so I told her what I knew about the history of Machu Picchu and Easter Island. We even looked them up on the internet so she could see what I was talking about. She said she'd never imagined anyone would spend that much on a vacation and that James must be really rich. I said that he was generous and that I was feeling a little guilty about him spending all that money. I told her I was thinking of paying my share and asked her if she thought he'd be insulted."

"And what did she say?"

"I don't think Tracey could fathom that amount of money, but she said she thought it was always a good idea for a woman to pay her share in a new relationship, at least at first because then she wouldn't be obligated. 'What if you end up not liking him?' she said."

"So you sent the money?"

"Yes."

As she spoke, the computer dinged.

Lydia glanced at her wristwatch. "Right on time. That should be a message from James."

She turned toward the monitor and squealed. Then she clapped and clasped her hands to her chest as if in prayer.

"Look, Sheriff. Look at this." She stepped aside so he could see the screen. "Perhaps this will convince you that everything is on the up-and-up."

"Good news, my lovely," the message read. "After much negotiating I have secured time off and am finalizing plans to visit you in Door County. Can't wait, my dearest."

A bouquet of blue dahlias appeared beneath the message.

"You see," Lydia said, smiling at the sheriff. "Everything I've said is true. I'll throw a party and invite everyone. You'll all meet him then."

In the foyer, Lydia kept up the happy chatter as Cubiak slipped his coat on.

"Thank you for coming, Sheriff. Regina just lectured and never gave me the opportunity to explain anything. But you listened and I appreciate that. You can tell my aunt that she has nothing to worry about."

The sheriff laid his card on the hall table. "In case anything comes up." He turned to leave and then stopped. "When you came to the door earlier, you said you thought I was Bobby. Who is that?"

She waved a hand. "Bobby Fells, he takes care of the snow for me. I send him a check every month, but once in a while if he's short, he'll ask for an advance."

"And he's married to your housekeeper?"

"Tracey? Oh, no, Tracey is his sister. She's been working for me for two years. I hired Bobby in the fall to deal with the leaves and after that to do the winter plowing and shoveling."

Lydia hesitated. "You will come to the party, won't you? You and Cate?"

"Of course."

Walking away, the sheriff glanced at the beat-up gray compact by the garage and then looked up, hoping for a glimpse of the cardinal. But the bird had flown away, taking with it the single splash of color from the front yard.

When he reached the jeep, Lydia was still in the doorway. As he pulled away, she waved triumphantly, but he didn't wave back. In the rearview mirror, the sheriff watched her step back into her fantasy world. Despite what she had said about James Dura, despite the message that had popped up on the computer, he couldn't help but wonder if Regina wasn't right: something was amiss.

Cubiak drove until he was out of sight of the house. Then he stopped and called the UW–Madison Alumni office. He figured it would still be closed for the holidays, so he left a message asking for someone to get back to him as soon as possible with the most recent contact information available for former student James Dura.

FATAL FALL

3

At ten on Wednesday morning, Cubiak's phone rang as he sat in the dentist's waiting room, paging through an outdated copy of *National Geographic*. He was scheduled for his annual checkup and was tempted to let the call go to voice mail when Mike Rowe's name popped up on caller ID. Rowe wouldn't call unless it was important.

"Sorry to disturb you, Chief. I know you took the morning off but—"

"What's up?"

"A call came in a few minutes ago from Lydia Malcaster's house-keeper—"

"Tracey Fells."

"Yeah, that's right."

The sheriff tossed the magazine to the table and pushed out of the chair. He sensed that whatever was coming would not be good.

"Tracey found Mrs. Malcaster lying at the bottom of the stairs." Rowe hesitated. "I'm afraid she's dead. I found your card on the hall table and—"

"I was there yesterday, talking to her. Hold on a second." Cubiak walked outside. "What time did Tracey call?"

"About ten minutes ago. She discovered the body when she came to work and called nine-one-one. The dispatcher knew I was in the area and passed it on to me."

"Any sign of foul play?"

"Not that I can see, but I just got here. It looks like she took a bad fall. Probably just an accident."

As soon as he finished with Rowe, Cubiak called Cate with the news about Lydia.

"I'll stop and talk to Regina later, but maybe you should be the one to tell her what happened," he said.

"I'll go there now. She'll be devastated. The poor thing, she was so concerned about Lydia. You don't think . . ."

The sheriff heard the worry in his spouse's voice. "At this juncture, I don't think anything. All I know is that Lydia fell."

The sheriff didn't want to alarm Cate but the domino effect surrounding Lydia's death was troubling. Three days ago, he had never heard of Lydia Malcaster. Two days ago, her aunt, Regina Malcaster, came to his house and told his wife that she thought her niece was in trouble. Yesterday he met Lydia face to face. Today, Lydia was dead. Most likely she died as the result of an accidental fall, as Rowe suggested. Falls were not an uncommon occurrence among people her age. But that was a huge category that included an elderly population with mobility issues and serious medical conditions. The Lydia Malcaster whom Cubiak had talked with was a vigorous and agile woman. He had a hard time imagining her taking a clumsy, fatal tumble, but still, if she was distracted, perhaps daydreaming about James Dura's pending visit . . .

Driving up the peninsula, Cubiak realized that he'd forgotten to ask Rowe where the body was found. The sheriff had seen two flights of stairs at the house, both with thick carpet runners. One led up to the second floor and the other down to the lower level. Had Lydia fallen down one of those or were there more stairs in the house?

The deputy met him at the door. His dusty brown hair had grown out for the winter and he sported a thick, reddish beard. "Tracey Fells is in the kitchen, waiting for you."

"How's she doing?"

"Well, she's young and pretty freaked out. I didn't get much out of her. She's drinking a cup of tea now, hopefully that will calm her down."

"The gray car outside is hers?"

Rowe nodded.

"You called Pardy?"

"Right after I talked to you. She was at a meeting, so I'd give her another forty minutes or so to get here."

"And the victim?"

"There, at the bottom of the stairs." The deputy glanced across the entranceway to the staircase that went to the lower level. "It looks like she's been dead for a few hours at least."

"It snowed again last night. Did you notice anything—footprints or tire tracks when you got here?"

Rowe shook his head. "The driveway had already been plowed and the walk was shoveled clean."

"Any signs of forced entry?"

"The front lock doesn't look jimmied, but I haven't had a chance to check any further yet. Tracey said the door was open when she arrived. Do you think it could have been burglary?"

Considering the four Remington bronzes in Zack's study and the jewelry Lydia had mentioned, burglarly was a definite possibility. Cubiak thought of his premonition about James Dura, but based on what little he knew, Dura was thousands of miles away. Just yesterday Lydia seemed so happy and lively, laughing about the burned cookies she had made. Now she was dead. What had happened to lead to this?

"It could have been anything. I'll take a look at the body and be back up in a minute. You wait with Tracey and then go check the grounds."

Cubiak crossed the foyer to the stairwell. To avoid contaminating the carpeting near the top step, he leaned into the wall and looked down toward the lower hall. A vine of blue flowers spiraled through the center of the carpet runner. Lydia lay directly in front of it, as if she had followed the floral path in flying to her death. Her body, clad in a white sweater and trousers, sprawled face down on the terra cotta tiles. Her head was twisted to the side, her face hidden in the shadows. One arm was tucked under her torso. The other stretched out in front of her as if she had been reaching for something. Viewed from above, her petite, slender frame appeared almost childlike. Like a crumpled snow angel, the sheriff thought.

He said something like a prayer. Then he stooped and examined the carpet, hoping the thick wool piling would reveal a clue as to how or why Lydia fell. Perhaps she had tripped on something or caught her foot in a loose thread of the rug. But he found nothing.

Descending, he pressed his shoulder to the wall and stepped along the bare wood next to the runner. The day before, when Lydia had led him to the lower level, she had fairly bounced down the stairs. She hadn't even used the handrail.

As Cubiak neared the last few steps, his perspective shifted, and he realized that Lydia wasn't lying flat on the floor. Her shoulders were hunched as if she had fallen awkwardly on her arm.

The sheriff pulled on a pair of latex gloves and checked for a pulse. Then he circled the body and snapped photos from a dozen different angles.

When he finished, he knelt and gently brushed the hair off her face. Her sightless eyes stared straight ahead, their color erased by death. Her pink lipstick had been worn off and her mouth gaped as if she were trying to speak. Against the whiteness of her skin, the smear of blush on her cheek seemed garish.

Cubiak turned away. He knew cops who took a macabre interest in investigating fatalities, but he had always found it hard to look upon death. For him, there was always that moment, that slice of a second, when he expected the deceased to make a sound, or when he wondered what he could do to help coax them back from the other side. Hard as it was to deal with the death of a stranger, it was even more difficult when the victim was someone he knew.

"What happened? Why were you going downstairs?" He asked the questions not of the dead woman but of himself because he knew that it was his job to find out.

Cubiak surveyed the hallway. The body lay not more than a few yards from Zack's study. "Why were you be going there? Or were you?" He leaned over and followed the trajectory of her outstretched arm. She wasn't pointing toward her late husband's office but in the opposite direction. "What were you reaching for?"

Despite overhead lights that illuminated the corridor's pale-gray walls, the dark tile floor and the deep-red baseboards lay in shadow. Using the light on his phone, the sheriff searched the area but came up with nothing. He was about to give up when he spotted a shiny object near the wall. Running his fingers along the baseboard, he felt a cold draft and then something small and hard. It was a ring. The sheriff picked it up with a tweezers and held it to the light. The ring was an unmarked, narrow gold band, small enough for a woman.

Cubiak dropped it in a small plastic bag and put it in his pocket. The ring could have been lying on the floor for weeks or months. Even years. Or only since yesterday. If Lydia was holding the ring when she fell and her hand had opened on impact, it could have rolled across the tiles. She might have been reaching for it, making a last desperate attempt to retrieve it, when she died. But why?

Upstairs, Cubiak found Rowe in the kitchen. The deputy was heating a kettle at the stove. Behind him, Tracey Fells perched on a stool at the granite island, her back to the door. The young woman was thin and tall. Her lank black hair hung over the shoulders of her thin leather jacket. During his visit with Lydia, Cubiak had heard the young housekeeper rattling around the house, but this was his first look at her.

He cleared his throat.

Tracey yipped and popped off the stool, knocking her phone to the floor.

"Shit," she said as she stooped and snatched the device. Straightening up, she shoved it into the back pocket of impossibly skinny jeans and turned a pale, scrawny face toward the sheriff.

He introduced himself and extended a hand. Her palm was damp and soft. Her fingernails were bitten to the quick.

"Please," he said, indicating the stool that she had vacated.

She glanced at it uncertainly and then slowly resettled herself.

He nodded toward the deputy.

"Sir," Rowe said. He set a mug of tea in front of Tracey and then left.

Cubiak pulled a stool to the opposite side of the island and sat facing the young housekeeper.

"How long have you been working for Lydia Malcaster?" he asked.

Tracey clasped her hands together and sat up straight. "A couple of years." She spoke quickly, her eyes blinking with each word.

"Did you like her?"

"I guess. She was all right. I didn't dislike her."

"What did you do?"

"I didn't do anything!" Tracey's eyes flashed, and the bright overhead light caught flecks of gold and brown in the gray iris.

"No, I mean, what was your job?"

"Oh, that. I did whatever. Ran errands on Monday, cleaned on Tuesday, and did laundry on Wednesday, plus tidying up and doing whatever else she wanted done."

"You were here three days a week?"

"Yeah. Half days." She brushed a strand of hair behind her ear and then clasped her hands again.

"Do you normally get here this early?"

"Only on Wednesdays. On the other two days, I go to Regina Malcaster's house first and then come here after lunch."

"Who else do you work for?"

"Right now, besides Regina—the other Mrs. Malcaster—I work for a couple of other women in the area."

"That sounds like enough hours to add up to a full-time job."

Tracey snickered. "Oh yeah. I'm working full time all right, busting my butt five days a week. They pay cash, which is good. But only twelve dollars an hour, which isn't good. And no benefits, either. Unless you count the hand-me-downs." She lifted her chin and chimed in a high-pitched voice: "'Here, dear, this sweater would fit you nicely. And these boots look your size. Why don't you try them on? They're Italian leather, so you'll need to keep them oiled.'"

The housekeeper picked at her nails and stared past Cubiak. "It's great. Perfect."

The sheriff waited. When her hands were still again, he went on. "Can you tell me what happened today?"

Tracey cleared her throat and swallowed. "I got here at nine, parked out front like I always do, and walked to the house. I had my key out but the door was already open, so I walked in and took my boots off in the hall. Then I came in here to talk to Mrs. Malcaster."

"She's usually in the kitchen when you arrive?"

Tracey nodded. "She sits over there"—she pointed to a small table along a rear window—"drinking coffee and making a chore list for me. This morning she wasn't there, which seemed strange, and she hadn't made coffee either"—Tracey turned and looked at the rear counter— "which was very odd because she was a big coffee drinker. For a minute I didn't know what do to. I looked around to see if she'd left me a note, but I didn't find anything. I went back to the front hall and called down to the lower level. When there was no answer, I went upstairs to her bedroom. I thought maybe she overslept or was sick or something. But she wasn't there, either."

"Had the bed been slept in?"

"I don't think so. It looked fine to me, all made up and everything. So at least I knew she wouldn't want me to wash the sheets today. She leaves it unmade when that's one of the tasks on the list." Tracey's eyes blinked steadily as she talked. "I thought, geez, maybe she sent me a text telling me that I shouldn't bother coming today. She did that sometimes. Anyway I wasn't sure what to do, and that's when I figured I'd go check and see if she was on the back patio. She goes out there sometimes, even in winter. I was halfway down the stairs when I saw her."

"You didn't see her from the upstairs foyer?"

Tracey shook her head. "The light was off . . ."

She twisted her hands into a knot. "I didn't know what to do. I thought maybe I should go to see if she was okay, if she was breathing or anything, but I was scared. She looked dead. I . . . I ran back up and called nine-one-one, and then I just walked back and forth by the front door waiting for someone to come."

"Did you hear anything?"

A frown formed on her face. "Like what?"

"A car door slamming or somebody driving by on the road."

"No, nothing. You can't hear anything from the road except in summer when the farmers drive their tractors from one field to the other."

"Which direction did you come from?"

"South, from Sturgeon Bay."

"Did you see anyone or notice any vehicles on the road when you got up here?"

Tracey shook her head. "There was just snow everywhere."

"The drive was already plowed when you arrived?"

"Yeah. Lydia insisted that Bobby put her first on the schedule."

"Bobby Fells, your brother," Cubiak said, remembering his conversation with Lydia.

Tracey started. "Yeah, that's right. How'd you know?"

"Doesn't matter. I'll need his contact information."

She frowned again. "Why?"

"He was here today before you and may have noticed something amiss."

The young woman tucked her chin down and batted her lashes at the sheriff. "I guess, maybe. But Bobby's not the most observant person in the world."

"Earlier you said the front door was open when you arrived."

"Yeah, that's right."

"Was it open or just unlocked?"

Tracey pursed her mouth into a thoughtful pout. "It was open," she said after a moment. "Just a smidge, but definitely open."

"You're sure?"

She looked at Cubiak. "I'm sure."

"And you noticed nothing else unusual?"

She shook her head. "No."

"I'll need you to come to the station later to give a statement."

She scowled. "But I've already told you everything."

"And I appreciate your help. It's just procedure, that's all. This afternoon if you can. Oh, and I'll need your key."

The young woman slipped off the stool and angled away from the sheriff. Lifting her jacket and shirt, she uncovered the orange carabiner key ring that hung from a belt loop of her jeans. A handful of keys dangled from the mechanism. Tracey extracted the one marked with a smear of bright pink nail polish and dropped it on the counter.

"Who else has a key to the house, besides you?"

"Beats me. Probably lots of people," she said as she reattached the key ring to her jeans.

"Why do you say that?"

Tracey shrugged. "I don't know. It's just that Lydia seemed very trusting."

The sheriff escorted Tracey to the door and watched her drive away. Uncertain of his next move, he turned around and found himself heading back to the kitchen. When there, he went directly to the small table by the window and sat in a chair—perhaps the same chair Lydia used when she drank her morning coffee. The table overlooked the snow-covered garden. In the warmer months, the garden would be awash in color, but now it slept under a thick white blanket. The wind had carved wavy ridges in the snow and left a shiny patina on the surface. The sheriff imagined Lydia musing about James Dura and projecting fantasies of a bright future onto the snowy canvas. He stared at the same field of white and projected questions about her death.

The open door indicated that someone had been at the house before Tracey arrived that morning. But who? Visitor or intruder? And when? Had they come to the house the previous evening before the latest snowfall, or this morning after Bobby Fells had cleared the drive and shoveled the walk? Tracey had been quick to downplay her brother's powers of observation, perhaps too quick. Cubiak opened his notebook and jotted down a reminder to ask the young man if he had noticed tire tracks or footprints when he came to plow.

It's possible that Lydia was dead when the unknown person arrived. She might have had a stroke or a heart attack while she stood at the top of the landing and keeled over instantly dead, or been sent reeling head-first down the staircase, dying as she fell. But if someone had seen her lying at the base of the stairs, wouldn't they have checked to see if she was breathing or at the least called 911?

What if Lydia was alive when the visitor arrived? Perhaps they had argued. Upset by the encounter, Lydia rushed toward the stairs and then tripped and fell to her death. It wasn't an impossible scenario.

Or worse, she had been pushed. And she died with the knowledge that the last pair of eyes she had looked into belonged to her killer.

No one should die like that. The possibility anchored the sheriff to the chair for several more minutes. Then he pushed up and returned to the foyer. For the second time that morning, he scanned the area at the top of the stairs, searching for imprints in the thick pile. But again, the rug revealed nothing. In the living room, the Christmas tree was dark and the furnishings appeared undisturbed. Upstairs, he checked to see if Lydia's bedroom had been ransacked in the search for jewels. The chamber was pristine. Still, he made a note to ask Regina to inventory her niece's jewelry, to be sure nothing was missing. When he finished with the upper floors, he went back downstairs to Zack's study.

As soon as Cubiak turned on the light, he knew something was wrong. Three of the Remington bronzes—*The Rattlesnake*, *Coming through the Rye*, and *The Outlaw*—remained in position, lined up in a historic parade of the Old West. But *The Bronco Buster* had vanished.

"Damn it to hell, it was a burglary," he said.

Then he paused. Who would steal just one of the bronzes? A professional thief would nab all four. Even an amateur would grab more than one.

Unless . . .

Cubiak swore under his breath and hurried back to where the body lay on the floor. He had assumed that Lydia had fallen on her arm, but when he lifted her head and chest off the red tiles, he discovered *The Bronco Buster* beneath her on the floor. Patches of dried blood smeared the statue and the front of her sweater.

"Jesus," Rowe said, coming up behind him. "What the hell happened?"

Cubiak moved the statue aside and lowered the body back to the floor.

"She must have been carrying it when she fell, like this"—he held his arm to his ribs to demonstrate—"and when she landed, the impact drove the rim of the hat or the horse's mane into her chest."

"Do you think that's what killed her?"

"I doubt it, but that's Pardy's call." The sheriff straightened up and glanced around. "What'd you find?"

"Nothing." Rowe pointed down the hall away from Zack's office. "There's a mudroom there that leads to the patio. The outer door was open but there are no tracks outside, although if there were any the wind could have covered them with snow. And no sign of forced entry anywhere either."

"An open door down here would explain the draft I felt when I found this," Cubiak said, taking the bag with the ring from his pocket.

"What does all of this mean?" the deputy said.

The sheriff shook his head. "Maybe nothing. Maybe everything."

He looked down at the dead woman on the floor. "What happened, Lydia?" he said.

The two men were standing over the body when Emma Pardy called out a cheery hello from the foyer.

"Down here," Cubiak said.

The medical examiner peered at them from inside the fur-trimmed hood of her gold parka.

"I'd better leave this up here," she said as she slipped off the jacket. "These too." She kicked off her boots and slipped into a pair of black flats. Then she pulled disposable foot coverings over the shoes and sidled down the edge of the stairway.

Cubiak ran through the details and the timing for the day's events: Tracey's call to 911, Rowe's response, and his arrival.

"And that? It looks kind of familiar," Pardy said, gesturing toward the blood-smeared statue.

The sheriff filled her in on the story behind the antique bronze. When he finished, Pardy dropped to one knee.

"Okay," she said, and unzipped her bag.

31

While Pardy conducted an initial examination, the sheriff checked in with Rowe and called the state tech office to request a team to come out and dust the premises for prints.

By the time he went back downstairs, the medical examiner was waiting.

As was her custom, she reported her preliminary findings in a straightforward, clipped manner.

"The deceased appears to be the victim of a fatal fall. Accidental from all appearances, although I can't rule out precipitating circumstances, such as heart attack, aneurysm, or stroke, until after autopsy."

"What about the bronze?" Cubiak asked.

"The statue appears to have pierced the dermis, presumably at the moment of impact. The presence of blood would indicate that the victim was still alive at the time. However, the small quantity of blood would also indicate that the puncture was not related to the death. Again, this is preliminary."

"Time of death?"

"I'd estimate between eight and midnight."

"She's been lying here for some time then," he said.

Pardy nodded and leaned against the wall. "I don't know, Dave, why do things like this have to happen? My mother's neighbor died from a fall down a flight of stairs. She caught her foot in her pant leg and tumbled headfirst. The same thing could have happened here. Look at the wide legs on the victim's trousers! She may as well have been wearing an evening gown!"

The medical examiner picked up her black bag. "At least she was wearing sensible shoes with no-slip soles, not that it mattered in the end."

"There is something else," Cubiak said, and showed Pardy the plastic bag with the ring. "I found this on the floor along the baseboard. It looked like she was reaching for it."

"And you think it belonged to the victim?"

"I don't know. I'm hoping you can tell me."

"Well, she has a ring on every finger, so I'm not sure where she'd find room for another one. However, it's a narrow band, so she might have been able to double it up with one of the others. I'll see if I can find any supporting evidence. That's more likely if she'd had the ring for years, even months, but if it were a new piece of jewelry, something she'd worn for a short time, I'm afraid I won't be able to come up with anything."

Pardy looked at the sheriff. "Did you know her?"

"Not really, why?"

"I know it sounds strange, but when I'm dealing with the dead, I sometimes get a sense of what they were like when they were alive. Today was one of those times," Pardy said as she started up the stairs. "And I have the feeling that Lydia was a good woman."

A VISIT WITH THE QUEEN

4

Cubiak and Pardy met the EMTs at the front door and watched as the team carried the gurney with Lydia Malcaster's body to the first floor and then down the walk to the ambulance. Neither the sheriff nor the medical examiner spoke until the medics drove away.

"Tomorrow, then?" he asked.

Pardy pulled her car keys from her pocket. "I'll have my report ready around noon."

Left on his own, Cubiak went back into the house.

Less than twenty-four hours had passed since he had listened to Lydia's bright chatter about her late husband, her new beau, and the wonderful days ahead. How quickly circumstances changed. The house was empty and quiet, weighted with the presence of death. Only his footsteps disturbed the oppressive silence.

Both Cubiak and Rowe had searched the premises and found nothing that could explain Lydia's death. Perhaps the fall was an accident, but the sheriff still wasn't convinced.

Taking his time, he revisited each room in the house.

He looked behind every closed door, checked every niche, scrutinizing the house for anything that seemed out of place, anything that he or his deputy might not have noticed earlier that would help him understand what had drawn Lydia to the top of the stairs and precipitated her fatal fall.

Again, he found nothing suspicious. There were no signs of a break-in or scuffle. Nothing missing or out of place. Pardy had taken *The Bronco Buster* to analyze the blood, leaving the three remaining bronzes undisturbed in Zack's office. Lydia's bed had not been slept in; her purse stood on the dresser, the wallet stuffed with twenties; a string of pearls nestled in a basket.

Cubiak was locking up when Cate sent a message saying that she was heading home after her talk with Regina.

He texted her back: *How is she?*

Stoic. But it would be nice if you can check on her.

Of course.

The sheriff needed to talk to the matriarch, so he may as well do it now. From Lydia's drive, he turned north. Regina lived ten minutes up the road. The first estate he passed had a gated entry. The second was marked with a large abstract sculpture that probably cost half of his annual salary. Given Regina's chauffeured Rolls, Cubiak figured her property would have an equally imposing entrance and was surprised to discover a nondescript gravel driveway with a simple wooden post marked by the Malcaster name etched into it. The understated entry belied the elderly woman's exalted status on the peninsula, and he suspected that the modest entrance was false cover for what lay beyond. Driving up the long lane through the heavily wooded parcel, he was reminded of the road that led to The Wood, the grand estate that Cate's grandfather had built. They had only just met the first time Cate took him to the old house. To her, the chalet and manicured grounds were familiar turf and didn't represent anything out of the ordinary, but to him the elaborate home was a harsh reminder of his low-ranking position in the world. A house like The Wood would match well with a Rolls. So too would a Tudor mansion with a steep, gabled roof and rows of leaded-glass windows. Or perhaps the woman who was known as the queen inhabited a faux castle.

Rounding the final curve, Cubiak anticipated a grand edifice. Instead, he pulled up to a contemporary, single-story structure at odds with his notion of a home fit for a dowager. He checked the GPS to make sure that he was in the right place. Perhaps another Malcaster lived in the area and he had gone to the wrong address. He hadn't met Regina Malcaster, but he found it difficult to imagine a woman of her age and pedigree residing in the sleek, glass and wood house that stood before him. Surrounded by towering trees, it appeared both fragile and exposed. The chauffeur-driven Rolls was nowhere in sight.

As the sheriff approached, the door swung open to a tall, silver-haired woman dressed in black slacks and turtleneck. She wore no jewelry or makeup, but there was steel in her regal posture and confidence in the way she extended her hand.

"Regina Malcaster," she said, her tone imperious. "Good of you to come so soon."

Only then, at this hint of the purpose for his visit, did Cubiak notice the strain in her face and the faint redness that rimmed her intense blue eyes.

"Very kind of Cate, as well." She started to say something else, but then she stopped and exhaled a puff of warm air that condensed into a small cloud and instantly vanished. Wordlessly, the dowager stepped back and let the sheriff pass. In the foyer, she pointed to a row of brass hooks on a brick wall. A plain wool coat hung from one. A silk scarf from another. He added his clunky parka to the collection.

Leaning on a cane that seemed to materialize from thin air, Regina led him through the wide entrance hall and into the house.

"Not what you expected, is it?" she said as they entered the living room, an indoor field of pale wood flooring, soft colors and light, and simple furniture heaped with pillows.

An awkward moment passed before Cubiak realized that she was referring to the house, either from a need to make polite small talk with her guest or a wish to delay the inevitable.

"It doesn't go with the car," he said.

"I suppose not," she said as she strode forward. "But then the grand old manse burned, and the Rolls kept rolling along. I appreciated the sedan for its roominess and ready accessibility—easy for me to get in and out of, a consideration in one's advancing age—so I kept it despite the absurd cost of repairs and maintenance. Do you know cars, Sheriff?"

"Not especially."

"I imagine that there's no reason you should. Like the car, the old house had its finer features, and I could have replaced it with a clone or something in the same vein, which is what people expected, but stairs had become the bane of my existence and the curlicues did nothing but collect dust, hence this." The dowager swung the cane like a pendulum, aiming it first at one glass wall and then the other.

"I told my architect that my time was limited and that as long as I was still on this earth, I wanted to be as close to nature as possible without having to endure any discomfort. The house is a tribute to her talent, not mine. I merely signed the checks."

As she talked, Regina proceeded toward a long ribbon of flame that danced in the wall at the far end of the room.

"It burns real wood," she said as they neared the fireplace. "I miss the sound of the crackling logs, but the glass front makes it more efficient, and with the vents it becomes a reliable source of heat. Fuel from the forest as it were."

The speech sounded rote, and she sounded tired.

She stared into the flames for a moment, and then she turned toward the pair of orange chairs that faced each other across the hearth.

"Go ahead," she said. "This will take me a bit of time." Cubiak remained standing and pretended to take in the view while she slowly lowered herself onto a thick upholstered cushion. When she was settled, he took the other chair.

"Poor Lydia," Regina said, cupping her hands over the top of the cane. "As soon as I saw Cate at the door, I knew something had happened."

"I'm sorry. I understand that you were close to your niece," he said.

The queen gave a soft, half smile. "She was the daughter I never had. Legally she was related to us only through marriage, but the connection always felt more direct than that."

"Zack was your nephew?"

"That's correct. His father and my husband were brothers. Lydia's mother died shortly after they were married and then her father passed a few years later. After her sister and Zack's parents died as well, we were the only family that he and Lydia had left."

"They had no other siblings?"

"No. I always wished that they would have a child but that was not to be."

Regina closed her eyes. When she opened them, the luster had dimmed. "Cate said that Lydia had fallen, that she was found at the bottom of the front stairs. Is that true?"

"That's correct. It appears that she may have tripped going down to the lower level."

The dowager nodded slowly. "It's so hard to comprehend, to take it all in. I realize that accidents happen, but we never expect them to involve those whom we know. Still, Lydia was always so careful. She'd lived in that house for nearly forty years and never had so much as a stubbed toe or a bruised elbow."

The muscles around her mouth tightened. "Lydia didn't deserve to die like that. I can't imagine the shock and horror of such a terrifying fall. How she must have suffered, even if only for a few seconds. Do tell me she died instantly. Allow me that small comfort."

Cubiak rested his elbows on his knees and leaned forward. "We don't know all the details, but many things are possible. If Lydia had a heart attack or a stroke, she might not have even been aware of falling. I should have a full report from the medical examiner soon."

"Yes, of course. I see." She paused. "You said she *may* have tripped."

"That's the most likely possibility."

Regina nodded.

"Lydia was holding one of the bronze statues when she was found."

Regina looked up, her face a question mark. "One of the Remingtons? Why was she carrying one of the statues around the house?"

"I don't know. When she showed them to me yesterday, I got the impression they were a permanent fixture in Zack's office. Do you have any idea why she would have moved one?"

"Me? No." The elderly woman seemed genuinely puzzled. "Which statue was it?"

"*The Bronco Buster.*"

"Ah, Rutherford's first acquisition."

"The one Zack's grandfather won in a poker game."

Regina gave a short laugh. "That's what he always claimed, but who knows? Rutherford was quite the raconteur. It could have been true, but he could easily have fabricated the entire story. In any case, over time he bought four more. He kept one for himself and gave the others to his sons. When Zack's father died, his bronzes came to my husband, Henry. Then Rutherford passed and we inherited his as well." She turned to Cubiak. "The idea was that my husband and I would bequeath our original two to our heirs and the other two to Zack, but since we had no children, all four went to Zack. But he and Lydia had no children and then Zack died and, well, you know the rest."

The fire flared and drew her attention again. "I can't imagine why she'd been walking around with it. She planned to sell them; did you know that?"

"No. When did this come about?"

"Not long after Thanksgiving, Lydia told me she intended to start downsizing and that she was considering the sale of the Remingtons. As a courtesy, she wanted me to have one of the statues. It was such a very thoughtful offer and I thanked her, of course. I also said that while I appreciated the gesture, I thought she was being overly generous. The truth is, I already own a Remington bronze—the cast that Rutherford kept—and don't need anything added to the estate. The whole business of sorting things out will be complicated enough once I'm gone. I suggested that instead of giving a statue to me, she select one to donate to the Miller Art Museum in our joint names. I told her she'd need to have it appraised first, and that to spare the museum from being saddled with the cost of insuring the sculpture, I would arrange for my estate to handle the cost in perpetua."

"Did she agree?"

"She thought it was a splendid idea but seemed a bit bewildered by the prospect of having to deal with the process. I assured her that she only had to ask John to help. I was sure he would be happy to handle the entire matter for her."

"John being?"

"John Overly. Her accountant and bookkeeper. We all use him. He's my financial advisor and also a longtime friend. He takes good care of all his clients and probably extra good care of Lydia.

"Nothing else was said leading up to Christmas and I thought she'd forgotten it completely, but last week she called and asked me over for tea. She said she wanted to continue our conversation about donating one of the bronzes and was anxious to discuss the details. When I arrived, the statues were all in place, lined up as usual with *The Bronco Buster* in the lead," Regina said, rubbing her hands together. "As you observed, Zack had pretty much enshrined them in his study and I doubt that Lydia ever went near them. Not her taste in art, I guess. That wasn't the case at my house. I was a student of art in my younger days, and while sculpture wasn't my purview, I admired the exquisite detail that Remington brought to his work. When *The Outlaw* and *The Rattlesnake* were still in our possession, I often carried one or the other to the window to study it in natural light.

"Without thinking twice about what I was doing, I picked up the cast of *The Outlaw*. As soon as I had it in my hands, I was struck with the odd sensation that something was not right. I knew what that statue felt like all those many years we had it, and the one in Zack's study seemed off." She rested the cane against the chair and tucked her hands into her lap. "Of course, it could have been my imagination."

"Did you say anything to Lydia?"

"No, I didn't want to alarm her unnecessarily. Besides, the notion passed immediately. I merely stressed once more that if she was going to donate the cast, she should have it appraised first. The museum is a nonprofit organization, and I'm sure there's a mountain of red tape that would have to be sorted through before the donation could be finalized. That's if the curator or someone on the board doesn't object because the museum's mission limits it to promoting Wisconsin artists and Remington could be disqualified on that account. Which would be unfortunate but understandable. Of course, there are other possible homes for it, like the Neville Public Museum in Green Bay."

"Where did you leave things with Lydia then?"

"Given my suspicions about *The Outlaw*, I went on to urge her to have the entire collection assessed. 'Just so you know what you're dealing with,' I said. One hates to think of such a possibility, but perhaps Zack had gone through a difficult spell and found it necessary to sell one or two of the bronzes. He was a proud man, too proud to ask for help if he'd needed to. He wouldn't have wanted anyone to know, so he'd have to put a duplicate in its place, a copy of lesser value, of course. In any case. Lydia said she was still waiting to hear from John about an appraiser."

"When you came to see Cate this week, it wasn't about the Remingtons, was it?"

Regina shook her head. "My visit had nothing to do with the bronzes."

"You were concerned about Lydia's relationship with James Dura."

The dowager looked up sharply. "She told you about him?"

"She said that telling you was a mistake, that you were upset and thought she was being disloyal to Zack."

Regina plucked at her trouser leg. "I was more surprised than anything. She should have realized that I would have come around to it eventually. It was just all so sudden, so secretive. And she was so different. About a week before Thanksgiving, I went to see her and when I got there, she was—how can I say this?—all dolled up. New hairdo, makeup, and wearing a pink angora sweater. All those years I'd known Lydia, I'd never seen her in anything pink."

"Did you say anything?"

"Of course I did, but she brushed it aside. She was all in a flutter, talking about new starts and second chances. When I asked her specifically what she had in mind, she became very elusive. 'I'm still young,' she said. She told me she was tired of sitting in that house by herself, alone, that she wanted to enjoy life. 'I deserve as much,' she said."

The dowager sniffed. "I may be old, Sheriff, but I'm not stupid. That only meant one thing to me, and I asked her if she was seeing someone."

"What did she say?"

"Her response was very precise and yet vague. 'Not exactly,' she said. When I asked what she meant by that, she shrugged and said it was too new to talk about."

Regina pressed her hands into the arms of the chair. "For those of us who live up here year-round, this is a very small world. Lydia had no obligation to discuss her private life with me, but I thought that perhaps she had confided to her friends about her mystery man. I made a few subtle inquiries with several women who I knew were close to her, but none of them had seen much of her for several months. Lydia had begged off from lunches and coffee dates. She'd even missed book club, which was highly unusual. One friend said she thought Lydia seemed distracted. But that was all they were able to tell me.

"I'd stopped hosting holiday dinners years ago. Instead, for the past five or six years, I invited Lydia to Christmas brunch. We'd always enjoyed the day, but this year it felt strained. I'd taken pains to prepare her favorite dishes, and she barely seemed to notice. She had little to say, and every few minutes she glanced at her watch. Normally we'd have spent the afternoon together, but shortly after we finished eating, she said she had to leave. I asked if she had other plans, and she said no, only that she needed to get home. She was in the hall putting on her coat when she asked me if I remembered one of Zack's old friends from school, a James Dura, one of the other boys on the team. I said no and asked her why. She shrugged and said it didn't matter. Then she was out the door. As I watched her walk to her car, I understood what was going on."

"You assumed she was seeing him, this James Dura?"

Regina tapped a finger in the air. "If Dura lived in the area, I would have known the name. No, I assumed she had somehow connected with him and that they were engaged in a long-distance relationship but one that was potentially serious, at least from her perspective. I even called John later that afternoon and asked him if Lydia had confided in him about this James Dura person, but he said no, that he'd never heard the name before."

She tilted her head toward the blazing logs and gave a small smile. "Poor John. He was sweet on Lydia for years. I imagine that it was hard on him when she married Zack, but John's a true gentleman. In fact, he was included among the few guests at their wedding."

The dowager looked at the sheriff. "I wish you could have known Lydia back then. She was a spirited young lady and an intelligent, kind woman. And loyal." Regina sighed. "Loyal to a fault."

"What do you mean?"

"If Lydia took to you, that was it; she never doubted, never questioned, took everything on faith. It was like that between her and Zack. She was her husband's greatest defender and would brook no criticism of him."

"Even if he deserved it?"

Regina sniffed. "Even when others thought he deserved it. No, it simply came down to the fact that our Lydia was a trusting soul. She embraced that rare optimism that allows people to go through life happy, even when circumstances don't warrant it."

The matriarch fell silent for a moment. "I trust that I can depend on your discretion, Sheriff. I never had any reason to doubt that Lydia and Zack were anything but happy and well suited to each other. There certainly was never any indication of impropriety here, but he traveled a considerable amount for his work, and so did my husband, and more than once he heard stories about Zack's drinking and philandering. Really, they were merely rumors, and if Lydia had become aware of them, she never let on that there was anything amiss. She never complained, so I never said anything to her either. People have their secrets, don't they? You never really know what goes on in someone's heart or in their marriage, do you?"

"No, you don't," he said.

Regina sighed. "Maybe Lydia put up with more than we ever realized and this business with Dura was her way of settling the score. Or perhaps everything was fine, and my suspicions were out of place. Maybe at this stage of her life, Lydia simply felt entitled to a little happiness. Is that so terrible?"

"No, but it could make her vulnerable," Cubiak said.

Regina smiled. "Under the right circumstances, we're all vulnerable."

He gave a nod of agreement. "You don't remember Zack ever talking about Dura?"

"Never, but that didn't mean anything. Zack had so many friends that we couldn't possibly have met or remembered them all."

"When you came to see Cate, you said you thought Lydia might be in some kind of trouble. What did you mean by that?"

Regina stiffened. "I'm not sure. An old woman's paranoia, I'm afraid. Or maybe I exaggerated the situation because I felt slighted that Lydia hadn't confided in me and had been so secretive about this new romantic interest in her life."

She hesitated. "The truth is that as soon as I heard that Lydia was dead, I wondered if Dura didn't have something to do with it. Believe me, Sheriff, I realize how absurd that sounds. Everything that went on between them was through the internet, that much she eventually admitted. He wasn't even here."

The dowager lifted her head high again but pain flashed in her eyes. "I do hope you'll forgive me for involving you in family business."

"There's nothing to forgive, but there is something else I need to ask you about." Cubiak handed her the bag with the ring.

"Do you recognize this?"

Regina pinched the plastic between her thumb and forefinger and peered at the gold band. "I don't believe I've ever seen this before. Where did you get it?"

"I found it at Lydia's house."

"Really? She was partial to rings, but I can't say that I ever saw her wear this one."

"What about other jewelry?"

"Most of the pieces Lydia owned were elaborate heirloom necklaces from her late mother-in-law." Regina placed her hand at the base of her neck as if she might conjure up a string of gems or pearls. "But she didn't wear any of them. They were old-fashioned and ostentatious and much too large and cumbersome for her."

"Are they in the house?" he asked. He hadn't noticed a safe but that might mean it was well hidden or disguised.

"Oh no. They're much too valuable to leave lying around. Lydia kept them in a safe-deposit box. Why do you ask?"

"Just curious, that's all."

Regina closed her eyes, and in the stillness she seemed to shrink into a smaller version of herself. Then she pulled herself upright and looked at him. "I can't believe all that's happened, and I can't help but wonder if I shouldn't have done something sooner. There are times I feel like everything that's gone wrong is my fault."

"You shouldn't feel that way," he said.

"It's hard not to."

"I know." Regina reached out and patted his arm. "Thank you, Sheriff. You're very kind."

In the foyer, Regina gave the sheriff directions to John Overly's house.

"He lives just past town, about twenty minutes from Lydia's," she said.

Cubiak took the hint and said that since it was on his way, he would stop there now. He was halfway to the jeep when Regina called to him from the doorway.

"Don't bother ringing the bell. John will be out back," she said. "I called him just before you arrived to tell him about Lydia. I thought it might be a small kindness that he heard the sad news from me. He thanked me and then he said he had to go out and take care of the birds. He feeds them through the winter. Poor John. Birds have been his solace for years, but at least he has them."

ONE FOR THE BIRDS

5

The snow and wind had picked up while Cubiak talked to Regina Malcaster, and both intensified during the drive to John Overly's house.
Figuring that the accountant had enough time to fill a couple of bird
feeders, the sheriff ignored Regina's advice. Instead of heading straight
to the backyard, he climbed the front steps and rang the bell.

Like the dowager's home, Overly's was surrounded by coniferous
forest, but the similarity between the homesteads ended with the trees.
The accountant's house was small and made of stone and stood about
fifty feet from the road, while her domicile was large and made of glass
and tucked far into the woods. With its small high windows and thick
walls, Overly's home squatted on the land like a miniature fortress that
was designed to keep either the world out or the man and his posses-
sions in. As he pressed the bell, Cubiak felt like he was storming the
citadel. There was no answer, only the faint scent of woodsmoke wafting on the icy breeze.

The sheriff waited at the door long enough to get cold. Then he
came down the stairs, tucked his head against the wind, and plodded
through deep snow around the corner of the house. He didn't realize the
extent of Overly's bird-feeding operation until he reached the back and
looked up. The yard opened up into a large field ringed by more than a

dozen feeding stations. They ranged from simple wood trays suspended from steel poles to bright yellow and orange tubes and structures shaped like miniature barns and houses. Against the backdrop of snow, they sparkled like a jeweled necklace.

On the far side of the loop, a man in dark-blue coveralls pushed a wheelbarrow loaded with several large, green buckets. Assuming it was Overly, Cubiak called out the man's name, but the wind carried away the greeting. He tried again but the birdman kept moving farther away. The sheriff had no choice but to start down the trail after him. On the shoveled path, he passed a wooden feeder in the form of a miniature cottage with a bright-green roof. The next two were slender orange resin tubes. Each one was filled with seeds.

Cubiak marched at a fast pace and was nearly out of breath when he caught up with the bird tender.

"John Overly? I'm Dave Cubiak."

The man set the wheelbarrow down and turned around. "The sheriff?" He peered out from behind his mirrored sunglasses. "How can I help you?"

"Regina Malcaster told you what happened to her niece. I'm talking to people who knew Lydia. Routine, that's all."

"Of course." Overly shoved a metal scoop into a sack and filled it with a mixture of grains and pips. "Do you mind?" he said as he poured the seeds into a short, wide feeder. "This is thistle seed for the goldfinches. There are three more like it here, as well as all the others. Do you know anything about birds, Sheriff?"

"No." Cubiak jammed his gloved hands into his pockets and flexed his toes inside his boots.

"That's too bad. We have a marvelous variety on the peninsula. If you're interested in learning more about them, you could join one of the birding groups. In fact, we have a meeting tomorrow evening."

"Another time, perhaps."

Overly chortled and then looked out across the field. "To continue with bird feeding one-oh-one. The first feeder contains shelled peanuts. That's for the blue jays, woodpeckers, chickadees, and nuthatches. The next couple carry mixed songbird seed, which all the visitors are partial to, except for the woodpeckers." The accountant swung his arm around the loop like a dial around the face of a clock. "There's a couple with sunflower seeds, as well. That's a real favorite for all the birds. The rest of the loop is pretty much a repeat. Oh, and I also scatter mixed seeds on the ground for the birds that don't like to perch and would rather graze on the ground or, in this case, the snow. That would be the juncos, grouse, turkeys, and mourning doves."

Overly finished filling the tube and screwed the top back on. "Damn cold out here, isn't it?"

Cubiak grunted.

"We're not all that different from the birds, you know. They need feathers to trap heat close to the body just like we need our coats and hats. But most of us don't go singing through the winter, do we?"

The birdman pushed the wheelbarrow forward. "Almost done. Just need to fill the last few and then check on the suet blocks and the water. The suet is for the woodpeckers, chickadees, and nuthatches. And the water's for all the birds. During winter, fresh water is a rare commodity, and for the birds it's as important as food."

The sheriff stopped. "You've got water out here?"

"Right there, in the birdbath. You can't see it from here for all the snow. It's there, in the middle of the yard."

"How the hell do you keep the water from freezing?"

"I heat it. With a generator and a long extension cord, it's simple."

By the time the feeders were full, the men were covered with fresh powder. "I'll have hot tea ready in a minute," Overly said as they stood on the back porch and brushed the snow from their shoulders.

Inside, the accountant led Cubiak through an arched doorway and down a short hall where a flock of small stuffed birds perched on a hodgepodge of wood and stone ledges. The passage led to a small living room that was more bird museum than a space meant for human habitat. A plaid love seat and barrel chair faced the fireplace, where a ribbon of flame nipped at a small stack of logs, but the furnishings seemed like an afterthought amid the stacks of bird books and magazines and the colorful avian mounts, wood carvings, and porcelain statues that roosted on every available surface. Dominating the room were three magnificent paintings of birds.

"My obsession," Overly said, tossing his hands open at the collection. He bent over the fireplace and adjusted a gas jet that sent the low flames dancing higher.

"Have a seat. I'll be back in a minute," he said, and disappeared back down the hall.

Cubiak moved a pile of *Nature* magazines off the chair and nudged it as close to the fire as he dared. While they were outside, the sheriff had wanted to come in and warm up. Now all he wanted to do was leave. Classical music began playing, and he focused on the melody and tried to ignore the claustrophobic clutter around him.

Several minutes later, Overly reappeared with two steaming mugs.

"It's already loaded with sugar," he said as he set a mug on a rough-hewn side table for the sheriff.

"You saw the Audubons?" Overly asked. "There, behind you."

Cubiak turned back to the three wild fowl images on the wall. The birds were large and startlingly crisp and vivid. One was bright white, another shocking pink. The third had a flaming orange body.

"I've never seen anything quite like them," he said.

"Credit goes to John James Audubon, who invented the technique. Over the course of his life, he produced four hundred thirty-five renderings of native fowl. Each one is an incredible piece of art." The birdman gestured toward the sketch of the oyster white bird. "That's an American ptarmigan. Next, the American flamingo and last but not least, the tri-colored Baltimore oriole.

"These are just prints, but they're more than anything my parents could afford when I was growing up. They were dedicated birdwatchers. As a kid, I couldn't imagine anything more tedious than wandering around with a pair of binoculars and searching for birds in the trees and marshes. But I grew up listening to them wax poetic about birds, and by osmosis I guess I absorbed their enthusiasm. I don't birdwatch per se, but I do enjoy looking out back at the ones that come here to feed. It's a nice hobby to have."

The accountant sat and set his warm brown eyes on the sheriff. "Sorry, I tend to get carried away. You're here about Lydia Malcaster." He picked up the cup of tea and then set it down without taking a drink. "I don't know what to say. It's such a shame, her dying like that. She was a wonderful woman, a good friend."

"When was the last time you saw Mrs. Malcaster?"

"Yesterday. She called around seven in the evening and asked if I'd come over. A storm was heading this way and I wasn't too keen about going out, but she insisted. I thought maybe she was ill or the kitchen sink wasn't draining—she'd sometimes phone and ask me to help with small repairs—but it was about the Remingtons again." He looked at Cubiak. "You know about the bronzes?"

"I've seen Zack's collection. You said she wanted to talk about the statues again. Was it a recurring issue?"

"She'd mentioned them twice before. The first time was around Thanksgiving. I was at the house going over her accounts, something I do . . ." Overly stopped and looked at his hands. "Something I did monthly for her when, out of the blue, Lydia said that she was thinking of selling the Remingtons. I was surprised, knowing how much they meant to Zack. Why? I asked. And she went on about decluttering. Some new trend, I guess. She said that Regina—that's her aunt, Regina Malcaster—"

"We've met."

"Ah, of course, well, she said that Regina suggested that she get the statues appraised first and said that I could help. That was a surprise to me. I don't know anything about Remingtons. I told Lydia that I'd look into it and left it at that."

"And did you?"

Overly colored. "Not really. It was almost Christmas, and everyone was busy. Me included. One morning about a week ago, she brought it up again and I advised her not to rush into anything. We ended up talking about a movie we'd both seen, and by the time I left, I thought she'd forgotten all about the idea. Then yesterday I got the third call. Lydia insisted that I come over immediately. She wasn't interested in listening to any advice. She said she'd made up her mind and was adamant that I help her," he said, getting up to stir the fire.

"She had this idea that she would give one of the statues to a museum here or in Green Bay and then sell the rest of the collection. Lydia wasn't a woman to rush into things. She was always very deliberate. None of this made sense. Why now? I asked her."

"What did she say?"

"That her life was moving in a different direction and she needed to downsize. Then start with the big pieces, I said. But she didn't pay any attention."

"You didn't ask her about this new direction she was taking?"

"I should have, maybe, but I didn't," he said as he straightened a stack of magazines that didn't need to be straightened.

"Was she in any financial difficulty?"

The accountant chuckled. "If Lydia had lived for another hundred years, she wouldn't have had any worries about money."

Then he looked at Cubiak. "Why are you asking all these questions? According to Regina, the poor woman fell down the stairs. It was a tragic accident." Overly hesitated. "Wasn't it? Are you implying that there was something sinister about her death?"

"I'm trying to understand her frame of mind, that's all."

Overly squinted at the flames. Then he sighed. "Lydia was always good natured and calm. At least until recently. The last couple of months she was often distracted and agitated. I asked her if anything was wrong, and she implied that some of her friends were being difficult. That didn't surprise me—some of the women do have their odd ways about them. Oh, please, don't let on that I ever said anything like that. I need the business."

The fire had faded, and again Overly got up and rearranged the logs. Once the blaze was going, he stood with this back to the flames, the poker still in his hand.

"There was one odd thing, come to think of it. Lydia was always confident about her appearance, not in a silly or obnoxious way but just, well, self-assured. But last night she said she was worried that she might be losing her looks. She even asked me if I thought a man would still find her attractive."

"What did you say?"

"I told her any man would be a fool not to."

"You knew both of them a long time, didn't you? Lydia and Zack?"

The birdman replaced the poker and slouched back in his chair. "Zack and I grew up together. We were next-door neighbors when we were kids, and back then there weren't many year-round families up here. So by default we were friends and as such practically inseparable through elementary and high school. After that we went to different colleges, and things changed—but we always kept in touch, and once he was back and married to Lydia, we saw each other often."

"According to Regina Malcaster, there was a time you were sweet on Lydia."

Overly shook his head. "The queen speaketh, huh? Lydia spent several summers up here when she was a teenager, and it's true that I had a crush on her back then. Hell, half the guys in the area did. Nothing ever came of it, though. Nothing ever does, nor should it."

"And now?"

"What do you mean now?"

"I mean over the past six years, the time that Lydia's been a widow."

The answer came like a whiplash. "I'm sixty-five and I've been a bachelor my entire adult life. No, Sheriff, you can put that notion aside. I had no romantic interest in Lydia. I was her accountant and her friend—a good friend—and that's all I wanted to be."

"When you saw her last night, how'd you leave things?"

Overly cracked his knuckles. "We ended up talking for a couple of hours. I got her to settle down a bit and cautioned her that it would probably take me some time to track down a reputable appraiser for the collection. The art world is very specialized. I know something about bird prints, but that's as far as my knowledge goes. Remington bronzes are in a class by themselves.

"The truth is, I was hoping to stall for a while longer and give her enough time to change her mind. Lydia's got a house full of art pieces that she could sell or donate and get rid of, if that was her goal. Downsizing or decluttering or whatever it's called doesn't mean you jettison a valuable asset like the statues. I was hoping she'd come to her senses."

"You told her this?"

"Not in so many words, but I think my feelings came across because she wasn't happy with me. We talked a little more about collectibles and that was it."

"Did you have anything to drink?"

"Lydia'd opened a bottle of sherry. I had a small glass but that was all. Given the weather, I didn't want to overdo it and then drive home."

"What time was it when you left?"

"A few minutes after midnight. I remember the clock chiming as we walked to the foyer. We hadn't heard the wind the whole time we were talking, but once we got to the front hall, we realized it was howling. When I opened the door, a gust brought in a wave of snow that dusted us both. The last thing I remember is Lydia laughing and brushing the flakes from her cheek."

"You didn't argue with her?"

"No! Not at all. I may have gotten a bit stern, but argue? There was nothing to argue about. I gave her my advice, but ultimately it was up to Lydia to decide what she wanted to do with the bronzes. Whatever she settled on I would accept, and she knew that."

The accountant rubbed his hands on his knees. "She told me to be careful driving in the snow and asked me to call or text when I got home. Normally I'd make it back in about twenty minutes, but last night it took more than twice as long because of the weather. It was nearly one when I walked in the door and I figured that by then she'd be asleep. I didn't want to wake her, so I let it go, thinking I'd touch base in the morning."

"And did you?"

"I called around nine, but she didn't answer."

"Did you leave a message?"

"No, I figured I'd try again later." Overly slumped back and stared at his hands. "I can't believe that I was the last person to see her alive."

Cubiak gave him a minute before he asked his next question. "Does the name James Dura mean anything to you?"

The accountant shook his head. "Should it?"

"He was one of Zack's college friends."

"Zack had a lot of friends. He may have mentioned him in passing but that was a long time ago."

"You never met him then?"

Overly shrugged. "Maybe. I don't know. Zack often showed up at Thanksgiving with one or another of his pals in tow. We'd get together and have a few beers but that was about it. I don't remember any of them."

"Lydia never mentioned him?"

Overly frowned. "No. Why would she? What's this Dura fellow have to do with anything?"

"Apparently he contacted her several months ago, and something of a friendship had developed. Regina Malcaster remembers asking you if you knew anything about it."

Overly slapped his knee. "Hah! That's right, I forgot. She did mention something about her niece's new friendship." The birdman put the word in quotes. "That explains a lot, doesn't it? Good for Lydia," he said.

There was a lively sense of bonhomie in the response. Too much, perhaps, Cubiak thought as he swallowed the dregs of the cold tea.

The sheriff was halfway out the door when he stopped. "Do you have any idea what the statues are worth?"

"The Remingtons?" The birdman whistled. "I wouldn't even hazard a guess. You need an expert for that."

Heading home, Cubiak called Cate and explained the situation. "Overly has had months to take care of this and he's done nothing. Can you use your contacts to find an appraiser?"

"I'll make a few calls and see what I can come up with," she said. "But no guarantees."

DETAILS OF DEATH

6

Cubiak was at his desk late Thursday morning when an email from the UW alumni office landed in his mailbox. The message listed two phone numbers for James Dura and a note explaining that both went back more than twenty years, probably were landlines, and might not be viable. With Lydia's death, the sheriff wasn't sure what would be gained by calling, but habit insisted that he follow through. The first number was disconnected; there was no answer at the second, so he left a message.

An hour later, he was at the end of a long line of vehicles crawling toward town behind a county snowplow. The jeep's speedometer registered a painful fifteen miles per hour but there was nothing the sheriff could do to hurry things up. He was late for his noon meeting with Emma Pardy. This would make him even later.

When he reached the morgue, it was 12:18. Even hurrying, it took him four more minutes to get from the parking lot to the building and down the long hall to the double doors.

As he walked in, Pardy looked up from her laptop.

"You're late," she said.

He unzipped his parka. "I was stuck behind a snowplow and didn't think it set a good example for the sheriff to go around it."

She laughed. "Welcome to winter in Wisconsin, the season when everything takes longer."

"You got that right." The sheriff worked his shoulders.

"Stiff?"

"The usual." Cubiak kept his head down to avoid having to look at the table where the body of Lydia Malcaster lay beneath a long, white sheet. Under the fluorescent lighting, everything in the room seemed to glow an eerie white. The sheet, the walls, Pardy's doctor coat.

The only spot of color was the red of the medical examiner's turtleneck. It peeked out from her coat like a bright red ribbon and reminded him of the cardinal in Lydia's yard. He took a deep breath.

"Are you okay?" Pardy said.

"Yeah. Let's do this."

The medical examiner lowered the sheet to the dead woman's shoulders. Despite himself, Cubiak flinched at the sight of the bruises on her face.

"You know the preliminaries. Lydia Malcaster: age, sixty-four; height, five feet and four inches; weight, one hundred thirty-five pounds. Cause of death was a combination of fracture to the upper cervical spine, C1 and C2, and rupture of the spleen resulting from a fall. Subject presents with contusions consistent with a fall, as down a flight of stairs," she said, indicating the discoloration on the forehead. "And internal bleeding caused by the ruptured organ."

"Death was not instantaneous?" the sheriff said.

"Sadly no. There's some slight bruising on her chest where she landed on top of the statue, which means she was still alive after she fell. But it's doubtful that she lived for very long. And if she'd been unconscious, which is a likely scenario, she wouldn't have suffered."

"Do you think it was an accident?" he asked.

"Given the circumstances, I can't provide a definitive answer. Falls are the primary etiology of accidental deaths in people her age and older, but whether or not this particular fall was an accident, it's not within my purview to determine."

As she talked, Pardy tucked the sheet around the torso.

"Then there's this." The medical examiner pointed to Lydia's arm. "Note the discoloration just above both elbows. The nature of the bruising indicates that someone had clutched her by both arms, hard, like this."

Pardy turned and pretended to take hold of Cubiak. "You can see the marks where the fingers pressed into her flesh."

"You mean that someone grabbed her and then shoved her down the stairs?"

"No, that's not it. Whoever was holding on to Lydia was standing directly in front of her. If they'd shoved her, she would have tumbled backward, but it's clear from the markings on her body and the way she landed that she fell face first. The more likely scenario is that the bruising occurred before she fell."

"Is there any way to establish a time sequence?"

"The discoloration on her arms is fairly recent, but I can't be more specific. The bruises might have been made anywhere from thirty minutes to three hours before death."

"Or thirty seconds?"

Pardy looked down at the body. "Possibly, but not likely."

"What if Person X took hold of Lydia in the hallway near the top of the stairwell? They argued and then she pulled free and walked toward the stairs. Just as she got there, the assailant came up behind and pushed her."

"There are no bruises on her back."

Cubiak leaned against the counter. "There wouldn't be any, would there? Not from a gentle shove. Lydia looked pretty fragile. A nudge would probably have been enough to send her reeling down the stairs."

"Perhaps," Pardy said. "The deceased had severe osteoporosis, which can affect balance. On the other hand, there are her pants to consider, the wide legs. She could easily have tangled a foot in all that fabric. And she'd been drinking."

"How much?"

"Her blood alcohol level was point zero seven percent, enough to cause impairment of speech and vision, so I'd say she had considerably more than she should have."

"Humph."

"What's that supposed to mean?"

"Her friend John Overly was with her the previous evening. He said they had a glass of sherry and talked until midnight."

"Either she'd been drinking before he arrived or she kept on after he left because she definitely had a lot more than one glass of sherry," Pardy said.

Cubiak paced along the counter. "What about the rest?"

"No indication of recent sexual activity. No sign of drug use. Stomach contents reveal a dinner of shrimp and pasta."

"And the ring?"

"I found nothing to indicate that she wore any rings other than the ones she had on when she died. And she'd worn all of them for a long time. I'd say for years, judging by the indentations in the skin."

The medical examiner repositioned the sheet over the body.

"What is it about this one, Dave?" she asked.

He rubbed his temple. "I don't know. I'd only met her the day before. Maybe it was the burned cookies she served. Or finding the ring on the floor. Maybe it's just too much winter . . . whatever. I realize that the circumstances point to this as an accidental fall, but I can't shake the feeling that there's more to Lydia's death, something I'm not seeing."

THE IMPOSTER

7

After he finished talking to Pardy, Cubiak stopped at the new west side deli for a sandwich and then headed to his office. At work, he tossed his lunch on the desk and was pulling off his parka when the red light on the phone console flashed. Still standing, he pressed the button.

"What is it, Lisa?"

"A call for you on line two." His assistant sounded amused.

The sheriff lobbed his jacket toward the conference table, but as usual he missed, and the jacket landed on the floor. He shrugged, picked up the receiver, and tapped another button. "This is Sheriff Dave Cubiak. How can I help you?" he said. There was no response, as if the words had floated into a distant void. He paused for a moment and then tried again. "Hello? Is anyone there?"

After a moment, the quiet was broken by a muffled cough.

"Who is this?" he asked.

"You left a message for James Dura?" The voice was female, slurred, and heavily accented.

"I did." Cubiak hooked his foot around the leg of his chair and rolled it away from his desk. "Are you Mrs. Dura?"

"That depends on whether or not you're looking for money," the caller drawled.

"I'm looking for information. But before we go on, I must ask again, are you Mrs. James Dura?"

"Was." The clipped response was followed by the sound of liquid being poured into a glass. "I've gone back to using my own name now. In another life I had the misfortune of being married to James for fifteen years. Now, if you are a spiritualist or conjurer with exceptional powers, it appears I might have the misfortune again. I surely hope that's not the case. I was out when you called but I heard the message when I got home. Since then I've been ruminating over the situation, considering whether I should return the call or not."

As she talked, Cubiak sat and reached for a pen. "I'm glad you did, but why wouldn't you?"

"Because I am tired of cleaning up the messes my dear Jimmy left behind. Creditors, bad debts, promissory notes to everybody and their grandmother, insurance scams, what have you. I had half a mind to ignore your call. But, sir, I was raised both a Baptist and an optimist, and I thought that maybe this time it would be different. Don't ask me why. I just had that thought in my mind."

She sipped her drink.

"Where is Door County anyway?"

"Wisconsin."

"Hah. How about that! Way up north, where James went to college. 'On Wisconsin, on Wisconsin . . .'" The caller's rendition of the UW fight song ended in a hiccup. "'Scuse me." More silence. Then "Are you or are you not going to tell me why you called?"

"Actually, I had hoped to speak with James Dura and would appreciate it if you would tell me how to reach your ex-husband."

"Oh, well now, honey, that's near to impossible. And he's not merely my ex. He's my once knight in shining armor, now deceased, and very dead former husband."

This time, Cubiak hesitated. "I'm sorry," he said.

"Don't be. James was a no-good son of a gun. I'd use a stronger word, but like I said before, I was raised Baptist and my parents did not approve of that kind of language."

"Nonetheless, I am sorry. And if you don't mind, I need to make sure that I haven't made a mistake. It's possible that I have confused your late husband with someone else by the same name. In which case, I offer my sincere apologies for disturbing you."

She coughed. "How tall are you, Sheriff?"

He frowned. "What difference does that make?"

"I like to talk to tall men." Ice cubes clinked in the glass. "I'll imagine that you're a tall man. Are you a handsome man as well, Sheriff?"

"No."

"Oh, I'll bet you are."

"Mrs. Dura," he said.

"It's Abigail Vanhausen, but you can call me Abby."

"Ms. Vanhausen, I need just a little more of your time."

Cubiak recited the date and place of birth that he had for James Dura.

"Check and check."

"Played football at the University of Wisconsin in Madison."

"Right again. A campus hero." She sighed. "That's my James."

"And there is no question that this James Dura, the one I just described, is deceased. No chance of mistaken identity, for example."

The voice on the phone grew hard. "It is the same James Dura who sat next to me and drove me home in the rain from a holiday party ten years ago that I was foolish enough to attend with him even though we were no longer wed. The same James Dura who swerved into oncoming traffic for God knows whatever reason and collided head-on with a produce truck. The James Dura who was killed instantly and who left me paralyzed from the waist down."

Cubiak stared at the receiver. After a moment of silence that was matched by her own deep quiet, he forced himself to speak.

"I am truly sorry. For everything," he said.

"I believe you are," she said. Her tone was brisk but not unkind. "Life happens, Sheriff. It happens to all of us. Now if there's anything else?" Instantly, she assumed a businesslike and formal manner.

"Just a couple more things, if I may?" He hated to go on but knew that he had to. "What was your late husband's occupation?"

"James majored in business and was working on his MBA when we got married. He was only into it a couple of months when his father died and he inherited the family supermarket. He managed to buy three more stores and then ran them all into the ground." The ice cubes tinkled again. "Tell me, Sheriff, this James Dura you thought you were calling, what did he say he was?"

"As I understand it, he said he was a petroleum engineer."

"Hah!" Abby Vanhausen guffawed. "Thank you, Sheriff. Thank you for that. You just made my day."

"Before, you said that you were tired of people asking about James. What did you mean?"

"Well, you're not the first is what I meant. Somebody else called inquiring about him. They said they went to school with him."

"Was it a woman?"

"Uh-uh. A man. I don't remember his name, but he said he was on the team with James."

After he hung up, Cubiak searched the internet for James Dura. A newspaper story about the accident came up first. The obituary, second. Both confirmed what Abby Vanhausen had told him about Dura's life and death as well as his own suspicions about Lydia Malcaster's internet suitor.

The man who called himself James Dura and who emailed his way into Lydia's life was an imposter. She had tied her dreams and sent money to someone masquerading as Zack's former roommate and friend.

Cubiak buzzed Rowe. "You're back," he said.

"Just got in. Why?"

"I'm heading up to Lydia's house and need you to come with me."

"Sure. I still got my hat on. I'll meet you outside."

The sheriff snatched his lunch from the desk and picked his coat up from the floor. As the two men drove north, he ran through what he had learned from Pardy about Lydia's death and from Abigail Vanhausen about the real James Dura.

"We've got a snowball's chance in hell of finding who's pretending to be him," Rowe said.

"Maybe," Cubiak said. "If the imposter was part of an international scam, you're probably right. But whoever was doing this knew an awful lot of personal details about Lydia. So much that it makes me wonder if it might not be someone local."

Rowe slowed to maneuver around a traffic circle. "Even so, it's not going to be easy. The internet's a big place to hide."

They were near Carlsville when Cubiak remembered his lunch. "Did you eat?"

Rowe shook his head.

"Here, then. Bon appétit." The sheriff unwrapped his sandwich and gave half to the deputy.

The driveway to Lydia Malcaster's house was unplowed, and coming in, they carved fresh tracks in the snow. Cubiak looked for the cardinal, hoping it had not forsaken the yard, but the bird was nowhere in sight. He ducked under the yellow tape and opened the door to the silent house.

"This way," he said, leading the deputy to Lydia's hideaway. In the small room off the kitchen, her computer sat on the glass-topped desk.

"Whatever went on between Lydia and Dura is in here," the sheriff said, indicating the laptop. "I need to read their correspondence. Can you open it?"

Rowe pulled up a chair and raised the lid. "I'll have to guess at her password but if I get it, I'm in." For several minutes, he tapped at the keyboard, and then the display screen lit up.

"Here goes," he said.

"How'd you do that?" the sheriff asked.

"Easy. I just tried variations of her birthday for the password."

Five minutes later, the printer whirred to life and spat out copies of Lydia's conversations with Dura. Cubiak carried the correspondence into the kitchen and sat at the table that overlooked the garden. To an extent, every death investigation was an invasion of privacy. But reading Lydia's most private thoughts felt close to sacrilegious.

The back-and-forth dialogue between the two started innocently. PD—Phony Dura—extended his condolences on Zack's death and spoke fondly of the university days the two had shared. Some of the stories he related were based on actual events, others were probably pure fabrications, the kinds of things young men said to each other in the middle of the night over one too many drinks, or at the end of a losing game. PD carefully lauded Zack and then began to console Lydia on her loss, subtly reminding her again and again of how much she must miss her husband.

You are a good man and too kind to take the trouble to comfort me, she wrote.

His response: he understood how she felt because he was lonely too. Perhaps, he wrote, by telling her what he was doing—his crazy job in this exotic location that he couldn't reveal—he could help distract her from her own pain. Would that be all right with her?

Of course, she replied.

What followed were colorful descriptions of sandstorms and sun-drenched landscapes, hints at tedious meetings, the challenges of high-level negotiations. Claptrap that painted PD as a successful professional, a man of standards and renown. A man like Zack.

After they had corresponded for a month, PD sent a virtual bouquet of roses. Lydia gushed her thanks. *But you mustn't,* she protested.

How can I not, when it gives me such pleasure to try and brighten your day? he countered.

A week later, more virtual flowers showed up. This time, Lydia's favorites, the blue dahlias.

How did you ever guess?

We are sympatico.

Soon, bouquets and poems arrived daily, and the shared sentiments became more intimate. The phony Dura caressed Lydia with promises, and she replied with such poignancy that Cubiak felt the heavy weight of her need. The scumbag PD would have felt it, too, and snickered.

"Bastard," the sheriff said, staring out from the kitchen window.

When PD mentioned travel, Lydia gleefully jumped on board.

Where would you like to go, my dear?

Lydia sent him her wish list. Easter Island, Machu Picchu, Amazon River . . . the same places she had rattled off to Cubiak.

Make sure your passport is up-to-date. I'll handle everything else, PD told her.

Within a week, the plans were laid and the reservations made. With each leg of the trip, the dollars added up until the sum reached the lofty ninety thousand total that Lydia had cited. Perhaps she felt guilty about the amount of money that this man—whom she had yet to meet in real life—had spent; perhaps she harbored a seed of doubt that fate would bestow such a bounty of good fortune and happiness on her at this stage in life. For whatever reason, Lydia asked to see the itinerary, and PD, confident that the hook was set, emailed her copies of the hotel reservations and the tickets that he had supposedly purchased from the various airlines and cruise lines. True, the imposter didn't ask for a dime, but then he didn't have to because Lydia, of her own volition and with Tracey's encouragement, insisted on paying her way.

The conversations went on, circling and repeating themselves, PD shyly admitting that he was falling in love with her. *Is this even possible?* he mused.

Oh yes, I believe it is. I know it is!!! Lydia said in return.

When he had read enough, Cubiak went to check on Rowe.

"Anything?" he asked.

The deputy shook his head. "Not a trace, but I'll keep trying."

"See what you can verify from these," Cubiak said, laying the travel itinerary on the desk.

He had his own suspicions, which Rowe quickly verified. The hotels that PD had booked were as fictitious as he was. The elaborate travel arrangements he claimed to have made were fabrications. There were no such flights, no such cruises.

"The fucker made up everything," Rowe said.

"True," Cubiak said as he stuffed the papers back into the folder. "But all that tells us is that this guy took advantage of Lydia. It doesn't tell us who he is or if he or someone else killed her."

FIRE AND ICE

8

In Friday's bitter predawn cold, Cubiak slipped out the side door to the deck. His breath came out in clouds that instantly disappeared in the frosty, brittle air. Beneath a charcoal sky, the icy black water scraped against the frozen shoreline like sludge. Cate and Joey and the dog were still inside, asleep and warm. Tempting as it was to stay under the covers, the sheriff had forced himself out of bed with the first alarm because the old-timers never surrendered to the weather. Hot or cold, rain or sleet, they would be at the historic downtown diner when the door opened, and if he wanted to hear what they had to say about local doings, he had to show up early, no matter the season or the conditions.

A hodgepodge of holiday lights glittered along the way into town and gave the ride a festive touch. In the country, the large, old-fashioned Christmas bulbs sparkled red and green and yellow and blue on trees and front porches. But in town, strings of delicate white lights hung in scallops from the eaves of the yacht club and the grand old homes along the frozen bay and laced the downtown shop windows. In a few weeks, the decorations would be taken down and packed away for another year, but until then, they twinkled day and night in defiance of the harsh winter.

For more than a decade, Cubiak had eaten his Friday morning breakfast at the old Sturgeon Bay café. During the early hours, the restaurant was an informal gathering spot for locals. Over black coffee and crisp hash browns they exchanged the kind of information that rarely made it into print or was broadcast on the air and never appeared in social media. It was the kind of talk that revealed people's attitudes and opinions; listening to the gossip was like eavesdropping behind closed doors. Mostly he overheard idle chatter, but he always left the wiser for it, and once, he had gleaned information that helped solve a murder case.

Inside he nodded a greeting to the venerated elders of Door County gathered around the corner table, and then he took his usual seat at the counter and ordered his usual breakfast—the early risers special of two eggs sunny-side up, sausage links, hash browns, and wheat toast. While he waited, a white mug of steaming black coffee was set in front of him with the usual "Morning, Sheriff, you're up early today" that the assistant manager never failed to deliver. Cubiak drank the coffee and listened to the old-timers speculate about the Packers' fading chances for a Super Bowl bid, grumble about the proposed highway expansion, exchange rumors about layoffs at the shipyards, and exclaim over orders for yachts costing upwards of ten million. What he wanted to hear were whispers about Lydia Malcaster and speculations about her death. But no one in the restaurant seemed to be concerned about her. And why should they be? They probably had never met her. Lydia Malcaster had lived in Door County for more than fifty years, but she had existed in a different world from that of the diner's customers.

Cubiak cleaned his plate and lingered over several more cups of coffee before he got up and dropped a ten spot and four singles on the counter. On his way out, he wished the elderly gents a happy new year.

"Another one for the geezers," quipped a wiry man in a red vest.

"Hardly recognized you in that fancy getup," another said. "Where are you going all duded up?"

Cubiak chuckled. He had forgotten that he was wearing a sports coat that day.

"I'm giving a lecture on firearm safety over at the yacht club," he said. "You're all welcome to come."

The men rolled their eyes. They were veteran hunters, experts when it came to handling weapons. "A waste of your time and our taxpayers' money," one of them said.

"You think so?" He reminded them about the three accidental shootings the previous fall: one that involved a novice hunter, one a child, and one a senior citizen.

"Nobody was seriously injured, but people want to know what they could do to protect their families," he said.

Coming from the warm restaurant into the cold was a shock and climbing into the jeep barely helped. The sheriff made a quick U-turn and headed back toward the bay. The sooner he reached the yacht club, the sooner he would be back inside a warm room.

The winter freeze had begun Thanksgiving weekend with the first major snowfall of the season, followed by twelve days of record-breaking cold. For nearly two weeks, temperatures hovered around twenty during the day and dropped below zero at night. By the middle of December, the ice on the bay was thick enough to support the winter fishing fans. The anglers drove their pickups and SUVs out onto the frozen surface, augured holes through the crust, and set up heated wood shacks to keep out the wind and cold. For them, life on the ice was a tradition.

The same ice that supported the winter fishing enthusiasts made it difficult for the lake freighters to reach the Sturgeon Bay shipyards where they lined up for their winter tune-ups and repairs. Several fishing shacks were already in place when the coast guard cutter *Mobile Bay* made its first pass through the Ship Canal and the bay. Gnashing and plowing through ice that was two to three feet thick, the cutter sliced a fifty-foot-wide gutter through the middle of the snow-covered ice field.

To Cubiak, standing at the yacht club's conference room window, the channel of open water looked like a strip of black tar.

"You're too close to the edge, get back," he wanted to shout to the anglers who sauntered casually on the ice and let their dogs run free on the slippery surface. No people or pets had ever fallen into the crevice of frigid water during his tenure as sheriff; no vehicle had ever slid over the lip into the frosty bay, but to the sheriff it seemed the ice fishermen were courting danger, even if it was only one that he could see from where he stood. To them it was business as usual.

"Looks like a toy village, doesn't it?" said a man who joined the sheriff at the large span of glass.

"Or a disaster waiting to happen," Cubiak said. "It's a wonder no one falls in."

The man guffawed and clapped his shoulder. "I wouldn't worry none about that. These folks have been going out there forever. They know what they're—"

Bam! An orange fireball exploded near the far shore. The window rattled. The walls and floor, the tables, the cups and saucers—everything in the room—shuddered.

Across the bay, a wooden fishing hut erupted in flames. Black smoke swirled into the blue sky.

Nearby a woman screamed. At the door, Cubiak yelled over the commotion. "Call nine-one-one."

As he raced down the stairs, the first sirens went off.

When he reached the ground, his phone dinged. Without looking, he knew that the emergency dispatcher was calling him.

"I got it," he said as he ran toward the jeep. "I'm on my way. Get Rowe and every available deputy out here."

The sheriff jumped the jeep over the curb. As he shot out of the lot, his siren joined the chorus of alarms screaming from town. Police. Fire. Ambulance.

In a crisis, with the Sturgeon Bay police chief on vacation, the Door County sheriff was de facto in charge of both departments. Swerving through traffic, Cubiak tore down the street and onto the bridge. Traffic had pulled off to either side, making way for the emergency responders. He was the first across. As he flew over the span, he watched as a handful of people scrambled toward the burning hut. One after another, they darted toward the flames and then fell back.

"Oh, Jesus, somebody's in there," he said under his breath. Then "Go, go," he cried, urging on the would-be rescuers as they struggled for purchase on the ice.

In the few minutes that seemed endless, he was back on land. Now where? It would take precious more time to follow the official road to the shoreline. Instead, he swung off the highway and onto the bumpy shortcut that the anglers had carved through the snow.

At the shoreline, he skidded to a stop and reached for his parka. The passenger seat was empty. He had run out of the yacht club without his jacket.

"Damn." He nabbed a pair of gloves from the console and a crumpled flannel shirt off the back seat.

On the bridge, onlookers massed along the rail and looked down. On the ice, men and women clustered together in stunned silence. Their faces were white from cold and shock. A woman knelt in prayer. Another wept but her sobs were lost in the cacophony of sirens descending on the bay.

In a torrent of shouts and cries, the half-dozen would be rescuers darted toward the burning hut, but each time they were driven back by the heat and the flames. City police and deputies from the sheriff's office joined the effort, but no one could get close to the burning hut.

"Someone was in there?" Cubiak asked.

A tall, burly man answered. "Yeah," he said. He kept his gaze on the wooden shanty. "Bobby Fells. Poor fucker."

Just then the fire truck and ambulance thundered to a stop near the frozen bay. The firefighters scrambled out of the truck and dragged hoses and equipment over the ice toward the blaze.

Within minutes, the fire was under control. Cubiak stood nearby with the fire chief and told him what he had seen from the yacht club and heard from the anglers.

"If anybody's in there, any chance they're gonna make it?"

The fire chief shook his head. Then he looked at the sheriff. "Where the hell's your jacket?"

Instantly Cubiak felt cold. "I'm okay," he said.

"Yeah, well, I wouldn't stay out here long like that if I was you," the chief said.

Cubiak went back to the group of six. "You did everything you could," he said.

"Wasn't enough." The man who had addressed him earlier spoke. This time he turned toward the sheriff. Under his hood, his wool cap was pulled down to his eyes. His cheeks were red from the heat, but ice crystals dotted his beard. His voice was deep and harsh, as if he were challenging the sheriff to sugarcoat the situation.

Cubiak nodded. "Sometimes, it's not."

The man grunted.

"You said Bobby Fells was in there?"

"It's his shack. I saw him go in there last night."

Cubiak stared at the smoldering ruins. A week ago, he had never heard of Bobby Fells; now it seemed he couldn't get away from him. "You're sure?" he said.

"It looked like him, but it was dark out, past midnight. It's his shed. Who else would be going in there?"

The sheriff reached for his pen and notebook and only then remembered that they were in his coat pocket and that the coat was hanging in the yacht club conference room. The full force of the frigid air hit him again and he began to shiver.

A woman in a blue snowmobile suit appeared from nowhere and handed him a cup of hot coffee. Orange curls framed her round face, a reminder of the orange flames that had engulfed the hut.

The burly fisherman nodded as a second cup was thrust at him. He wrapped a thick gloved hand around it and held out the other.

"George Landis," he said. He leaned forward and peered at Cubiak through the cloud of steam that floated up between them. "Jesus, man, look at your face. You're getting frostbite. We gotta get you inside somewhere. My shack's right here. Let's go."

There was no use in protesting. The rest of the small crowd encircled the sheriff and escorted him across the ice behind Landis. Before the sheriff knew what had happened, he was in the shelter sitting in a worn red-plaid recliner. The heat stung his cheeks. The air stank from the smoke and sweat that the anglers had carried into the packed room. The sheriff had lost his cup of coffee on the ice, but his host gave him another—spiked, he said—and went on with his spiel as if there had been no interruption.

"People tend to set up in the same spots every winter. That was Bobby's father's for years. Bobby took it over when the old man died."

The mention of death cast a pall on the room.

"What time was it that you saw him?" Cubiak asked Landis.

"Past midnight. One, two o'clock. I was out here late and fell asleep."

"What about the rest of you?" he asked.

A dark-haired woman spoke up. "I saw some guy there when I was pulling up this morning. It looked like Bobby." She glanced around the room. "Hard to tell though, seeing as how we're all dressed pretty much the same. Plus, it was snowing like the dickens."

"Does anyone else ever use his shack?"

"Not that I know of." Landis pivoted to the others. One after another, they shook their heads.

"Did any of you notice anything unusual this morning?" the sheriff said.

Again, the answer was no.

"What about Bobby's vehicle?"

"The only thing I ever seen him in was an old green pickup, but it ain't here now. Maybe he left it on shore or his sister dropped him off. I seen her do that a couple of times," Landis said.

"Did anything like this ever happen before?" Cubiak said.

"No. We're all real careful." Landis's response was echoed five times over.

Using a borrowed pen and the back of an old receipt from someone's pocket, the sheriff recorded the names and phone numbers of the people who had tried to save Bobby Fells.

"I suppose you're gonna want us to give statements," Landis said.

"It's a matter of procedure, and I know this has been a tough day for all of you." In the cramped quarters, Cubiak shook hands with each of the four men and two women.

He was at the door when Landis handed him a black parka. Strips of camo duct tape sealed several holes on the front. "It's a spare. Take it, you'll need it," he said.

Outside the hut, Cubiak was grateful for the jacket. A heavy layer of clouds had blown in from the west, and without the sun, the temperature continued to drop. Bobby Fells's shack was a heap of smoldering timber when Emma Pardy arrived. In another ten minutes, the fire was out.

The body of a man was found inside.

Also found: a space heater and propane generator.

"This was either an accident or arson," Cubiak told the medical examiner.

He reported the incident to the Appleton Field Office of the state Division of Criminal Investigation. Due to the holidays, the office was short-staffed. It would be at least forty-eight hours before anyone could be sent to examine the body, assess the site, and analyze any items recovered with the body or from the shed to determine the cause of the explosion and fire.

In the meantime, Pardy would conduct an autopsy and prepare detailed drawings of the burns on the victim's body. Before the corpse could be moved, the scene had to be photographed and every detail carefully recorded. By midafternoon, Cubiak and his deputies had completed the work, erected a canopy to protect the burned-out shelter from the elements, and cordoned off the area.

Cubiak watched as the EMTs prepared to move the body to the morgue.

"You okay, sir?" Rowe said, coming up behind him.

The sheriff crossed his arms against his chest and rocked back and forth. He couldn't remember ever being this cold. "I'm fine. Better off than that poor bastard, Bobby Fells," he said, indicating the charred hut.

Cubiak kicked a chip of ice and sent it skittering across the frozen bay. "I don't like it. Two suspicious deaths in one week."

"Could be a coincidence," Rowe said.

"Maybe," Cubiak said, rubbing his arms. "But you know what I think of that kind of thing."

The sheriff looked up at the handful of onlookers who remained on the bridge. "What I want to know is, where's Bobby's sister? Why isn't she here? By now, word must have gotten around that it was Bobby's shed that burned. Someone would have called Tracey, don't you think?"

"She could be working up north."

"Still, she'd have heard by now. If it was your brother, you'd drop whatever you were doing, job or no job. I'd expect her to race down here to see if he was okay."

"Maybe she's sick. She could be home in bed with the phone turned off."

"That would be another coincidence, wouldn't it?"

Cubiak turned toward his deputy. "There's nothing more we can do here. I'll go see if I can find her."

THE OAK TREE ARMS

9

Stiff with cold, the sheriff staggered over the ice. Everything hurt. His knees buckled. His fingers tingled. His cheeks burned and his lips cracked. Despite the borrowed parka layered over the old flannel shirt, the cold seeped into the very marrow of his bones. The jeep cut the wind but that wasn't enough. Even with the heat on high, he felt a flood of ice pebbles coursing through his veins. Beads of sweat rose along his neck, but his body refused to thaw.

Cubiak stabbed Tracey's number into his cell. No answer, and her mailbox was full.

Maybe he was being too cynical. Maybe Rowe was right, and she was at home, sick in bed. He wished he could go home. He would take a long, hot shower and drink a hot toddy in front of a roaring fire. But when he reached the highway, instead of taking a right and heading for Jacksonport, he turned left and drove toward the Oak Tree Arms, a new apartment complex on the other side of town, where Tracey lived. He would tell her the sad news first and then fix a cup of tea for her. He would sit with her for as long as necessary. He would ask if there was someone he could call and make sure she was okay, or as okay as she could be under the circumstances. He would be gentle but would ask the questions that needed answering: How often did Bobby use the shack? Had he had any problems out there before? Was he in any kind of trouble? Did he have any enemies? Was there anyone she could think of who would want to hurt her brother?

In town, he passed the shop windows with their holiday decorations and twinkling lights, but the gaiety escaped him. Death dulled the world, and now he had two deaths to investigate. In life, Lydia Malcaster and Bobby Fells were linked by a tenuous relationship, and although each had died as the result of an apparent accident, Cubiak sensed a connection, a link he hadn't discovered yet.

He was mulling over the situation when he reached the Oak Tree Arms, a U-shaped complex stuck in the middle of a barren, wind-swept field. Tracey lived at the west end in Unit 312 of Building A. Her car wasn't in the lot. He cruised the other parking areas as well, but the gray compact wasn't in either one. Undeterred, he circled back to the first structure. A sign on the outside door warned against soliciting. One inside read Manager on Site.

Ringing the bell for Apartment 312 was like calling her number: no answer. Tracey's physical mailbox was stuffed as well. A half-dozen catalogs lay in disarray on the floor beneath it. The inner door was propped open. Cubiak slipped through and started up the stairs. On the second-floor landing, he stopped and massaged his left hip. He wished he could blame the cold for the discomfort, but this was a different kind of pain, one he had been experiencing for several months.

The previous fall, when Evelyn Bathard had shown him the X-ray results and suggested that he was a candidate for a hip replacement, Cubiak had waved off the notion. If it came to surgery, surely it wouldn't be for years, he insisted. His doctor friend had smiled. "There is no predicting," he said.

On the third floor, the sheriff rubbed his hip again. After he caught his breath, he started down the long gray hall to Tracey's apartment. The door of 312 was decorated with a Welcome plaque and a green plastic wreath. He knocked, but again there was no response. Save for the soft murmur of a distant television, the building was quiet. He leaned into the door, hoping to catch a hint of movement inside, but all he heard was the whine of a truck accelerating on the highway. He called her number again, and again there was no answer and no way to leave a message.

He needed to get inside the apartment.

The building manager was at his desk unwrapping a piece of apple pie when Cubiak stepped in from the hall. He glanced at the visitor's shabby jacket. "No vacancies," he said, despite the sign to the contrary on the front door.

Cubiak flashed his badge and asked him to unlock the door to the missing woman's apartment.

"Now? It's my break time." The manager eyed the pastry sitting in front of him on a piece of wrinkled waxed paper.

"Yes, now." Cubiak read the name plate on the desk: L. Abels.

"You got a warrant?" Abels said, running a hand through his thinning hair.

"Mr. Abels, I got an emergency. Tracey Fells's brother was killed this morning, and I have reason to believe her life may be in danger. Do you want that on your hands?"

"Jesus, no." The pie forgotten, Abels scrambled to his feet.

The manager was a complainer. Trudging up the stairwell, he grumbled about the job, his boss, and the tenants—not Tracey, never a peep from her. When they reached the door to 312, he grew serious and rubbed his hands vigorously.

"First time I ever had to do this," Abels said as he inserted the key into the lock.

Before the manager could turn the key, the sheriff grabbed his arm and motioned him away from the door. "I'll go first," he said.

"Why?" Abels looked puzzled and disappointed to have his grand adventure aborted.

"Because I said so."

Because this morning her brother's shack exploded on the bay. Because there's no way to know what will happen when I open the door to her apartment . . .

The sheriff stood at arm's length and grabbed the knob.

"What's wrong?" The manager pressed his face forward as far as he dared.

"Nothing."

"Why aren't you going in?"

"I will."

Cubiak held his breath and twisted the knob.

The moment passed and he exhaled.

"Wait here," he said to Abels as he stepped into the cramped entrance.

The apartment was hot and filled with the kind of quiet that an empty space envelops. When he was sure it was safe to proceed, he moved past the jumble of shoes and boots that littered the floor.

Three steps took him to an oblong, sparsely furnished living room. It had a crumpled, forgotten look. A row of droopy plants lined a plastic wall shelf. Dust motes danced in an errant ray of sunlight that poured through uncurtained windows. A red sweater and black bra hung over the arm of a torn leather sofa. Jeans and leggings draped the back of the only chair in the room. Dirty dishes and piles of magazines and discarded mail littered the chipped coffee table. There was a similar mess in the kitchen. In the bathroom a worn toothbrush lay on the sink, and a ridge of black mold rimmed the edge of the tub.

The bedroom stood in contrast to the rest of the apartment. The bed was made. Polka-dotted curtains covered the window. A rainbow of scarves hung from a rack of wooden pegs.

Prints of waterfalls and sunsets decorated one wall. Framed photographs filled another. The largest showed a freckle-faced young woman and two small children sitting on a beach. Tracey and her brother, most likely, with their mother or perhaps an aunt. There were graduation and prom pictures of Tracey and of a gangly teenage boy he assumed was her brother. He snapped pictures of the images with his phone.

"Well?" the manager asked when the sheriff reappeared. His parka was still zipped.

"There's no one here and it looks like she's been gone for a few days," he said.

Abels grunted. "Doesn't surprise me none. Who knows what these kids are up to these days. Half the time they're not even here."

"What makes you say that?"

"I count the cars in the lot before I turn in for the night."

"You live here?"

"I got a studio downstairs; it comes with the job."

"When's the last time you saw Tracey Fells?"

The manager shrugged. "Can't say, Sheriff. I only know the people by what they drive. Her car comes and goes a lot, but it's usually here at night." He scratched his chin. "Though now that I think about it, I can't remember the last time I saw it. Only thing I can tell you is that it's not here now."

From the apartment complex, it was a short drive to the justice center. Lights twinkled on the faux Douglas fir in the lobby, and silver streamers looped the hall, but the usual cheerful chatter had given way to silence. Even the phones had stopped ringing. In the break room, a trio of deputies sat at the table and stared into cups of coffee. They looked up as the sheriff walked past and then dropped their gaze.

In the radio room, Cubiak issued an APB for Tracey Fells. Then in his office, he buzzed Lisa and asked her to come in.

As soon as he saw his assistant, he knew that she had heard the news about the explosion and fire.

"Are you okay?" he asked.

She nodded and slipped into one of the two chairs that faced his desk.

"You look tired," she said.

Cubiak smiled. Lisa was young enough to be his daughter, but she spoke with motherly concern. "Just cold," he said, and flexed his fingers. "I only hope to hell it was an accident."

Lisa blanched. "What else . . . ?" She stopped.

"Just me being paranoid," he said.

"Right."

"I need everything you can get on Bobby Fells. Current address, his mother's name and address or that of the nearest living relatives. Friends, coworkers. You know the drill."

"Doesn't he have a sister?"

"Yeah, Tracey. I went to her apartment to tell her about the fire, but she wasn't there. She hasn't answered my texts either."

"She must know about Bobby by now."

"You'd think so."

"If I was her, I'd go straight to the emergency room, hoping he was there, hurt but alive."

Cubiak gave Lisa a long, steady look. "You're wise beyond your years," he said as he reached for the phone.

"Who are you calling?"

"The hospital."

But Tracey hadn't been there either.

It was dark by the time the sheriff left for home.

Cate waited at the door.

"I heard what happened," she said as he came in. She reached for his parka. "What are you wearing?"

Cubiak held his arms out. His parka was blue but the one he had on was black. Then he remembered. "One of the fishermen loaned it to me. I left mine at the yacht club."

He stood under the hot shower for so long that he worried the steam might melt the paint off the walls.

When Cate ladled out bowls of barley soup for supper, he figured that his wife had previously undisclosed telepathic abilities.

She told him that she had been working all day and apologized for the light meal.

"It's perfect, exactly what I need. This and a hot toddy," he said.

MISTAKEN IDENTITY

10

On Saturday, the day after the explosion and fire that killed Bobby Fells, Cubiak headed back to the morgue. Two days earlier, he had been in the ice room listening to Emma Pardy's report on the death of Lydia Malcaster. He had dreaded that visit, and he dreaded this one more. He arrived to find the medical examiner standing over the charred body that had been found in the burned shack.

"You're here, good," she said. Pardy's manner was more clipped than usual, but under the circumstances the sheriff didn't take umbrage. He averted his eyes from the corpse and tried not to imagine the horror of having to work on it.

Pardy made a quick note in a chart. Then she dropped it on the counter and turned a grim face toward the sheriff. He always thought of her as young and was surprised by the wisp of gray hair along her temple. The morgue's bright light playing tricks, he thought.

"I'll give you all the particulars later," the medical examiner said. "But for now, the most important fact is that this not the body of Robert Fells."

Cubiak started. "What?" His gaze automatically shifted to the table. He winced and then looked back to her.

"What do you mean it's not Bobby Fells?"

"The body was burned beyond recognition, and I had to rely on dental records to make a positive identification," Pardy said as she pulled off her gloves. "I've had cases where it took weeks to track down the information but, in this instance, I was lucky. Bobby's dentist was a local practitioner, and her office forwarded the records immediately."

The medical examiner tossed the gloves in the trash. "There's no match, Dave. This isn't Bobby."

"You're sure of that?" Cubiak gave her an apologetic nod. "No offense meant."

"None taken. I know you have to ask. And under the circumstances I'm as surprised as you. Poor man, whoever he is," she said.

Pardy picked up the chart. She had barely glanced at it before she put it down again and looked back at him. "There are times it gets to me. So much unnecessary death."

She retrieved the chart one more time and then picked up three plastic evidence bags from the counter. "Would you mind if we continued this discussion somewhere else?"

The medical examiner was at the double doors when she spoke. Cubiak followed, grateful to be out of the cold and away from the disfigured corpse.

"You wouldn't happen to have a cigarette, would you?" the sheriff said as they walked down the hall.

Pardy glanced back and rolled her eyes. "I don't smoke."

"I know. Neither do I. Not anymore. But at times like this . . ."

"There are always times like this," she said.

The exchange ended and they were silent until they reached a small, vacant room at the end of the corridor.

"This'll do," Pardy said as she settled behind a chipped table.

She scanned her notes and returned to the business at hand.

"The deceased presents as a healthy adult male. Five feet, eleven inches. Approximately one hundred seventy-five pounds. Between the ages of twenty-five and thirty-five. No sign of underlying diseases. Blood alcohol level point two four. Cause of death, asphyxiation as evidenced by the presence of soot in his lungs. Time of death . . ." She faltered and looked at the sheriff. "You'd know that better than I."

Cubiak rested his elbows on the table. "The shed exploded and burned at nine a.m. I guess that makes it the approximate time of death."

Pardy made a quick notation.

"No signs of foul play?"

"Not as far as I can determine."

"And he was alive when the fire broke out?"

"Alive, yes, but judging from the amount of liquor he'd consumed, I'd guess that he was passed out cold. He probably died without ever regaining consciousness."

The sheriff exhaled sharply. "Still a lousy way to go."

Pardy brushed a strand of hair off her face. The lock of gray was real. "What's wrong with these guys? Why do they have to drink so much? What the hell are they trying to prove?"

"Their manliness?"

"More like their stupidity." She sighed. "I have a son. I worry . . ."

Cubiak's phone chirped but he ignored it. "What else?" he said.

Pardy indicated the plastic bags in front of them. "Here are the victim's keys, wallet, and cell, or what's left of them. I don't know if you can get anything off the phone, but the case is singed, as are the wallet and the contents, so no legible IDs either," she said as she slid the evidence bags to the sheriff.

"We won't get any prints, but the state tech team might be able to pull something off the phone, and we can use the keys to try to find the victim's vehicle. All the cars and trucks at the bay that morning were accounted for, so it's got to be somewhere else."

Pardy nodded. "There is one more thing," she said. "His footwear."

"What do you mean?"

"Most people who spend time out on the ice dress for the cold. They're especially careful about keeping their feet warm. Most of them prefer insulated boots, the kind you'd use for snowmobiling. The victim was wearing steel-toed shoes."

"Work shoes?" the sheriff said.

"That'd be my guess."

"Maybe that's all he owned or maybe he wasn't planning on being out on the ice. It could also mean that he worked construction or had a job at the shipyards, anywhere really, maybe at one of the factories around here or in Green Bay. We'll start asking around to see if anyone didn't show up for work yesterday. It's not much by itself, but it's a start."

THE TRAILER
IN THE WOODS

Pardy's discovery added new urgency to the situation. Cubiak needed to recruit extra hands. As soon as the medical examiner returned to the morgue, he started calling his staff to see who was available to work that Saturday afternoon. Lisa and Rowe and several other deputies all signed on.

"I'll meet you in an hour," he said.

As Cubiak headed back to the justice center, a towering ridge of dark clouds stretched along the western horizon like a mountain range. For a moment the sheriff imagined that he was driving toward the Rockies. The snow would start soon, and he wondered if the people out west were skiing in the same snow that was heading toward Door County. Maybe some day he would go skiing.

In the incident room, he told the skeleton crew what he had learned from Pardy. The reaction was a mix of relief and shock. Those who knew Bobby Fells were relieved that he wasn't the man killed in the explosion and fire, but they were all stunned by the news that they were dealing with a John Doe.

"We need to find out who died in the fire and how he was linked to Bobby Fells," Cubiak said.

He tasked a junior deputy with combing through recent missing persons files and another with tracking Tracey Fells's movements since

Wednesday, when the sheriff had talked to her at Lydia Malcaster's house.

Rowe was assigned to help the Sturgeon Bay Police search for the vehicle that belonged to the man who died in the fire.

"It's possible, but unlikely, that the victim drove there himself and someone else drove away in his vehicle using a second set of keys. But an eyewitness is pretty sure he saw Bobby Fells at the shack last night, so the most likely scenario is that the two men drove to the fishing shack together. For whatever reason, Bobby left and the John Doe stayed. If we can find his vehicle, we'll be able to identify him. Knowing who he was may help us locate Bobby as well. If they were hanging out together, someone would have seen them."

Rowe asked the question that was on everyone's mind: "Why wouldn't Bobby come forward on his own?"

"If the two of them argued about something, Bobby might think he'll be blamed for the man's death. Even if the explosion was accidental, he could feel guilty about what happened." Cubiak paused. "Or Bobby's got another reason to hide from us, in which case, we need to find out what it is."

At a few minutes after two, Lisa texted Fells's address to the sheriff.

The location was southeast of town, far from the glittery world of festivals and fish boils that attracted two million visitors annually to the area. He entered the address into the jeep's GPS and pulled out of the lot. He was barely half a mile away when the snow started to come down.

In a normal winter, the department would be dealing with traffic accidents caused by the bad weather, a scattering of domestic abuse cases, a half-dozen drug deals gone bad, and a few reports of petty theft or burglaries.

This was not a normal winter. This was the January of a body found at the base of a staircase, an unidentified corpse pulled from a charred fishing shack, and two missing siblings.

Less than nine days after New Year's Eve, when the three-hundred-pound cherry dropped in Sister Bay to celebrate the holiday, Lydia Malcaster tumbled to her death. Her fatal fall appeared to be accidental, but for Cubiak there were too many unsettling circumstances.

Most suspicious was Lydia's internet relationship with the person pretending to be James Dura, a man who had been dead for a decade. The sheriff registered other irregularities as well: the unlocked front door and the open downstairs door the morning the body was discovered, the Remington bronze clutched to her breast, and the bruises on her arms. Separately each could be explained away, but taken together they formed a puzzling web of circumstances that became more tangled when the recent events involving the brother and sister duo of Bobby and Tracey Fells were added to the mix.

He had to take the siblings into consideration because both had worked for Lydia. There was no connection between her death and the death of the unidentified man found in a burned-out ice-fishing hut—except that the hut belonged to Bobby Fells. There was no way to link Lydia's fall with the fire or with Tracey's apparent disappearance, but that didn't mean the incidents weren't intertwined. It only meant that he hadn't uncovered the link yet.

Cubiak was five minutes from his destination when conditions disintegrated. Heavy sheets of snow whipped across the road and cut visibility to less than an eighth of a mile. Hunched over the wheel, he crept down one county road and then another, heading toward the southeast portion of the county.

When he arrived at the address Lisa had given him, Cubiak inched onto the shoulder and set the flashers on the jeep. He was only six miles from Sturgeon Bay, in a part of the county that was filled with dairy farms and cherry orchards, but the frozen, forlorn landscape around him felt a world apart. As he stepped out into the storm, a howling wind caught his breath. Frozen snow pellets peppered his cheeks and clouded his glasses.

Half blind, Cubiak trudged back and forth through the snow, searching for a sign of life. There was no mailbox, no overhead power lines, nothing to indicate that anyone lived there. He was about to give up when he spotted a fire sign nearly buried in a drift. Ducking beneath the low-hanging branch of a sprawling cedar, he waded to the sign and dug it out of the snow. The numbers confirmed that he was in the right place. So where was Bobby's house?

The sheriff retraced his steps to the road and scanned the woods again. There was a break in the snow and as he looked, he noticed an opening in the trees, a gap just wide enough for a small vehicle. There weren't any tracks in the snow, but given the way the wind was blowing, it wouldn't have taken long for a trail to be covered.

The sheriff started forward again. Within minutes he was enveloped by the forest. In the distance, a cow bellowed. The mournful cry shivered through the icy air and then faded to a heavy silence. In the stillness, the crunch of his boots on the snow sounded like the rumble of an invading army, but Cubiak felt very alone. He patted his jacket to make sure he had the search warrant. The document gave him legal access to Fells's premises, and while he had no reason to fear the young man for whom he was searching, caution made him slip his gun from the holster and into his pocket.

Trudging through the woods, he lost track of time and distance. Walking was an effort. He had no idea how far he had come or how long he had been slogging through the trees when he saw a splash of red between the bare branches. The sheriff pushed forward several more yards and emerged in a small clearing where the snow fell quietly on a faded red trailer. Perched on stacks of gray cinder blocks, the trailer looked like an old boxcar that had been stripped of its wheels and put out to pasture. Snow mounded the metal steps and piled halfway up the door and drifted against the jumble of wooden crates underneath the structure. A small rusty shed stood at the far end of the trailer, nestled close like a baby hedgehog that was trying to hug its mother for warmth. The shed was too small for a pickup but large enough for a snowmobile. Again, there were no tracks, but wind and snow would have covered those.

It was a lonely spot made more isolated by the snow and cold.

A padlock hung on the trailer door. Either no one was home or someone was locked inside. The stairs shook under his weight. He knocked but there was no answer. When he tugged the handle, the door gave way unexpectedly, tipping him backward against the flimsy railing.

"Damn." He caught his breath and recovered his balance. Then he ducked his head and stepped into the dim interior.

The air inside was stale and felt colder than the frigid outdoors. The sheriff shivered and took shallow, quick breaths. As his eyes adjusted to the light, the living room came into focus. The furnishings, scaled to fit the cramped quarters, were chipped and worn. Tattered yellow curtains hung over the frost-layered windows. Tangles of clothes and carryout trays and food bags littered the floor and chair. Cubiak shoved several large trash bags off the compact sofa, hoping he wouldn't find a body hidden beneath them.

Wary of the black mold that climbed up the wall like decorative lace, he moved through the confined quarters. In the miniature kitchen, he opened a cabinet to two dishes, three cups, and a pair of shot glasses. Behind another door, he found open boxes of cereal and macaroni and cheese. A serrated knife and handful of plasticware lay scattered in a drawer. A dented pot and a rusty cast-iron skillet nearly filled the tiny oven. The trailer was a homage to careless living. A pair of boots lay in the corner of the bedroom and a pair of torn boxer shorts were on the floor of the miniature closet. More mold was flowering on the torn plastic curtain in the tiny shower stall.

Cubiak returned to the living room and flipped the light switch. The overhead fixture didn't respond. He opened the refrigerator. The interior light was dark and the carton of milk on the middle shelf was frozen. He tried the kitchen faucet. Nothing. He went back to the bathroom and lifted the lid on the toilet. The bowl was empty.

Bobby Fells had been absent for some time. For certain he hadn't been there after he left his friend in the ice-fishing shack.

The sheriff stepped outside. The wind had shifted and was blowing off the lake. Even with the water a half mile away and the grove of trees to buffer the force, the breeze stung but he was grateful for the fresh air. Tightening his hood over his wool hat, he tromped around the perimeter. He found a generator near the water pipes, but there was no juice running through the meter and the pipes were intact. Without heat in the trailer, they would have frozen and burst by now unless they had been drained. The shed was filled with the same tomblike damp as the trailer, but it was empty.

By the time Cubiak reached the jeep, he was colder than ever. Leaning into the warm air that blew from the vents, he wondered if the ordeal on the bay had permanently chilled his body. Bathard would scoff at the notion, but he would ask him anyway. The sheriff pulled off a glove and tried Rowe's number. The phone rang several times and went to voice mail. He left a message. "Looks like Bobby shut the place down before the first hard freeze. He hasn't lived here all winter."

Where the hell are you? What are you hiding from? Cubiak wondered. He texted Lisa with instructions to check local motels for the missing man. His deputies were looking for the vehicle that belonged to the unidentified dead man, but maybe they should be searching for Fells's pickup as well. If he was sleeping in the cab, he could freeze to death.

Just as Cubiak shifted into drive, his phone dinged with a text from Rowe. *Abandoned vehicle found.*

Where?

Old Gray Mare. Rowe typed in the address of a bar in Southern Door.

The sheriff checked his GPS. The tavern was less than five miles from Bobby Fells's trailer. *On my way.*

THE OLD GRAY MARE

12

Cubiak made an awkward turn on the snow-packed road and followed the directions to the Old Gray Mare. Door County was home to some sixty bars, taverns, and saloons. The businesses ranged from upscale establishments that catered to tourists to the kind of down-home, hole-in-the-wall joints many locals preferred, where food was an afterthought limited to peanuts, pickled eggs, and microwave pizza. He was familiar with many of the businesses, but not the low, sprawling building that sat at the junction of two county roads like a giant domino piece. The walls were painted black and festooned with murals of white-spotted gray horses. The marquee was dark but smoke streamed from the chimney and light radiated from a ceiling fixture that glowed through a high front window. A sign on the red door read Good Food, Cold Beer, Friendly Folks.

Just as Cubiak pulled up alongside Rowe's cruiser, the door banged opened and the deputy stepped out into the gray light. He was bare headed. His jacket flapped open, and he wore only one glove. Ah, youth, thought the sheriff, who was busy trying to zip his parka shut.

With his bare hand, Rowe gestured over his shoulder. "It's out back," he said.

"Can't we drive?" Cubiak muttered to himself.

But Rowe was striding toward the corner, pulling his hat over his ears as he walked.

Cubiak sighed and got out. After a few more seconds of fiddling with the zipper, he gave up and with his parka open trailed after his deputy.

Wisps of fresh powder blew off the top of the five-foot-high wall of plowed snow that rimmed the large parking lot. The two vehicles up front belonged to the sheriff and his deputy. The rear lot was empty except for four dumpsters and a large snow-covered hump. The aroma of grilled meat hung heavy in the air.

"The owner got a call this afternoon from the guy who does his plowing to ask what he should do about the truck parked in back. I was getting lunch when I overheard the snowplow guy talking about it. When I asked, he said the proprietor told him to talk to the manager about it. It sounded like a wild goose chase, but I came over anyway to check, and it turns out it's the one we've been looking for."

"How do you know?"

Rowe pulled a key from his pocket and depressed the unlock button. There was a click and then the vehicle's antitheft system beeped, and taillights flashed red through the layer of snow.

"I'll be damned," Cubiak said. Hunching his shoulders, he grappled with the zipper again. "Damn nuisance," he said, and let it be. "Get the plate number and we'll call it in."

They were sweeping snow off the vehicle when the back door of the bar swung open and a stout, bearded man stepped out. "That thing yours? About time you moved it. I was going to call the sheriff if it wasn't outta here by this evening."

"You own this place?" Cubiak said.

"Nope. I just run the joint."

"Well then, Mister, we saved you the trouble of the call," Cubiak said, uncovering the badge on his belt.

The manager grinned. "My lucky day, huh? Hell, man, you guys better come inside before you freeze your balls off," he said.

In the small rear hallway, Cubiak radioed for a tow while Rowe called in the plate number.

"Let's wait here, until you hear back," the sheriff said as he stomped snow from his boots.

A few minutes later, Rowe's phone dinged with the reply.

"The truck belongs to a Kyle Murphy," he said.

"Where does he live?"

"Algoma."

"Ah," Cubiak said. "Let's go find out if this is his usual watering hole."

At the bar, the bartender had cups of hot coffee waiting. "I put a little something extra in there, to take the edge off," he said as he slid the mugs toward the lawmen. "Yeah, yeah, I know you're on duty. But it's damn cold out there."

Cubiak gave a nod and he and Rowe picked up the drinks.

"Thanks," the sheriff said, grateful for the burn down his throat. With his hands wrapped around the hot mug, he studied the reflection of the room in the bar mirror. The place had a warm, friendly feel, candles on tables and walls made of old pallets. Hundreds of names and inscriptions were scrawled in ink or etched into the soft wood. It was the kind of place where even a stranger would feel welcome.

"That truck out back is registered to a Kyle Murphy. You wouldn't happen to know him, would you?" Cubiak asked.

"Kyle? Yeah, sure, he's a regular, more or less. What's this all about? He's not in some kind of trouble, is he?"

The sheriff explained why they had been searching for the vehicle.

The bartender spread his large hands on the bar and leaned into them. "Oh man. No, no. I heard about all that. You think it's Kyle who died in the fire?"

"We don't know who it is."

"Yeah, okay. I wouldn't wish that on anybody, but when it's maybe someone you know . . ." He let the thought trail off.

"What can you tell me about Kyle?"

The barman shrugged. "He's just a regular guy. Kinda quiet. Kept to himself mostly."

"When's the last time he was here?"

"Thursday night."

"You're sure?"

The manager swiped a white rag over the mahogany bar. "I had a full house that evening. The joint was packed with people watching the game, and both rooms were taken too." He nodded to twin private rooms off the back. "When it's that crowded, I'm usually too busy to notice much of anything, unless there's trouble."

"And was there?"

The bartender frowned. "It didn't exactly get that far. But Kyle was with two other people, and the three of them were making quite a racket. At least the other guy was—the woman with them kept trying to get him to shush up."

"Do you know who the other guy was?"

"Naw."

"What about the woman?"

"She seemed kinda familiar, but I can't say for sure."

"Were the men arguing?" Rowe asked.

"Not really. In fact, Kyle didn't seem to be saying much of anything. It was the other guy who was shooting off his mouth. They were sitting down there." He lifted his chin toward the end of the bar. "The loud-mouth friend was ordering rounds of top-shelf stuff, too—I tend to notice things like that. Anyway, the more they drank, the louder he got."

"Louder like how? Belligerent?" Cubiak asked.

"No, loud like he had the world by the tail. Bragging that he'd found an easy way to get rich quick. Lotta hot air, if you ask me. Finally some guy in the back room came out and yelled for him to shut up."

"What happened then?"

"The windbag quieted down for a few minutes, but then he started up again, even louder than before. After a while someone from the other room got up and slammed the door."

Cubiak showed the manager his phone with Tracey's prom photo. "Do you recognize her?"

The bartender pulled a pair of glasses from his pocket and slid them over his nose as he bent toward the image. "It sure looks like the woman who was here that night," he said.

"How about him?" Cubiak clicked to the photo of the man he believed to be Bobby Fells.

The manager snickered. "Oh yeah, no doubt. That's the asshole who was making all the noise."

"You didn't happen to overhear anything else he said?"

The barkeep laughed. "Are you kidding, Sheriff? I got six TVs blaring, and with all the other yapping going on, I wasn't paying much attention to them. A couple of times that I glanced that way, Kyle was just sitting there and grinning like a drunk fool. Then I looked and they were gone."

"Did you know the man who told them to be quiet?"

"I couldn't see who that was, but the guy who shut the door on them was John Overly."

Cubiak almost spilled his coffee. "The accountant?"

The manager went on. "The only John Overly I know. My folks used to have a business up north, and he took care of our books for us. John's one of those bird lovers. There's a whole group of them that get together every couple of months. I think John steers them here occasionally out of a sense of loyalty, which I appreciate. They don't drink a lot, but they always order wings and a couple of pizzas and go about their business in a civilized way. I like having them here, gives the place a bit of polish, you know."

By the time the tow truck arrived, a half-dozen customers had filed into the bar, and the bartender was busy taking orders for burgers, beers, and shots. Cubiak laid down a twenty and then he and Rowe slipped out the back. The thermometer by the door registered zero.

"Maybe it's broken," Rowe said.

Cubiak laughed.

"What do you think happened after Kyle and Bobby left?" he asked as the truck was loaded onto the flatbed.

"I assume that they drove off together in Bobby's pickup and eventually ended up at the fishing shack. Bobby had to be there to unlock the door, right? My guess is that once they got inside, Kyle passed out. Bobby left him there to sleep it off and then went home—wherever that is—to do the same."

The sheriff nodded.

"Would he have left the heater on?"

"Sure. He didn't want his friend to freeze to death."

"Yeah, well . . ." Cubiak looked up into the falling snow, struck by the irony of what his deputy said. "I'll have Kyle's vehicle dusted for prints tomorrow."

"Why bother?"

"Why not? We may find something helpful. You never know. Sometimes you get lucky."

"I thought you didn't believe in luck," Rowe said.

"I don't." Cubiak scooped a handful of snow and tossed it in the air. "If we find anything useful, it's because we looked."

LADIES IN WAITING

13

The report on Kyle Murphy's truck arrived a few minutes before noon on Monday. The tech team's findings confirmed the sheriff's predictions. The technicians hadn't pick up any prints on the outside of the vehicle, which was expected because it was winter and people wore gloves. Inside, however, the investigators recovered a full set. Two hands. Ten digits. Given the extent of the victim's injuries from the fire, forensics wouldn't be able to pull any prints from the body, and without any on file, there was nothing with which to make a comparison. Until anyone proved otherwise, Cubiak had to assume the prints from the truck belonged to the dead man.

He saved the file. So much for luck. At least the snow had stopped and the sun was out. He took his jacket and headed for the door.

Twenty minutes later, he was at a nearby restaurant, crumbling oyster crackers into a bowl of steaming clam chowder. He was about to dig in when his phone rang. The call was local. The sheriff answered.

"Sheriff Cubak?" The high-pitched voice of L. Abels, the manager of the Oak Tree Arms apartment complex, streamed out at him.

"Cubiak."

"Right, like I said, *Cubak*. You know how you told me to call if I thought of anything else?" Abels rattled on, not trying to hide his excitement. "Well, after you left the other day—you know when you came here looking for Tracey Fells? I got to thinking and I figured that if Tracey wasn't in her apartment maybe she was at her brother's place. I mean, Tracey's car wasn't here when you come by, but that doesn't mean she wasn't here, does it? Anyways, that's what I got to thinking."

"I've already checked his place," the sheriff said. He couldn't imagine Tracey seeking shelter in the trashed trailer and didn't think it was necessary to tell the manager that it had been vacant as well.

"Where'd you get the key?"

"I didn't need one."

Abels made a noise. "You can't get into any of the apartments here without a key."

Cubiak pushed the bowl of chowder aside. "Bobby Fells has an apartment at the complex?"

"Yeah."

"Why didn't you tell me this when I was there last Friday?"

The apartment manager cleared his throat. "You didn't ask me, did you? You asked about Tracey and didn't say nothing about Bobby. Besides, he's only been here a few months. I can't keep track of everybody."

"Have you seen him recently?"

"Not that I can recall, but like I said, I can't—"

Cubiak was on his feet. "I'll need to get in there," he said as he dug for his wallet.

"You have to have a warrant."

"I already do." He was fudging the details. The warrant in the glove box was for the address for the trailer in Southern Door, but he could have it augmented.

"Glad I could be of service," Abels said, his voice puffed with importance once again. "I'm here until three if you want to come by."

The sheriff reached the complex at one thirty. He had the expanded search warrant in his pocket and Mike Rowe at his side.

They found the manager waiting in his cramped, overheated office. At the sight of the lawmen, he sat up straight and grinned.

"Expecting trouble?" he said, eyes bright at the prospect.

"Not especially," Cubiak said. It was another masked truth. He wasn't anticipating problems, but he couldn't rule out the possibility that Bobby was involved in the explosion and fire at the fishing shack. Better to have backup than not.

The manager pulled his parka off the back of his chair and herded the visitors down the hall and out the rear exit into the cold.

Bobby Fells's apartment was in Building B, Abels explained as he led them across the parking area. Cubiak glanced at the half-dozen vehicles in the lot. Judging from the amount of snow on them, none of the six had been moved recently.

"Bobby drives a pickup, doesn't he?" Cubiak said.

"Mostly. But I've seen him go off in Tracey's little compact too."

"Do you keep that close a watch on all your tenants or just the young women?" Rowe asked.

"I see what I see," the manager said.

Cubiak shot a warning glance at Rowe. "My deputy was just commenting on your keen powers of observation," he said.

They made the rest of the short trek in silence.

According to the manager at the Old Gray Mare, Tracey left the bar before Bobby and Kyle. At some point, she was gone. It was just the two guys sitting there, he had told Cubiak.

Was Tracey responsible for the explosion? What if she and Bobby had had a falling out? What if her brother often slept at the shack after a night of heavy drinking? She could easily assume that Kyle would leave the bar and go home and that Bobby would be out on the ice alone. She could have gone to the shack to set a trap for him.

"Bobby's got a studio on the ground floor." Abels made the announcement as they approached the next building over. It was identical to the one they had just left but faced the highway straight on.

"I looked up the paperwork after I called you, and according to my records, he moved in eight months ago."

In the lobby, Abels opened the security door to a hallway that smelled of fried chicken and stale cigarette smoke. When he reached the last unit, he stopped. The door was blank. No welcome sign. No holiday wreath.

"Damn, look at that. The stupid idiot."

"What's wrong?" Cubiak said.

"What's wrong? This fucker added two more locks. Look, they're drilled right through the door. He ain't allowed to do that. It's a violation of the lease."

Cubiak leaned in past Abels and banged on the door. There was no response.

"Can we get in?" he asked.

The super held up a key. "Not with this, Sheriff. I gotta get a locksmith to open this bad boy."

Forty minutes later, a young woman in a black jumpsuit showed up and handed the sheriff her card.

"I'm Shirley. I took over the business from my father," she said.

"Sure Lock?" Cubiak read the company name out loud.

"Sure thing." Shirley grinned as she pulled off her wool cap and shook her hair loose.

The sheriff stepped aside and the locksmith knelt down to inspect the door.

"This is some serious business you got here. It's not often that people put in extra deadbolts, but they'll do it. But these? These were installed upside down. It could have been someone made a dumbass mistake, but if they did it on purpose, it means they were serious about keeping people out. Upside-down locks will stop the average burglar cold. Anybody trying to rob the place wants to get in and out fast. They wouldn't bother taking the extra time needed to unpick them. Makes my job harder too."

"But you can open it?" Cubiak said.

"You betcha. It's gonna take me a little longer than usual, that's all. Cost you extra, of course."

Cubiak waved Rowe into the hall.

"What the hell does Fells have in there?" the sheriff said.

"Drugs? Maybe Bobby's dealing."

"It could be. He's up to something, that's for certain." The sheriff lowered his voice. "It's possible he's in there."

The deputy gave Cubiak a sideways glance. "Right."
They left the rest unspoken.

On the walk to the building, Abels had bragged about his stewardship of the Oak Tree Arms, but when the locksmith finished and Rowe kicked open the door to Bobby Fells's unit, the stench of mildew and rotting food billowed into the hallway. Stepping into the dimly lit room, Cubiak felt like he was back at the red trailer. Piles of damp laundry and black trash bags and an avalanche of carry-out containers speckled with the dregs of spoiled food evoked the same sorry mess that he had found in the young man's abandoned home in the woods. Then the sheriff saw the black curtain hung across the middle of the studio apartment.

"What the hell is going on here?" Cubiak said.

He pulled the thick fabric aside, revealing a tidy home office space complete with an elaborate computer setup.

"Young Mr. Fells appears to be something of a Jekyll and Hyde. What do you make of all this?"

The deputy let out a low whistle. "That's about ten grand worth of electronics, all top of the line. I'd say Bobby's made himself a gaming paradise. My gamer buddies would go apeshit for this kind of setup," Rowe said.

"Gamers?"

"Yeah, you know, the geeks who'd rather play video games than eat or sleep. A few of my friends have gotten into e-sports as well, but they're strictly amateurs. The pros are the ones who play for big bucks."

"People make money playing video games?" Looking at his deputy, Cubiak felt old. What else had he missed as time and the world slipped by him?

"They can. Some players are on salary. They even get benefits and vacation. But the really big money's in competitions. A couple of years ago, a sixteen-year-old kid entered a gaming tournament and walked off with the three-million-dollar jackpot. Maybe that's Bobby Fells's thing."

Cubiak stepped behind the curtain and looked at the walls. One was papered in travel posters. There was a picture from Machu Picchu, another from Easter Island, and a brochure with a photo of Katmandu, the same exotic locations Lydia Malcaster thought she would be visiting with James Dura.

An oversized corkboard hung nearby, and this too was filled with familiar images. One was a photo of the painting Lydia's friend had done of her garden. Another, a picture of her workroom. In fact, there were photos of every room in the house. A second corkboard held handwritten notes and messages. The sheriff removed a piece of pink paper for a closer look.

"I think our boy's playing a very different game. Take a look at all this," he said, indicating the garden shot. "That's a picture of a painting in Lydia's house."

Then he handed the note card to Rowe. "See what it says."

"Blue dahlias. Don't tell me. Lydia's favorite flower."

"Not just that. Look at the tiny heart over the *i*. This is the second time I've seen it. It was on a note that Tracey Fells left for Regina Malcaster."

Cubiak put the note back in place. "I don't think Bobby Fells is a gamer. I think he's the homegrown scam artist we've been looking for. Pretending to be James Dura, he used all this"—the sheriff indicated the computer equipment—"to connect with Lydia Malcaster. He romanced her, and after he gained her trust, he took money from her. This was the scheme he was bragging about at the Old Gray Mare."

"I can't believe something like that would happen here," Rowe said.

"Why not? It's a problem all over the world. Why would Door County be immune? Lydia Malcaster sent forty-some thousand dollars to a man she never met after he promised to take her on the trip of a lifetime to places like those." The sheriff nodded toward the posters. "He even sent her copies of the plane tickets and hotel reservations. You already proved that the itinerary was phony, but Lydia didn't realize it and insisted on paying for her share of the expenses. Why? Because she trusted him and probably was falling in love with him. She believed that he was one of her late husband's school friends and that he loved her too."

Rowe rubbed his jaw. "Where does Tracey come in?"

"She had access to the kind of personal information Bobby needed to get close to Lydia. She was at her house three days a week and could easily have listened in on Lydia's private phone conversations or chats with visiting friends. She cleaned for her, which means she knew what Lydia owned and treasured. Tracey even ran her errands and did her shopping. She knew what foods Lydia liked, what kind of wine she drank. She knew everything about her from her shoe size to her favorite color. And what she didn't know, she could find out. Imagine her asking Lydia how she'd met her husband. The lonely widow would relish the opportunity to share her memories. Over time she'd see Tracey as a confidante, someone she could talk to about anything."

Cubiak glanced at the bank of monitors on the desk. "If you can get into his files, I'm sure you will come up with plenty."

While the deputy checked out the equipment, the sheriff continued searching the apartment. There was little of interest until he opened the closet and found an antique metal file cabinet shoved in the corner. One drawer was crammed with unopened packages of tube socks, briefs, and T-shirts. In the other he discovered a book of poetry and two thick manila folders. Instinct and a bad feeling told him what he was going to find in the files. He sighed, hoping he was wrong, and opened the first folder.

Gazing up at him was a color snapshot of a smiling Lydia Malcaster. The picture was a close-up, but there was enough background to know it had been taken outside against a backdrop of blooming rose bushes, perhaps in her own garden. There were more photos, as well as articles clipped from the Door County *Herald* and the Green Bay *Press-Gazette* and newsletters from several local organizations reporting on her charitable and community activities for the past twenty years. There was even a copy of a speech she had given at a fundraising event for the Nature Conservancy a decade prior. Included in the folder were her email address and cell number and lists of her favorite foods, favorite movies and books, and her dream vacation spots. The most personal details were documented: favorite makeup, lipstick color, sizes of the clothes she wore—sweaters, blouses, pants, dresses, shoes, even her bra and underpants.

"Oh, Lydia, if only you'd known," he murmured.

Cubiak put the folder aside and reached for the second one.

He was even more certain that he knew what the contents were, and he wasn't disappointed. Another smiling face, only this time, male. On the far side of middle aged. Square jawed, full lipped, squinting warm eyes, and a full head of curly silver hair. The kind of man many women would find attractive.

"I'll bet I know who you are," Cubiak said quietly. He turned the photo over and read the neatly typed label: James Dura. The sheriff was two for two that afternoon and not happy about it.

The real James Dura had been killed in an auto accident ten years ago, but the fictional Dura in Bobby Fells's file was alive and well. Photos showed him riding horseback in Montana, sipping espresso in a Paris café, and lounging poolside at a mountain retreat in an undisclosed location. Had Dura done any of these when he was alive, or had the pictures been photoshopped? Cubiak wasn't sure.

Not everything in the folder was suspect. Most of the material that could be verified was from the time when the real James Dura was a student at the University of Wisconsin–Madison and he and Zack Malcaster played football together. Several of the team photos were the same pictures Cubiak had on the wall of Zack's study. He tried to imagine Bobby Fells standing in front of the big desk, ostensibly waiting to pick up a paycheck or to get Lydia's signature on a work contract and surreptitiously snapping pictures while she focused on the paperwork. It was possible but risky. So much easier for Tracey to do the dirty work.

Suddenly Rowe laughed. "Bobby sure had a lot of faith in those upside-down locks of his."

"What makes you say that?" Cubiak asked.

"He taped his password to the back of one of the monitors."

A few minutes later, the printer whirred to life and the deputy handed his boss a single sheet of paper.

"It looks like Fells has a weird sense of humor."

The printout was titled "Ladies in Waiting" and listed the names of five women. Lydia Malcaster was one of them.

Cubiak looked around. "We need to impound all this equipment—computer, external hard drives, whatever you think is relevant. There may be more on it yet."

While Rowe assembled the devices, the sheriff paced back and forth in the hall. As he worked the stiffness from his knees, he called the circuit court judge and requested search warrants for the cell phone and bank records for both Robert Fells and his sister, Tracey Fells.

Then he called Abels.

"All done here, for now," he said.

By the time the manager showed up to lock the door, Rowe had strung yellow police tape over the doorway.

The super protested. "What are you doing with that? You're gonna give the place a bad name," he said.

"It's temporary," Cubiak said.

It was after six when the sheriff and the deputy emerged from Building B. It had been daylight and cold when they went in empty handed, and it was dark and colder when they came out toting a half-dozen pieces of computer equipment. Buffeted by a fierce wind, they carried the confiscated equipment to Rowe's vehicle.

When they were done, the deputy left for the station, and the sheriff went home.

THE QUEEN'S COURT

14

Cubiak liked the look of winter—the lacey pattern of frost on the window, the ripples of snow in the trees, and the ice floes on the lake. But he didn't like the feel of the season. He was bothered by the cold, by the early darkness, by the hazards of being on the road in the kind of near-blizzard conditions that came up as he drove away from Bobby Fells's apartment. Nearly half the evening was gone by the time the sheriff got home. Joey had already eaten his dinner and finished his homework. He was back at school for play rehearsal.

"Who drove?" Cubiak asked.

"One of the older boys. I can't remember his name," Cate said as he shrugged off his jacket. "Don't worry. They'll be fine."

The sheriff dropped his coat on a hook and scratched Bear between the ears. "It's getting bad out there. If they run into trouble, they'll end up stranded in the cold."

"They all have phones. They'll call for help," she said.

Cubiak rubbed his hands together. "You're right, as usual."

"I thought I was right as always," she said with a quick teasing smile. "Speaking of cold, we better eat what's left of the lasagna before it cools off anymore."

While the sheriff made a fire in the living room, Cate uncorked a bottle of Chianti and carried their food in on a tray.

Once they were settled on the sofa with their plates, she told him about her search for an appraiser for the Remington bronzes.

"I made several calls but I eventually found someone who can help. His name is Vincent Yaync. He has a gallery in Madison that specializes in Southwest art. He wanted me to bring the statues there, but when I told him about the collection, he said he'd gladly come here. He has an appointment in Sheboygan in the morning and will drive up afterward. He'll need to stay overnight, so I booked a room for him downtown."

Cate brushed a wisp of hair off her face. "We were almost finished talking about the arrangements when Yaync said that it had been years since he'd been to Door County and that he looked forward to seeing some of the familiar sights and catching up with John Overly, whom he described as another collector of note."

"Overly? The birdman?" Cubiak said.

"It seems so. I didn't know what to say except that I quite admired John's Audubon prints. Yaync chuckled. 'Is that what he calls them?' he said. I asked what he meant, but instead of explaining, he changed the subject. Then he said he had another call coming in and hung up."

Cate sipped her wine. "I can't explain it, but I had this funny feeling that he felt like he'd spoken out of turn and wanted to end the conversation before it went any further."

"Sounds like the art world is as secretive as the confessional," Cubiak said as he got up to stir the fire. "It probably has nothing to do with any of this. Still, I may have to talk to Overly again."

He reached for Cate's glass, but she put up her hand. "No more for me tonight. I have a bit of a headache." He refilled his and sat down again.

"Can we stop talking business now?" Cate said, nestling into his shoulder.

Cubiak gave her a quick squeeze. "I wish, but there's one more thing."

In his nearly twenty years as sheriff, Cubiak had come to rely on Bathard and Cate for their store of local knowledge. The retired doctor was an expert on the history and folklore of Door County. Cate knew the people, and through her own personal experience and the accumulated stories passed down through several generations of her family, she understood them as well.

He showed her the list of names that Bobby Fells had compiled.

"Besides Lydia, what do you know about these women?"

Cate held the paper up to the light and squinted. "Where'd you get this?"

"First, tell me what you know about them."

She rolled her eyes. "Simply put, if Regina Malcaster had a court, they'd be in it, and if Door County had a social register, they'd be on it. They're all from old money and lots of it. Their families were the bedrock of Door County. Even today these women are among the biggest donors to many of the local charities and community organizations. Gladys Ingersoll is widowed. I've met her a few times at various events. Same for the last two. Helen Yaeger was in one of my drawing classes a couple of years ago. She comes around the arts center regularly. I think she's divorced."

"I'm assuming they're all up in years?"

"Since seventy is the new fifty, I'm not sure what you mean by that, but yes, they'd range in age from the late sixties to the mid-seventies. Now, your turn. Why is Lydia on this list? What's this all about?"

Cubiak described the computer setup and paraphernalia that he and Rowe had discovered in Bobby Fells's apartment. "Based on what happened to Lydia, it looks like he was running a homegrown internet scam," he said.

Cate hugged a throw pillow and stared at the fire. "I can't believe he'd do that. Poor Lydia."

"It's all about money. She had it. Bobby wanted it and thought he had a surefire way of getting it from her."

A log popped and a bright-orange glow lit Cate's face. "But that doesn't explain her death. Why would he hurt her? Why would anyone want to hurt her?" Cate tossed the pillow to the end of the couch. "And Tracey? Was she a part of this?"

"I'm afraid so. It certainly looks that way."

"Oh geez, what the heck is wrong with people? And these other women, do you suppose they're targets too?"

Cubiak drained the last of his wine. "Given that they're on the list, I'd say they are."

"Do you think Regina knew anything about this?"

"She had her suspicions but not about this. I think that if she knew about the scam, she would have said something."

Cate slumped into the sofa. "Tracey and Bobby Fells. I just can't believe they'd do something like that. They were such sweet children."

"You knew them when they were kids?"

She had taken care of them for a couple of summers while their mother helped Ruby in the weaving barn in exchange for free lessons and time on one of the smaller looms, Cate explained. "Aunt Ruby often did that, hoping to encourage women to explore their creative instincts."

"Did anything come of it?"

"Unfortunately, not. Mrs. Fells stopped coming by after she and her husband split up. The last Ruby knew, the poor woman was working two jobs just to keep a roof over her head. It's hard enough for a single mother with one child, but with twins . . ."

Cubiak was about to put another log on the fire. He turned toward Cate. "Bobby and Tracey are twins?" he said.

"Yes. Sorry, I thought I'd mentioned that. Maybe that explains things." Cate sighed. "The family had money once, too, but the story was that their great-grandfather Peter Felton made a mess of things and lost it all."

By the time the fire burned down, Cate had gone to bed and Joey was still out.

Left alone, Cubiak opened his notebook and listed the things he needed to check on: Regina/list. Fells/family money. Bronzes/value. Overly/collection.

The appraiser was due the next afternoon. Cubiak would listen to what he had to say and then he would talk to both the queen and the birdman again.

The sheriff was nodding off when a car pulled up outside. A door slammed and then the vehicle drove off. He walked into the kitchen just as Joey slipped in from the deck.

"It's past eleven. Where have you been?" he said. He meant to sound concerned and was surprised by the harsh tone.

"Play practice." The boy was defensive.

"How come you're home so late?"

Joey bent down to unlace his boots. "We kept messing up a big scene."

"It's a school night."

"Yeah, I know. I'm beat. Can I go to sleep now?" he said, ducking along the counter.

As he hurried past, Cubiak caught a whiff of a familiar smell.

"Were you smoking?" he asked.

The door to the boy's room clicked shut, leaving the sheriff alone in the silent kitchen.

For a moment, he wondered if he should follow his son and demand an answer. Then he sighed and plodded back to the living room. Kids. Had he been like that? he thought as he turned off the lights and went to bed.

THE REMINGTON BRONZES

15

Late Tuesday morning, a squall blew in off Lake Michigan. The surprise storm cut visibility to under a mile and pelted the area north of Sheboygan with heavy snow. The appraiser was due at Lydia's house at two, but at one he called Cate to tell her that he was on the interstate, crawling toward Door County in a long line of vehicles, and would be late. Cubiak reached the house at four and parked behind an unfamiliar silver SUV. The driveway hadn't been plowed, but the walk had been cleared recently and Cate's car was pulled up to it. She met him at the door.

"You shoveled?" he asked.

"I had to, for Regina."

"Of course. What about the appraiser? Is he finished yet?" he asked as they moved into the hall.

She shook her head. "He just got here half an hour ago. The poor man was exhausted from the drive and asked if he could sit a bit. I made him a cup of coffee and let him rest by the fire for a while. He didn't start looking at the bronzes until a few minutes ago."

On Cubiak's first visit to the house, Zack's study had been flooded with morning sunshine. This time it was a dreary day and he was there late in the afternoon. The only light in the room came from three halogen lamps that had been placed strategically around the edge of the desk to illuminate the four bronzes. The empty shelf behind them lay in the shadows, as did the rest of the room.

In her trademark black, Regina Malcaster was nearly invisible in the dim corner, where she sat in an oversized leather chair, buffeted by pillows and clutching her cane. With a half nod, the matriarch acknowledged Cubiak's entrance and then turned her full attention back to the man at the desk.

This was Cubiak's first encounter with an art appraiser. He had imagined him to be an academic type, a stooped, slight fellow with elbow patches on his jacket, wire-rimmed glasses, and billows of hair spilling onto his collar. Someone with smooth fingers and a delicate touch.

Not the burly, bald man who leaned over Zack's desk. The man whose Packers sweatshirt strained at his linebacker's neck and the seams of his wide shoulders.

"You must be the sheriff," the art expert said in a booming voice as he came around the desk. "Vincent Yaync." He extended a thick hand whose grip matched its size.

"You know," Yaync went on, with a glance at the statues, "Remington started out as an illustrator and was a damn good one, too, but now he's mostly remembered for his bronzes. There's even one of his statues in the White House."

"My wife mentioned that," Cubiak said.

The appraiser gave Cate a nod that threatened to segue into a bow.

"Now, if you don't mind, I must apply myself to the task at hand." Yaync arched his eyebrows. "All I ask—require, in fact—is your patience and your silence. Or your absence."

Regina scowled and crimped her mouth. She wasn't going anywhere.

Cubiak and Cate retreated to the hall.

"Well?" he said.

She shrugged. "After he'd rested for a few minutes, he was very chatty, but once we were in the study, he barely said a word. Just the occasional 'aha.' He left to make a phone call and I went up to the door to eavesdrop, but I couldn't hear anything."

"How's Regina doing?"

"It's hard to get a reading on her. We came early to make sure everything was in order, and she was very subdued on the way. The first thing here, she went to the top of the stairs. 'I have to see it,' she said. She stood there for so long that I began to worry that she'd lose her balance and tumble headfirst like Lydia did. But she snapped out of it and got very businesslike, insisting that we move the bronzes to the desk for the appraiser. We were waiting for Yaync when he called to say he was delayed because of the weather. That seemed to distress her and she started walking around the house and talking about Lydia and Zack. She said it was almost as if they were here with her."

Just then the study door opened and the appraiser stepped out. "Excuse me." He dipped his head and waggled his phone at them. "Another quick call," he said as he hurried down the hall.

When they were alone again, Cate took Cubiak's hand. "This can't be easy for her, Dave."

"I'm sure it's not." He glanced after Yaync. "What about the appraiser?"

"Oh, him! She grilled me on his credentials and references. I went over everything with her until she was satisfied. When he got here, I could tell she was put off by his appearance. To tell the truth so was I, but he was quite charming over coffee and was positively tickled when Regina told the story about the poker game—"

She was about to go on when Yaync thundered back toward them.

"A few more minutes and I'll be ready," he said as he swooped past.

Cubiak waited until the office door closed. "He doesn't seem to be taking a lot of time with the assessment. Is that bad?"

"I don't know."

They went back in as the appraiser circled the desk and scrutinized the sculptures. When he finished, he moved *The Bronco Buster* toward the front of the desk and arranged the other three—*The Rattlesnake, Coming through the Rye,* and *The Outlaw*—in a row behind it. Frowning, he sat and shuffled his notes into a neat pile. Another moment passed and he stood.

The wall clock ticked. The appraiser turned away and coughed into his fist. When he looked back, he was nodding, more to himself than to his audience, as if organizing his thoughts.

Regina thumped her cane. "Mr. Yaync, I do believe we're ready to hear whatever it is you have to tell us," she said.

The art dealer cleared his throat and gave a small, sad smile.

He began slowly. "Before I agree to take on an assignment of this magnitude, I gather as much information as I can. Based on what Ms. Wagner told me"—he glanced at Cate—"I came to believe that the four bronzes in this collection were authentic Remingtons."

Regina sniffed. "As these most certainly are." She spoke as if challenging the appraiser to prove her wrong.

Yaync went on unperturnbed. "Use of the term can be confusing when evaluating the Remington statues. It goes without saying that the term applies to bronzes that were cast during the artist's lifetime. These are the most valuable for the simple reason that he would have had a hand in making or altering the casts that were used. And because the bronzes were numbered sequentially, the lower the number, the greater the value. But bronzes that were cast posthumously and authorized by his widow are also termed authentic, although of lesser value, as are those made posthumously with estate approval."

"Assuredly the statues in this collection are lifetime casts," Regina said. Head high, she ran through the titles and the cast numbers: *The Bronco Buster*, six; *The Rattlesnake*, nine; *Coming through the Rye*, five; and *The Outlaw*, six. Again, she spoke as if daring Yaync to disagree.

The appraiser pinched the bridge of his nose and then looked at the dowager. "*The Bronco Buster* was cast in 1902, seven years before Remington died. There is no question of its authenticity. However, this was the most popular of Remington's bronzes, and with hundreds produced while he was still alive, it is not as valuable as some of the bronzes that were more limited. The other three in the collection appear to be genuine, but"—he paused and took a deep breath—"they are spurious castings. In other words, they are fakes."

The matriarch gasped. "How dare you stand there and tell us that except for the statue Rutherford won in the poker game, the bronzes in Zack's collection are fakes, and that we've been made fools of for all these years. I don't believe it. It's impossible. I gave you the papers that substantiate the statues' provenance, each one of them. Have you bothered to look at them?"

"The papers appear genuine . . ."

"Then what are you saying?"

The appraiser clasped his hands together and pressed them to his chin. "These are delicate matters, indeed. And I don't want to misconstrue the circumstances, but I assume that when the papers came into your family's possession, they did so accompanied by the authentic bronzes"—Regina glared at him—"and because I have no reason to presume this was not the case, then I am afraid that at some point . . . how shall I put this? That at some point, substitutions were made."

Regina pulled herself to her full height. "Don't mince words, Mr. Yaync. The papers substantiate the provenance of the pieces and prove that the ones my husband, Henry Malcaster, owned, statues originally acquired by his father, were authentic Remington bronzes."

Yaync squared his shoulders. "Forgive me, madam, while I have no reason to question the integrity of the bronzes that were originally in your family's possession, I do have reason to believe that, with the exception of *The Bronco Buster*, the figures on display lack that integrity."

"Unless you are mistaken in your assessment." The dowager's voice cut like barbed wire.

Yaync said nothing.

Cate stepped into the fray. "Could you tell us how you arrived at your conclusions?"

The appraiser shot her a grateful look and picked up *The Bronco Buster*.

"Details mean everything. They were crucial to Remington and remain critical in assessing his work. In the case of *The Bronco Buster*, I would check to see if the right stirrup wiggles back and forth, like this . . ." He demonstrated the movement. "I would also note the horse's tail. Does the tip of the tail loop around and connect to the leg or flank, or does it extend out at full length behind the horse, as is the case in the number six cast that you have here. Both characteristics—the movable stirrup and the extended tail—indicate that this is a lifetime cast."

Like a professor giving his students time to absorb the lecture, the appraiser paused and surveyed his audience. "Okay?" he said. Then he carried the statue over to the light.

"In addition, the Roman Bronze Works foundry stamp is clearly marked here on the base, another important detail. Then, there is the matter of the patina or glaze, a characteristic that Remington took great pains with. The patina on this bronze displays a notable color mixture. There is a vibrancy to the finish, a glowing quality, that speaks to its authenticity."

Yaync stepped away from the desk, leaving the four statues in clear view. "It was the difference in the patina between this bronze and *The Rattlesnake* that first made me suspect about the other statues."

"I don't understand," Cubiak said. "The coloring looks pretty much the same to me."

"As it does to most people." Yaync turned to Cate. "You're a professional photographer. Can you tell the difference?"

"Until recently I'd only seen them once or twice before, and they were on the shelf away from the light," she said, approaching the desk. "Looking at them now, I understand your concern. The veneer on *The Rattlesnake* exhibits no luminescence; the color is flat and darker than on the others."

Yaync moved beside her and picked it up. "That was my assessment as well, and as soon as I realized the difference, I knew I had to take a closer look. When I did, I noticed the problem with the foundry stamp. If you look carefully at the base, you'll see a faint remnant of the first stamp and then a fresh stamp on top of it. See here." He showed the statue to Cate and then to Regina and Cubiak.

"Which means what?" the sheriff asked.

"The obvious answer is that the copy was made from a cast taken from the original statue in the collection. When the foundry stamp didn't come out clearly, the forger redid the stamp, believing this would make the piece appear authentic. I found the same problem on *Coming through the Rye* and *The Outlaw*. Although the patina on those two was much improved, the double stamping marked them as fakes. Good copies, but—"

"Bah, worthless junk, or so you say." Regina banged her cane on the floor and then jabbed it at Yaync. "If you are correct, it would appear that the authentic statues were spirited away and replaced with counterfeit copies. My niece was robbed."

"Perhaps." The sheriff tread carefully.

"What do you mean, perhaps?" Regina redirected her rage toward the sheriff.

"Perhaps Lydia sold the bronzes."

"Never. She would never do such a thing."

"Or Zack. You said yourself—"

"I've changed my mind." Regina took a deep, angry breath. "I'm sure this has to do with that James Dura fiasco."

"Lydia's relationship with him started a couple of months ago. I don't think the timing works."

Cate turned to the appraiser. "Assuming someone else has the authentic statues, what good are they to anyone without the papers?"

Yaync tugged his sleeves down. "Unfortunately, not everyone cares about the documentation. Besides . . ." He cast a quick glance at Cubiak. "Papers can be forged."

Regina clutched her scarf and made a strangled sound.

Cate hurried across the room and knelt alongside the matriarch's chair. "Is there any way to trace them?" she asked as she took the elderly woman's hand.

"That depends. Art is acquired and sold through innumerable channels. A legitimate transaction creates a paper trail. But between the back-room and black-market deals, much is under the radar. The situation is complicated by the fact that we don't know when the statues were replaced. Were all three switched out together, or one at a time over the course of years?"

The appraiser wiped his brow. "It's possible that whoever made the switch kept them for himself, or herself. Dozens of authentic bronzes are unaccounted for."

"And the authentic bronzes, how much are they worth in today's market?" Regina asked.

"*The Bronco Buster* that you have here, approximately half a million. *The Outlaw*, between seven hundred fifty thousand and a million plus. *The Rattlesnake*, roughly two and a half million. *Coming through the Rye*, ten million."

A stunned silence fell on the room.

Leaving them to their own thoughts, Yaync gave the bronzes a final glance and then packed his briefcase. When he finished, he came around the desk and stood quietly staring at the rug for a moment. Finally, he squared his shoulders and approached Regina. She stared straight ahead, ignoring him, her hands curled in her lap.

"I am so sorry. I had hoped to be the bearer of good news." Yaync made an awkward bow. "I remain at your service."

The dowager closed her eyes and unfurled her hand with a dismissive wave. "Thank you."

The women stayed together in the study while Cubiak walked the appraiser upstairs. In the foyer, Yaync touched the sheriff's arm and spoke with quiet urgency.

"I didn't want to get the old woman's hopes up, but there is a possibility that the person who bought one of the authentic bronzes loaned the statue to a museum for a show. If that's the case, it could well open the door to discovering the thief. I have a vague recollection that the number nine casting of *The Rattlesnake* was in just such a show some years back, hence my phone calls earlier. It's a long shot but I'll continue trying to check that out . . ."

Yaync sighed and reached for his coat. "So sad," he said as he rammed his right arm into the empty sleeve of the parka. "You'd think that by now I'd know better. I had such grand expectations . . ."

Suddenly, the appraiser stopped and frowned. "Hold on a minute," he said, reversing his movements. He tossed the jacket to Cubiak and hurried toward the stairwell.

Still holding the coat, the sheriff trailed the art expert back down to the study.

Cate gave him a puzzled look as Yaync again took up his position in front of the dowager.

"I was told that there were five bronzes. But I've only seen four. Where's the fifth one?"

Regina harumphed. "You were engaged to evaluate the statues in my niece's collection. The fifth bronze was never meant to be included. It was my husband's favorite, and although it's not to my particular liking, I kept it in his memory and honor. I'm not sure why I mentioned it earlier. Perhaps I was simply curious to know its value. But after this fiasco, why would I even bother discussing it with you?"

"As long as I'm here, I'd like to see it." Yaync looked from Regina to Cate and then to Cubiak. "If it's not too much trouble," he said, softening his tone.

After much back and forth, Regina reluctantly agreed. Thirty minutes later, the four left Lydia's house and under a frigid, starry sky drove up the road to the dowager's estate.

Once inside, Regina announced that she would not be present when Yaync evaluated the fifth bronze.

"Sheriff, I would be much obliged if you accompanied our guest to the library." The dowager nodded toward the glass wall. "It's along there, at the end of the hall. You can't miss it. Cate will wait with me in the living room, won't you, dear? Perhaps we can have a fire," she said.

The Stampede depicted a lone cowboy frantically struggling to control three rampaging steers and was the largest of Remington's bronzes. Some twenty inches tall and nearly four feet across, it dwarfed the four statues in Zack's collection.

At a signal from Yaync, the sheriff retreated to the sofa and leafed through a copy of *Smithsonian*. He was about to toss it back on the side table when the appraiser gasped.

"What is it?"

Yaync dropped into a chair and gaped opened-mouthed at the sheriff. "I need a minute," he said. His face glistened with sweat. He pulled several papers from his satchel and poured over them. Then he opened his laptop and began tapping the keys.

Suddenly he sat up. "Oh my God, I don't believe it," he said.

"What?"

The appraiser mopped his forehead and exhaled. He reached out toward the bronze and then pulled his hand back as if he was reluctant to touch it.

"It's the real thing? The statue's authentic?" Cubiak asked.

"More so than you can imagine." Yaync exhaled and pressed his hands to his knees. "Of course, my findings will have to be substantiated, but still . . ." His voice dropped off and he staggered to his feet. "I have to tell Regina."

The art expert made the trip back down the hall to the living room with a jaunty step. For the third time in as many hours, he positioned himself in front of the dowager. Regina appeared to be asleep.

Yaync coughed softly and she jolted up.

"Madam," he said.

She blinked. "Oh, it's you. Out with it, then."

"You have the papers for the statue?" he asked.

"Yes, I already told you I did."

"Do you mind if I sit?" As he looked around, Cate got up and pushed her chair toward him. He pulled it within a few feet of Regina and sat facing her. Light from the fire lit his face with a boyish glee.

"Remington finished working on *The Stampede* just months before he died. It was the last model that he crafted, and only three statues were cast from it. The third is at the Remington Art Museum in upstate New York. The second is at the Gilcrease Museum in Tulsa. The first cast is officially designated as 'unlocated.' "

Yaync reached out and took Regina's fragile hands in his. "There are literally thousands of copies of *The Stampede* in existence. But you, my dear lady, own the first cast that was made of it. This rare and highly valuable Remington bronze, the 'unlocated' cast that has long been coveted by collectors around the world, has been in your possession for decades."

Regina did not respond.

The appraiser went on eagerly. "A lifetime cast of another Remington recently sold for more than ten million dollars at auction. I suspect that your sculpture would be valued much higher. As for a private sale, well . . ."—he lifted his eyes toward the ceiling—"there really is no limit. It depends on what a collector or investor is willing to pay for it. At the very least, *The Stampede* wouldn't be worth less than—"

"Get out!" Regina jabbed her cane at him.

Bewildered by the outburst, Cate and Cubiak looked on as the dowager raged at the startled man.

Yaync stumbled to his feet. His face white, his arms outstretched, he whirled on them. "What—?"

"You pompous fool. How dare you tell me my statue is worthless," Regina said as she grabbed the arms of the chair and pushed to her feet. Stiffened to her full height and brandishing the cane like a weapon, she advanced toward the appraiser.

"Regina!" Cate stepped between them. "Stop it, this instant. What are you talking about?"

"What he said, the utter gall . . . saying the statue was worthless."

Cate caught her by the wrist. "I'm afraid that you misunderstood. Vincent Yaync didn't say that."

"I heard him . . ."

"He said it wasn't worth less than a cast that had sold for millions." Regina sagged. "Oh." She blinked and reddened. "Oh my, I seem to have made quite a spectacle of myself, haven't I?" she said, clutching at Cate.

Struggling to regain her composure, the proud matriarch shuddered and then faced Yaync. "I apologize, sir." Her voice cracked. She pressed a hand to her heart and inclined her head. "If you'd be so kind, perhaps you could repeat what it was you were telling me before."

After Regina recovered from the shock of the news, she insisted that they have something to eat before Yaync left. The four ended up in the kitchen supping on soup and sandwiches. As they ate, they talked about books and movies and touched on the weather.

The Stampede wasn't mentioned until the table was cleared.

"One thing I am curious about is how you came to be in possession of such a rare artifact," Yaync said.

Regina laughed. "That's the stuff of family lore. My husband's father already owned four Remingtons when this one was cast. As the story goes, he'd closed a deal on a southern rail line and was feeling particularly flush. I believe he paid two thousand dollars for it, which back then, in 1910, was an unheard-of sum to spend on what many would consider a frivolity. He brought the bronze back to Wisconsin and it's been in the family since."

"Well, now it should be kept under lock and key. Do you have a safe large enough to accommodate it?"

"I do, indeed."

After the bronze was secured and Yaync had driven off into the night, the three of them returned to the living room, where Regina took her favorite chair by the fire.

"I'm still finding all this difficult to process," she said, staring into the flames. "All these years that statue was in this house, I had no idea it was so valuable, no one did. The only time anyone mentioned the Remington bronzes, they were talking about Zack's collection."

She accepted a glass of sherry from Cubiak. "I can't believe he sold them, but it's the only scenario that makes sense to me. Lydia couldn't have or she wouldn't have agreed to having them appraised."

"There's another possibility," Cubiak said.

"What do you mean?"

"Who else had access to the house over the years that the statues were there?"

"I'm not sure I know all those to whom they'd have given a key, but certainly John and the twins' mother. She used to clean for Lydia. That poor woman was afraid of her own shadow. I doubt she'd have the moxie to steal an old pot, much less a work of art. And then to find a credible duplicate? No, no, not her."

"Anyone else?"

"The caretaker perhaps. Zack and Lydia traveled quite a lot, and when they were gone, he kept an eye on the place. I always assumed he checked the grounds, but maybe he went inside as well. You'd have to ask him. Anyway, that would have been years back. Since Zack passed on, Lydia's only taken short trips, long weekends, that sort of thing."

"What about the twins, Tracey and Bobby?"

"Tracey's only been working for Lydia for the past couple of years. She started there the same time she started here." Regina shook her head. "She doesn't seem to know much about anything, and less about art. She wouldn't have had the slightest idea how to buy or sell a Remington bronze. You give her too much credit."

"And Bobby?"

Regina arched her brows. "That oaf. You think that Tracey told him about the statues and that he engineered the switch? Bobby does a decent job snowplowing and cutting the lawn, but I doubt he has any other expertise."

"He knows his way around the internet," Cubiak said.

"Stuff and nonsense," she said.

"And John?" Cate asked. "He's quite open about his Audubon prints. But Vincent Yaync implied that his collection encompasses much more than a few relatively inexpensive prints. He'd know his way around the art world."

"John Overly is one of the finest people I know. He would never have done anything to hurt Zack or Lydia or any of us. No, it couldn't be John. He's been a friend to all of us for so long. I'd trust that man with my life."

THE VAULT

16

John Overly hadn't answered his phone the previous evening, and on Wednesday morning when Cubiak tried to reach him, the call went straight to voice mail. The storm had continued through the night, and the sheriff assumed that the birdman was out clearing the path to the birdfeeders. The sheriff left a message asking him to call, and then he helped Joey shovel the deck.

Heavy snow was still falling when Cubiak walked into the justice center.

"You look like a snowman," Lisa said as he shrugged out of his jacket.

"It's pretty bad out there. You should think about leaving early," the sheriff said.

"Maybe I will." The assistant picked up a a handful of papers and trailed him to his office. "I got the information you wanted on Bobby Fells."

She pulled a paper clip from the top set of papers and handed them to the sheriff. "First, here's his cell phone history. The only person Bobby routinely called was Tracey. I highlighted her number in yellow, and you can see that during the past couple of months, he contacted her five or six times a day. But for the last several days, he hasn't made any calls from his cell." She hesitated. "He could be using a burner."

The sheriff put the first report aside. "What about his finances?"

Lisa gave him another set of papers. "I listed his credit card charges first. Most of them are pretty routine—gas, groceries, some clothes, plenty of bar charges."

Then she laid out a third set of documents. "This is everything I got from the bank on his checking account. It looks like Bobby pretty much spent every nickel he earned. At the end of November, he had thirty-three dollars and change in the account, and at the end of December he was overdrawn by twelve bucks."

"What about a savings account?"

The assistant shook her head. "No savings, at least not locally. I checked banks in Manitowoc and Green Bay, too, but nothing there either. I doubt that Bobby stuffed money into his mattress. So, I asked myself: if I had a lot of cash and wanted to hide it, where would I put it so it would be secure but out of sight?"

"In a safe-deposit box," Cubiak said.

"Bingo." Lisa grinned and sat down. "I called all the banks again but got nowhere until I tried the Wisconsin Bank of Green Bay, where, it turns out, Bobby Fells opened a safe-deposit box last June. That's the good news. The bad news is that you need another warrant and have to be present before they can open it."

Cubiak slapped the desk. "Lisa, you're golden. Call them back and tell them I'll be there at eleven."

With the storm, traffic on the divided highway was down to one lane in each direction. Despite leaving early, Cubiak didn't reach the outskirts of Green Bay until nearly eleven. From there he still had to wend his way into the heart of the city.

Green Bay was incorporated in 1855, and four years later the Wisconsin Bank of Green Bay opened. Ole Wis, as it was affectionately known, occupied the first floor of a five-story stone citadel four blocks from the Fox River. While other financial institutions modernized with drive-up windows and walk-up ATMs, the grande dame continued conducting business in the subdued hush of its ornate, gold-leafed fortress.

Cubiak's appointment was with a Katherine Kensey.

"Sheriff Cubiak," the bank manager said when he appeared in her doorway. Before he could apologize for being late, she glanced at her watch. "I understand the weather is terrible," she said as she rose from behind an obsessively neat desk to shake hands.

Kensey was a youthful forty, smartly tailored in a charcoal gray skirted suit, and with the trim figure of a runner. The financial world's equivalent of Emma Pardy.

Cubiak presented her with the warrant and his credentials.

"You don't mind," she said as she reviewed the documents.

"I appreciate it."

She gave a half smile. "Not everyone does," she said, and handed the packet back to him.

"I assume that you're familiar with the procedure we need to go through to open the box? Two keys are required. I have the master"—she pulled back her sleeve to reveal the key dangling from the coiled bracelet around her wrist—"and the client has the other. That's the reason to have a safe-deposit box, security is guaranteed. No one gets in. The warrant changes everything," she said as she tugged her sleeve back into place.

"Shall we?" Kensey pressed a button on her phone console and then motioned toward the door. "The vault is downstairs."

She led the way, her heels clicking smartly on the gleaming black-and-white marble floor. Trailing behind, Cubiak wondered if he should apologize for the annoying and unprofessional squeak of his boots as they processed through the lobby and down the elegant, curved stairwell to the lower level, where they were met by a weighty silence that felt as old and somber as the bank itself.

The vault gaped open. "It's a bit of a dinosaur, but our clients appreciate its gravitas," Kinsey said, drawing his attention to the door. The steel slab was three-feet thick and outfitted with a complicated network of locks and levers.

Through the arched entryway, Cubiak glimpsed the beehive of metal compartments that lined the inner walls. Each compartment held a safe-deposit box, and each had a door that was punctuated with two key slots.

The bank manager kept talking. "The room is surrounded by concrete, and the walls are armored. It was built first, before the rest of the building went up."

Cubiak half-listened. He was trying to guess which door hid Bobby's box and how he was going to get up the nerve to step inside the vault. When he was eight, his friend Tony had accidently locked him in a hot, dark closet during a game of hide-and-seek and then forgot about him. He wasn't found until hours later, when his mother discovered him huddled in the corner, weak from thirst and dripping with sweat. Ever since, he had avoided small, enclosed spaces. He imagined the door swinging shut and . . .

Kensey stepped inside. "Sheriff?" she said.

As if she could read his mind, her expression softened. "The vault is equipped with an emergency button that activates an alarm. We can't be trapped inside."

Bobby Fells had rented safe-deposit box number 1109. It was a medium-sized box, located toward the rear of the south wall. "This is the one we want," she said.

"How are you going to unlock it?" Cubiak said.

"Without the customer's key, I can't. The locksmith will drill it open."

Half an hour later, Cubiak huddled in a small room with Kensey and a trio of other bank officials. Safe-deposit box number 1109 sat on a table in front of them.

When Kinsey lifted the lid, her professional manner momentarily faltered. "Well," she said.

The box was crammed with neat stacks of twenty-, fifty-, and hundred-dollar bills.

Kinsey fed the money into a counting machine, and then read the tally.

"Seventy-five thousand dollars," she said.

The bank manager looked at the sheriff. "May I ask what this young man does for a living?"

"He shovels snow."

By midafternoon, the roads were clear and Cubiak made good time on the return trip to Sturgeon Bay. His first stop was at the coffee shop, where he bought an extra-large mocha latte for Lisa.

"A small token of my appreciation for your work," he said as he handed her the drink.

"For my lucky guess, you mean," she said, lifting off the lid to a mound of whipped cream.

"You should take more credit for what you do. That wasn't a guess and there was no luck to it," the sheriff said.

He left her blushing and went off to tell Rowe about Bobby Fells's stash of cash.

"That's a helluva lot of dough," the deputy said.

"It's more than enough to account for what Lydia paid him for her share of the bogus vacation, but it's nothing compared to what he'd have if he'd stolen the Remingtons."

"Only if he'd sold them. Maybe he's got those tucked away somewhere. The bronzes could be stored in bank boxes all over the country."

"True, but if Bobby didn't take the statues, where'd he get the additional dough? And where is he? Tracey too? Any more leads on either of them?" the sheriff asked.

"Nothing yet. It's like they just vanished."

Cubiak grunted. "No one vanishes. Keep looking for them and take as many people as you need," Cubiak said. "There were five names on the list we found at Bobby's apartment. My hunch is that he started at the top and was working his way down. Lydia was victim number three, so we can assume the scams stopped with her. I'll talk to the first two. If he finagled anything from them, that would account for the rest of the money in the box."

DEAD END

17

Gladys Ingersoll was the first woman on Fells's target sheet. Before Cubiak left to meet her, he tried to reach Overly again, but the birdman didn't answer. This time his voice mail was full, so the sheriff couldn't leave a message. Overly had drawn his attention to the three Audubon prints on the wall but didn't hint that there was more to his collection, much more if Cate had understood the appraiser's implication. Was he secretive by nature, was he purposely hiding his true treasures, or was Cate mistaken? In any case, the birdman would know who else had access to Zack's house and the Remington bronzes over the years.

The previous afternoon, Cubiak had called Mrs. Ingersoll and spoken to her private secretary. He was circumspect about his reasons for his visit but the secretary wasn't fooled. "It's about Lydia Malcaster, isn't it?" The secretary set the appointed hour, and when the sheriff dropped the brass knocker, she opened the door.

"You're right on time," she said as she let him into the grand foyer. "Mrs. Ingersoll appreciates punctuality."

He was taken to a small parlor flooded with the bright winter light. A petite, birdlike woman sat in a floral wingback chair that was angled toward the windows and a view of the frozen bay. She wore a bright-red sweater and pants, a match for the poppy stencil that rimmed the walls near the ceiling. Her hair was silver, the color of the tea service that was laid out on the table near her.

"Sheriff." The elderly woman inclined her head when he introduced himself. "It's not every day I get a visit from local law enforcement," she said, motioning for him to sit. "You're here to talk about Lydia Malcaster and her unfortunate liaison with that rogue James Dura."

"You've heard of him?"

"Lydia let the name slip once. Lydia and I were friends for many years, and while I've always known her to be a sensible woman, I'm afraid that in this instance her better judgment was lacking. I don't say that lightly. I want you to understand that Lydia was a fine woman, certainly not one given to frivolousness. But when I became aware of how rapidly the relationship with this man had developed, I was alarmed. I may be old, but I can add two and two, which I assume still equals four," she said, peering over her glasses at him.

"Had you ever heard of Dura before Lydia became involved with him?"

"No." She moistened her lips. "Men like this James Dura target women of means who live alone and therefore are presumably lonely. Am I correct?"

"That's often the case," he said.

"They prey on their weaknesses, and of course we all have them."

"Even Lydia?"

The elderly widow tilted her head in acknowledgment. Then she trained her pale-green eyes on Cubiak. "I don't judge Lydia harshly, Sheriff. None of us should. Since she died, I've had to ask myself how I would have fared in her situation. Perhaps if I were so unlucky as to have contact with a lothario of Dura's ilk, I too might be susceptible to his charms or promises. I assume he made promises?"

"He did."

"Well," she huffed. "I am spared that humiliation, perhaps for no other reason than that I despise computers. It is my firm belief that modern technology has destroyed civil discourse and is quickly debasing society. I own such a device—one must in this day and age or risk being left out of the loop—and I even have something called a Facebook page, but my private secretary is my buffer. She handles both my business matters and my very limited social media presence."

"You seem very in touch with modern communication."

"I stay current, Sheriff. There's a difference." Mrs. Ingersoll lifted her hand off her lap. "And to save you the trouble of asking, yes, there have been overtures. My secretary has shared the more interesting specimens with me. It's a bit of a sport between us. Several of the men who have attempted to make my acquaintance were quite dashing, but I'm aware that they may well be the same sorry individual operating under different guises. Someone who is nothing more than a heartless thief.

"I cautioned Lydia as soon as she mentioned James Dura, but it wasn't enough. I was too late and she didn't listen. 'You wouldn't understand,' she said. The truth is that I would understand well enough, but she didn't believe me. And you?"

Gladys Ingersoll turned her gaze on Cubiak again. "Do you know who the culprit is?"

"We have identified a person of interest."

"Really? Presumably someone operating from foreign soil," she said.

"I'm afraid not. If we're correct, the culprit is a local man."

The old woman grimaced. "That's impossible. Something like that wouldn't happen here."

"But it has, hasn't it? And not just with Lydia." Cubiak held out the sheet with the names he had copied down. "We found this list of local women who we believe were potential targets. Your name is included."

Mrs. Ingersoll took the paper with a trembling hand. "Those overtures I mentioned, you think they're the work of this miscreant?"

"It's possible, especially if there have been any recent messages."

"My secretary hasn't said anything lately, but that may be because she knows how distasteful I find this sort of thing."

The elderly widow pressed a button on the side table and sat back. From outside, a shriek pierced the stillness. She turned to the window. "It's the wind moving the ice around. You've seen the ice shoves, of course. The piles can grow to great heights over the winter. I've seen shoves that were more than ten or twelve feet high, spectacular ridges of them along the edge of the bay."

Looking out the window, she smiled. "Fantastic, aren't they? People tell me I should go south for the winter. Stuff and nonsense. I'd miss all the action."

Amid the cacophony of sound, a door opened and closed behind them. Footsteps approached and the secretary appeared.

"The sheriff needs to ask you about those . . . those requests." The old woman barely spat out the word.

"Of course." The assistant gave a month-by-month report. The first request came in the previous May, she said, and the most recent just before the New Year. "There have been twenty in all, a veritable barrage." She paused. "I couldn't help but notice that the requests always came from fine-looking older men who claimed a variety of impressive credentials," she said, coloring slightly.

"You deleted them, I assume?" Cubiak said.

"Yes, as instructed. But the three most recent messages arrived within the last thirty days and will still be in the spam folder. I can forward them to you, if you think they'd be of any use."

"Everything is potentially of use," he said.

Cubiak was about to leave when Mrs. Ingersoll stopped him.

"I saw Helen Yaeger's name on the list. If you haven't spoken to her yet, you must. Helen is a good friend, a smart woman, and I am sorry to say that she was fleeced of a goodly sum. If you don't mind, I'll call and tell her you're on your way."

COOKIES AND CRUMBS

18

Based on the list, Helen Yaeger was Bobby Fells's second target. Half an hour after the sheriff left Gladys Ingersoll's mansion, he stood at the door of a modest, white two-story colonial. Given the prestigious address, the house was a surprise.

So too was the pleasant, gray-haired woman who answered the bell. She had a grandmotherly look that went with her blue, flour-dusted apron and the aroma of freshly baked cookies that wafted out the door.

"Sheriff Cubiak? I'm Helen. Gladys called to tell me you were on your way," she said, brushing her hands against her apron. "Please, come in." She stepped back to let him into a foyer cluttered with shoes and boots.

"I've been baking," she said as she led him through an unpretentious living room to a sleek, modern kitchen where a rack of chocolate chip cookies cooled on a white tile counter.

Two placemats were set on a small table near the window.

"Please, sit. Coffee?"

Helen was already filling a mug, complaining about the weather as she poured. By the time she had set out cups and dessert plates, the cookies were cool enough to move from rack to platter and then to the square butcher block table in front of the sheriff.

"Gladys told me about her conversation with you," she said, as she untied her apron and hung it from a wire rack.

"You know why I'm here then," Cubiak said.

Against the backdrop of the robin's-egg blue of the walls, her pale-green eyes glistened. She nodded and nudged the plate of pastries toward him. "Please," she said, and sat. In an instant, an enormous orange-striped cat jumped on her lap.

"Do you mind? Some people get upset if animals show up anywhere near food."

"I have a dog," Cubiak said, and reached for a cookie.

Helen stroked the cat. "I suppose Gladys told you what happened?"

"She suggested I talk with you, that's all."

"Ah," she said, and stiffened. She tucked a loose curl behind her ear. "Well, I'll be blunt then. I was a fool."

"Can you tell me what happened? What you mean by that?"

Helen opened her mouth and then closed it. She kept one hand on the cat, and with the other she pulled her yellow turtleneck to her chin and slumped against the back of the chair.

Cubiak rested his elbows on the table and leaned in. "I'm investigating potential internet scams. The kind that involve men who establish romantic liaisons with women and—"

"Con them out of money." Helen finished the sentence. She scratched the cat between the ears one more time and then eased the animal from her lap. "That's exactly what happened to me. I understand it happens to a lot of women." Averting her eyes, she broke a cookie in half and arranged the pieces on her plate.

"Of course, I thought my situation was different." She gave a bitter laugh. "I thought I was special."

"How did it start?"

"How do these things usually start? We met through an online dating service." Helen gave him a sheepish look. "People do meet this way, it does happen. I know of two couples, so why not me? Why couldn't I be lucky, too? Why did I have to go on alone?" She spoke with a hard edge.

Cubiak said nothing.

"He claimed that he was a widower. His wife died in a car accident ten years ago and left him to raise their daughter alone. He managed to get on, focusing on the child and on his job. He was a financial manager with an international firm headquartered in London. I looked it up to make sure it was real.

"He was from Connecticut originally, but he was living and working in England when he met his late wife. After they married, they decided to stay, good jobs and all that. The firm was expanding, and several months ago he was sent to open a branch in Milwaukee. The move made him realize how happy he was to be back in the States. His daughter was studying at Oxford so she stayed on in England and he found himself on his own again. Somehow, he said, it seemed like the right time to meet someone here. And wasn't he lucky to find my profile on the site."

Helen ate a piece of cookie from her plate and snapped the other half in two. She continued breaking the segment until her fingers were smeared with melted chocolate and crumbs littered the dish. "Lucky? I'll say he was. We exchanged several email messages telling each other about ourselves, and then he gave me his phone number and suggested we start texting. It would be easier, he said, more like talking. We did that for a week or so, but I found it awkward to type anything of length on my phone, and when I said as much, he suggested we move to a chat site. I'd never done that before, but I caught on quickly. It was like texting but on a real keyboard, not that miniature thing on the phone."

"If you had each other's phone numbers, why didn't you talk?"

"We tried but it didn't work. He was constantly on the road, traveling, back and forth to London and Singapore. We'd arrange a time to talk, and then he'd be on a plane or in a meeting. Once he said that he'd fallen asleep and didn't hear the phone. The company was leaning on him, he said. When he got the new assignment, he'd been in the middle of important negotiations, and the department head expected him to see those through as well as organize the new office here."

"You believed him?"

"Why wouldn't I? It was a legitimate company, and I understood the demands of that kind of position. My ex-husband was a corporate lawyer in Green Bay, and there were days he stayed in the city overnight, weeks when I barely saw him. When you're in a high-profile profession, the job always comes first. He said his dream was to work another couple of years and then retire to someplace quiet. He'd never been to Door County but he'd seen pictures of it online and thought it looked like a piece of heaven on Earth." Her voice cracked as she added, "With an angel waiting there for him."

Helen pulled a piece of tissue from her pocket and pressed it to her eyes. "I'm sorry."

"It's okay. Take your time. You're okay," Cubiak said.

"Okay? I need to have my head examined," she said, her voice thick. "I was stupid enough to give money to a man I'd never met." She attacked the tissue as she had the cookie and shredded it as she talked. "It was a stock deal, an opportunity that was too good to pass up. Something he'd stumbled on when he was in Asia. He'd feel derelict if he didn't share it with me. He told me that he'd already invested ten thousand on his own. He said he knew how suspicious that sounded and that he didn't expect me to trust him without proof. The next day, he emailed me a copy of the transaction along with a tweet confirming the rumor that the start-up was set to be listed on the New York Stock Exchange within days. When that happens, he said, the price would go through the roof. There wasn't much time and I had to act quickly to have any chance of getting in on the windfall. He was buying another twelve hundred shares, and if I wanted, he'd put my order in along with his. For some complicated reason that I didn't understand, I couldn't buy the stock directly from here. I had to give the money to him, and he'd invest it for me."

She made a sound like a laugh and tugged at her sleeve. "The next morning, I authorized a wire transfer for thirty thousand dollars to his account. I sat here for hours watching the clock, calculating the time difference, and waiting for a response. But there was nothing. It started to rain, I remember. And that's all there was. Just rain."

"Did you ever hear from him again?"

"No." She stumbled up from the chair. "Wait here, I'll show you," she said.

Cubiak heard her in a back room. When she returned, she handed him a copy of the stock transaction the scammer had sent her. "I've bought stock before. I'm not a neophyte. It looked legit."

"And you didn't report this to anyone?"

"To whom?"

"To me, for one."

"What would you have done?"

"To start, I would have contacted the FBI."

Helen got up again and switched on a light. "What would they have done besides ask me a lot of questions like you are now? No, I was too mortified to tell anyone. You have to understand, Sheriff, that it wasn't just about the money, not then anyway, it was about me. I had concocted a marvelous fantasy about how my life was going to change. It felt so real, I couldn't let go of it.

"For the next couple of days, I refused to believe that I'd been duped. I made excuses for him. He'd had a heart attack and couldn't contact me. He'd been hit by a car and was lying somewhere in a hospital, all alone. I was desperate to find him. Finally, I did what I should have done in the first place. I called the company's London office and talked to the human resources director. I gave her his name and babbled on like an idiot. I said it was an emergency, that I had to get in touch with him. I told the director that we met while he was in the States organizing their Milwaukee branch but that the last time I'd heard from him, he was working in their Singapore office. I had to reach him. Do you know what she said?"

Helen Yaeger took a deep breath and in the best British accent she could muster, she relayed the rest of the conversation. "'I'm sorry, madam, but you must be mistaken. We do not have a branch in Milwaukee. Furthermore, there is no record of anyone by that name employed by the firm in either our London or Singapore offices.'"

The cat leapt onto her lap again and nuzzled its head into her hand. "I hung up and crawled into bed and stayed there all day. I was so emotionally devastated that I couldn't process what this woman had told me. It sounds absurd but it felt like I'd lost something real. I even searched for his profile on the dating site, but it had been removed.

After I finally faced the fact that I'd been conned, that everything I'd dreamed of was an illusion, I became physically ill.

"When I woke the next morning, I called my banker and asked him to trace the funds. The transfer had gone through, and the money deposited as directed. I asked if I could get it back and was told very politely that it couldn't be done. The money was gone. I'd been played for a sucker."

Helen stared out the window. "Afterward, I was too humiliated to face anyone, so I stopped going out and refused to talk to any of my friends. One day Gladys pried the whole miserable business out of me. She had her secretary check out his story. There was no obituary on his wife, no news reports of a fatal auto accident around the time of her alleged death, no daughter by that name at Oxford. Everything he had told me was a lie. Gladys was kind enough not to say so, but I could have done all that myself right at the start: called the company, searched the internet for all the details that should have been there."

Helen swallowed a sob. "My husband had left me for a younger woman. I was hurt and desperate to be loved again, and somehow this man knew it. There must be hundreds of profiles for women like me on that dating site. What lousy luck that he came across mine."

Cubiak waited a moment before he spoke. "Bad luck may have had nothing to do with it," he said as gently as possible.

The distraught woman looked up sharply, her expression caught between anger and confusion. "What do you mean?"

"I'm investigating an internet scam that targeted several women on the peninsula. There was a list and your name was on it."

"My name?" Helen sank back into the chair. "Oh my God. I can't believe something like that would happen here."

She stood and glanced around the room as if she wasn't sure where she was or what she had meant to do. Then she retrieved the coffee pot and refilled their mugs.

As soon as she sat down again, the cat returned.

"Do you remember why you enrolled in online dating?"

"Why does anyone do it? I was lonely and wanted a companion. I told you I knew two couples who met that way. Then one morning my housekeeper started talking about her neighbor and how she'd met a wonderful man online. 'It's how people your age meet. You should try it,' she said. I pooh-poohed the suggestion and told her I wouldn't know where to begin. I didn't think any more about it until a week later when the housekeeper was here again. She said she'd asked her neighbor for the name of the dating service she'd used. 'It's top rated. Why not give it a whirl? What have you got to lose?' she said. She even offered to help."

Helen gave a rueful smile.

"I fretted about it for days. I'd always been reticent about trying anything new, but this seemed safe, right? If my housekeeper's neighbor could meet someone decent online, maybe I could too."

"Did you discuss this with any of your friends?"

She shook her head. "They equated online dating with loose behavior and would have been appalled. And to be honest, I wasn't ready to own up to it. If nothing came of it, then I'd never have to admit that I'd tried it, but if I met someone and things worked out, then it wouldn't matter. In the meantime, it was my little secret. The next time my housekeeper came, I told her I was ready to get on board. She gave me a high-five. She even helped me write my profile and select the photos to post on the site. Before I knew it, I was enrolled.

"The first day or so, I got several 'likes' but they were from men with whom I had nothing in common. Then I got a message from *him*. He was educated and polite, a real gentleman, and I was drawn to him immediately." She gave a short, bitter laugh. "I thought it was kismet."

"You were supposed to," Cubiak said.

Helen looked up inquiringly. "You said earlier that maybe I'd been set up. But by whom? Who would do . . . ?"

She reddened with a flush of rage. Jolting upright, she shoved the startled cat off her lap. "Tracey! It was she, wasn't it?"

"There's a possibility that she had a role in the scam," he said.

"That little bitch. Always so friendly. So interested in my life, now that I think about it. She's the one who talked me into it. I would never have signed on if it weren't for her." Tears welled in Helen's eyes. "I can't believe she'd do that to me. I've known her family since I was a kid. Her mother used to clean for me."

Helen pressed a fist to her chest. "I'm sorry, Sheriff, but I feel sick."

Cubiak filled a glass with water for her. "It's not your fault that you were tricked."

She drained the glass. "Are you telling me that all the time I thought I was communicating with the scammer, I was talking to Tracey? That I sent the money to her?"

"I think that Tracey was just part of the scheme. In your case, it was her job to set you up and then feed information to the person hiding behind the dating profile."

"So who was her accomplice?"

"Most likely it was her brother."

"Bobby Fells?" Helen patted her lap and the cat leapt back up. "I always thought he was a bit slow, but maybe that was a put-on." Her eyes widened. "That's why we never talked! He was afraid I'd recognize his voice. Damn. I hope you've arrested him. Tracey too."

"I'm afraid that we're still looking for them. I've already checked her apartment and Bobby's place as well. You said you were familiar with the family. Do you know if any of them are in the area?"

"I have no idea. The parents are both deceased. There was a grandmother—Sarah Felton, if I remember correctly."

"Felton? Not Fells?"

Helen frowned. "Maybe I have the name wrong. At any rate, I haven't heard anything about her in years. She may be gone as well. As for other relatives, I don't believe there's anyone else."

She shivered. "Oh my God, this is all going to come out, isn't it? I'll be the laughing stock of the county."

"If you have the courage to tell your story, you'll be a heroine."

"What do you mean?"

"Think of the women you can help. The women who will learn from your experience that this kind of thing can happen anywhere."

"But how could I do that?"

WRITTEN RECORDS

19

The sheriff left Helen Yaeger sitting at the kitchen table and let himself out. It was only a few minutes past five, but he was surprised by how dark and cold it was. Not a glimmer of light or a speck of warmth awaited him on the other side of the door, only his frozen breath and the inky black of the wintry night.

As he drove the back roads across the peninsula, light from the high beams splashed against pearly drifts and cast eerie shadows into the trees where deer foraged for food in the subzero temperatures.

At home, Cate and Joey waited for him in the bright, warm kitchen.

"Sorry I'm late," he said.

"You're fine. We've got time." Cate stood and took his jacket.

Cubiak spied the container on the counter. "What's on the menu?" he said.

"A bowl of your famous chili. You made enough last week for an army. I was working and didn't have time to cook so I pulled a batch from the freezer."

"I hope the old doc likes it."

She smiled. "He will. He doesn't like to cook so he'll enjoy anything he doesn't have to prepare himself, and after the holidays I think we'll all appreciate a simple meal."

"How about you? Did you eat?" Cubiak asked his son.

"Yeah."

"Homework all done? Bear fed?"

"Check and check. I walked him too."

"Good," Cubiak said.

"I have another reheasal tonight," Joey said.

"Right." Cubiak hesitated. Should he say something about the boy's behavior the other evening?

"I'll be home early."

"Good," Cubiak said again.

The sheriff took a few minutes to clean up and change into a fresh shirt before the three of them left. After he and Cate dropped Joey at play practice, they stopped at the bakery for a baguette and then headed north for their biweekly dinner with Bathard. Cubiak met his friend for lunch once a month, but Cate had suggested the occasional evening meals as well. They provided the entrée, and Bathard supplied the wine and dessert.

The table was set when they arrived at the doctor's condo in Egg Harbor.

The former coroner watched Cate serve. "You make this new place feel a little more like home," he said.

She passed him a bowl of chili. "You've been here long enough to make it feel like home yourself. It's been four years now, hasn't it, Evie?"

Bathard smiled at her. He had been widowed twice, and Evie was the pet name favored by both his wives, Cornelia and Sonja. "I like when you call me that. It's the name all my favorite women use."

He set the bowl down and raised his glass. "To old friends and new condos. And to new hobbies as well. I've taken up birding. Something to keep myself sharp. I even joined the birdwatchers club. In fact, I attended my first meeting last week."

"At the Old Gray Mare?" Cubiak said.

Bathard looked up, surprised. "Yes, how do you know about that?"

"Kyle Murphy, the young man who died in the fire, was drinking at the bar with Bobby Fells that night. He left his truck in the lot, and when we went to pick it up, the bartender mentioned the birders' meeting."

Cate scowled at Bathard. "How'd you get there? I thought you'd stopped driving at night."

"I got a ride." Bathard paused. "Such a lovely evening and then hours later there was that terrible explosion on the bay killing that young man. The fishing shack belonged to Bobby Fells, did it not?"

"Yes, and now he's disappeared." Cubiak went on to describe what they had found in Fells's studio apartment and his safe-deposit box in the Green Bay bank.

"He must know that we're looking for him. I think he panicked and went into hiding before he could get to his money, which means he's stuck. He's probably down to his last few dollars and won't chance using a credit card because he knows it will lead us to him. I put out an APB on his truck but there've been no sightings. His sister, Tracey, is missing as well. My guess is that they both hunkered down somewhere in the area."

"Do you think they are hiding out together?" Bathard asked.

"It's possible."

"To be honest, I am having a hard time placing those two," the old doctor said.

"They're twins," Cate said. "Does that help?"

"I cannot remember every infant I delivered, but I am almost certain to recall twins, and judging by their ages, it is very likely that I brought them into the world."

"Helen Yaeger mentioned a grandmother, but she remembers her last name as Felton. Does that ring a bell with either of you?" Cubiak said.

Cate shook her head.

Bathard surveyed the empty plates on the table and then pushed his chair back. "We can have dessert later. Come with me," he said.

Leaning lightly on his cane, Bathard led them down the short hall to the library. When he sold his house, he said it was the room that he would miss the most. To smooth the transition, he replicated it as much as possible, installing bookcases on three of the walls in the second bedroom and adding an electric fireplace to substitute for the real thing. He even managed to squeeze his old desk and two leather chairs into the space.

"For whatever reason, I retained my patient files through the years. When I retired, I moved them from the office to the house, and then again to here. They are in the closet behind you," he said. "If you would be so kind as to find the carton marked with the letter *F* and bring it here"—he tapped the desk—"perhaps I can retrieve some useful information."

The closet was wedged full of cartons, just as the box that Cubiak dislodged from the stack was crammed with folders.

While Bathard combed through the material, the sheriff turned the fireplace on and poured a round of sherry, another one of the doctor's traditions. Then he and Cate settled in and waited.

Several minutes passed. "Ah, here they are." The elderly physician opened a green file. "Tracey and Bobby Fells." He scanned several pages. "According to this, the parents were the primary emergency contacts, and the secondary contact was a Sarah F. Fells, who is identified as their paternal grandmother."

"F for what? Frances? Felton?" Cubiak asked.

Bathard gave a gentlemanly shrug. "I cared for the twins for a number of years—perhaps something will come up in their immunization charts or school records," he said as he pulled a paperclip off several yellowed forms. "I wrote everything in longhand back then, and the ink has started to fade but I can still make out enough." After a few moments went by, he looked up.

"The year that Tracey and Bobby went into third grade, I put down the grandmother's name as Fells, but then I crossed that off and wrote Felton instead."

Bathard handed the page to Cubiak. "I would not have done that of my own accord. She must have accompanied the children on the visit and instructed me to make the change."

"I wonder why?" Cubiak said.

"Perhaps her husband died, or she divorced him and didn't want to use his name. It was not my place to inquire."

"I guess not. But this means Helen Yaeger was right. The twins' grandmother was Sarah Felton," the sheriff said.

Cate peered over his shoulder. "Hearing the name earlier didn't mean anything, but seeing it is different. I don't know why, but it looks familiar. I'm almost sure I've seen it somewhere before."

Cate was subdued on the ride home.

"Tired?" Cubiak asked.

"No, just thinking about Bathard and how his life has changed now that he is on his own again. There's a good chance that will be one of us someday. Statistically, it will be me and I'll end up like Lydia Malcaster or one of those other women. But statistically it should have been Cornelia or Sonja, not Evie. Just as it shouldn't have been you before."

She squeezed Cubiak's arm. "Life's not fair, is it?"

He glanced at her in the moonlight. "It never has been. But it's all we've got."

OLD MAPS

20

On Thursday, Cubiak woke to a room crowded with shadow and filled with the aroma of freshly brewed coffee. The house was still. Joey was asleep in his room, but Cate and the dog were gone. In the kitchen, the sheriff drank a cup of coffee and looked out at the lake. The offshore breeze had pushed the ice pack out half a mile, where it stretched from one end of the bay to the other, like a long white stripe drawn along the horizon. He was at the window when the back door opened, and Cate and Bear tumbled in on a wave of frigid air. The dog trotted to his water bowl while Cate leaned against the wall and kicked off her boots.

"What are you doing up so early?" Cubiak asked, pouring a cup of coffee for her.

"I couldn't sleep." She took the warm mug and pressed her frosty cheek to his. "I woke up thinking about last evening and got tired of staring at the ceiling and trying to remember where I saw the Felton name before. I hoped a brisk walk would help jog my memory."

"Did it?"

"I'm not sure. But I have an idea." She undid her scarf and parka. "When I was a kid, my grandfather used to let me look at his collection of old Door County maps. I was just learning to read, and I'd sound out the names on the parcels. Some were impossible but others were easy. If the name Felton was there, it would have been one of the words I could actually read. When I was older, I asked him why he kept the maps. He said that they told the real history of the peninsula and that they explained a lot of things about the present that people needed to understand."

"Your grandfather's 'present' is ancient history now."

Cate shrugged. "True, but maybe the maps can tell us something."

"Us?"

"You said yourself that you've run out of leads trying to find Bobby and Tracey. They belong to the Felton clan, and finding the name on one of those old maps may be helpful. You've got nothing to lose by looking. Besides, it gives us the chance to spend the morning together."

Most of the land that Cate's grandparents owned had been converted to a wildlife preserve, but she still owned The Wood, the elegant European chalet that her grandfather had built, as well as the house's contents.

Inside, Cate headed directly for the treasure trove of old books and historic documents in the second-floor library. The antique tomes filled two walls of floor-to-ceiling bookshelves. The records were kept in the wide shallow drawers of the handcrafted cabinet that stood behind her grandfather's desk.

"If there's anything, it'll be in here," Cate said, pulling open the top drawer of the cupboard to the original plans for The Wood. The sketches were detailed and precisely rendered on blue paper.

"It's why they're called blueprints," she said.

The next two drawers were filled with certificates that marked births, deaths, and marriages. But there was nothing with the Felton name.

They found the first old maps in the fourth drawer. The sketches, hand drawn in black ink on thick rag stock, documented the existence of Clay Banks, Lily Bay, Graceport, and the dozens of other waterfront villages that sprang up during the boom years of the logging trade and then faded from existence when the industry died.

Cubiak was checking his text messages when Cate got to the bottom drawer. "Sorry for wasting your morning," she said as she reached for the brass handles.

"It's fine, I—"

"Dave, look at this," Cate said as she laid a large parchment sheet on top of the cupboard.

The document, dated 1925, was a land survey of the fledgling town of Fish Creek. In addition to the lots that were carefully noted within the town limits, the survey showed three large adjacent swaths of land that started at the village limits and stretched more than halfway across the peninsula. The segments were approximately equal in size and each was labeled with the name of its owner. Rutherford Malcaster. Oscar Hanson. Peter Felton.

"I wonder where this will lead," Cubiak said.

There were several more drawings in the drawer. In each one, the parcels that belonged to Malcaster and Hanson remained intact, but Felton's holdings diminished. By 1932 his claim had shrunk to a small corner of the original parcel. The rest of the land had been divided into a patchwork quilt of plots, each with a different owner.

The last map in the batch jumped ahead four years. By then Felton's crumb had vanished. The patchwork quilt had disappeared as well. The individual bits of land that Felton had sold off now belonged to Malcaster and Hanson.

"Rutherford Malcaster, Zack's grandfather?" Cubiak said.

"Looks like it."

"What about Hanson?"

"There's a bunch of them around. It's another old family," Cate said. "Do you think maybe this is all just a coincidence?"

"I doubt it, especially if either of the other women on Bobby Fells's list is connected to the Hansons," Cubiak said.

Cate swiped a finger across her phone screen. Her manner was quick and efficient, and with her head down, it was impossible for him to read her expression.

After a moment, she looked up. "Got it. Gladys Ingersoll, née Hanson." She continued swiping the screen. "Daughter of Ingrid and Johan Hanson. Granddaughter of Alice and Oscar Hanson."

"And Helen Yaeger?"

Cate took another minute. "Helen is Gladys's cousin."

By late morning, Cubiak was back in the office in front of his computer. Using the two-finger method he had perfected on an old Underwood in high school, he pecked at the keyboard, slowly entering the information he had jotted down at The Wood. The method was a study in inefficiency, but when he finished, he had inputted the approximate dates that Felton had sold his parcel of land and the names of the buyers. He sent a copy to Lisa.

"I need you to search county records and get everything you can about these transactions. The more information, the better. See if you can track down what Felton originally paid for the land, what he sold the parcels for, and the full names and addresses of the buyers."

"That it?" she asked as she reached for her purse.

"That's step one. Eventually Rutherford Malcaster and Oscar Hanson snapped up all of the pieces and put them back together. Step two is to find out what they paid for them. Oh, and there's a third step as well."

His assistant sighed. "Go on."

"See if you can find anything owned by a Sarah Felton."

Lisa studied him from under her brow. "And you want this when?"

"It's one thirty now. By three would be good," Cubiak said, glancing at his watch.

"Miracle worker isn't part of the job description."

"As soon as possible will do, then. And get yourself lunch, on me," he said, laying a ten-spot on her desk.

From Lisa's desk, the sheriff detoured to the break room for a cup of coffee and then went back to his office to call Bathard.

"You haven't been shoveling snow, have you?" Cubiak said as he set his mug on the desk.

"I live in a condo, remember. All the amenities of home but none of the work." Hearing the lightness in his friend's voice, Cubiak was glad that he and Cate hadn't bailed out on dinner the evening before. "And you? What have you been up to?" the old doctor asked.

"More on the Felton business."

The sheriff told him about the morning's foray at The Wood.

"Cate took pictures of the old maps, which I am emailing to you now. I have Lisa checking into county records for information on land sales, but I wonder if you'd be willing to see if there's anything in the library history room?"

Bathard chortled. "As in give the retiree something useful to do? In fact, I already have plans to visit the library this afternoon. While there, I will try to unearth whatever documentation I can find. You would be surprised at the array of interesting material the library historian has rescued from either the trash heap or the jaws of the shredder."

The argument about what to keep and what to discard was a standing joke between them, and Cubiak played along. "So I've been told," he said.

"Good. What precisely am I searching for?" Bathard asked.

"Anything related to the land sales."

"I will do my best. Wish me luck," Bathard said.

Shortly after two that afternoon, the retired coroner ambled into Cubiak's office. He carried a worn leather briefcase in one hand and dusted the snow from his shoulders with the other.

Wordlessly he took off his coat and folded it over the back of a chair by the conference table. Then he balanced his Russian fur hat on top of the coat, patted down his thinning gray hair, and approached the desk.

"Your wish came true. I was lucky," he said.

"How lucky?"

"That is for you to determine."

Bathard popped the brass latch on his case and removed several sheets of paper, which he arranged in a neat row on the desk.

"What you have here is a copy of a page one article from the October first, 1937, edition of the Door County *Herald* about the dispute between Peter Felton and his former business partners Rutherford Malcaster and Oscar Hanson. Go ahead, read it."

The doctor angled one of the visitors' chairs toward the window. "While you are doing that, I will watch the snow fall."

In the article, Felton claimed he had been defrauded by the two men, "whom he had come to look upon as brothers." By his own admission, Felton had fallen upon hard times in the early years of the previous century. In need of funds to support his family, he applied for bank loans, which were denied. Desperate, he appealed directly to Malcaster and Hanson.

In the article, Felton recalled, "I did not ask for a handout. I asked to borrow small sums from each." The men declined, said Felton, citing what they described as their own reduced circumstances. Instead, they advised Felton to sell his holdings, which he did, bit by bit and year by year. "They told me it was useless dirt," Felton said, and they even helped line up buyers, as a favor to their colleague.

Like the map at The Wood, the accompanying sketch showed the original parcels that the three men had owned. From north to south, the names appeared in the same order: Malcaster, Felton, Hanson.

Claiming that his former colleagues had conspired against him, Felton sued for fraud. He argued that both were privy to inside knowledge about plans for development on the land, information that they kept from him. Twenty-six months after he sold the final parcel, they purchased all the segments that he had once owned. Six months later they consolidated the three segments into one massive holding. Soon after, they sold the portion nearest Fish Creek to the town for a park and other large segments to a large cherry producer and several developers, all for a tidy profit. "They reaped financial benefits while my family was reduced to penury," said Felton.

Cubiak reached the end of the article and looked up. "According to this, Malcaster and Hanson refused to talk to the reporter."

"That is correct. And no follow-up stories were ever published," Bathard said. He turned back to the desk. "What you see there is not the half of it. Would you venture to hazard a guess as to who sat on the boards of directors of the Sturgeon Bay banks that denied his loan applications?"

"Oscar Hanson and Rutherford Malcaster, the man who had recently spent two thousand dollars on a bronze statue."

"Really? I did not realize that. But you are correct, both men were on the boards. Both of them could have helped Felton secure the loans but were also in positions to make sure that his applications were denied."

"And the lawsuit?"

"The judge dismissed it as frivolous. Then, to complicate matters further, Malcaster and Hanson countersued for damages." Bathard retrieved another sheet of paper from his briefcase and gave it to the sheriff. "Eventually they settled out of court, but I cannot imagine that they got much out of Felton because by then he was nearly destitute."

"While Malcaster and Hanson went on to prosper," Cubiak said.

"Indeed. Which only goes to prove that there is truth in the saying that it takes money to make money. As development progressed on the peninsula, they were able to take advantage of numerous investment opportunities while Felton was forced to file for bankruptcy and subsequently was shut out of any future financial benefits."

They were still talking when Lisa arrived with more damning evidence.

According to the official records, she explained, the three men bought the land at a premium, but by the time Felton was forced to sell, the market was spiraling downward. "The price per acre dropped each time he sold. Overall, based on my rough calculations, he was out nearly sixty-five percent of the original purchase price."

Cubiak whistled under his breath. "What about the buyers?"

Lisa arched her brows. "That's where things get really interesting. There were ten altogether. One was a transient who ended up in jail on a vagrancy charge. But I couldn't find any trace of the other nine. It's as if they never existed."

"Or they used phony names and fictitious addresses," Bathard said.

The sheriff had been taking notes, but he stopped. "No one checked this out at the time?"

"There was no need to. The sales were all cash transactions," Lisa said.

"Really? I wonder where they got the money for that." Cubiak tossed his pen down. "What about Sarah Felton?"

"For the past twenty years, there's no record of anyone by that name living in Door County. I even checked *Felten* and *Fellton* and a couple of other spellings but came up with nothing. However, twenty-two years ago a woman named Sara Felton—that's *Sara* with no *h*—bought twelve acres up around here." Lisa stabbed at a spot on the map near the junction of two county roads. "It's mostly scrub and was probably going dirt cheap back then. Taxes are low and have been paid on time every year since."

"She lives there?"

"Who knows? There's no fire number or address."

"She may just own the land. More important, are the two women—Sarah and Sara—one and the same?" Bathard asked.

"I'd put money on it. What about you?" The sheriff looked at Bathard and Lisa.

They both nodded.

Cubiak was certain that Regina Malcaster would know all there was to know about Sarah Felton. A visit to the dowager would take him several miles out of his way, but he needed to question her and see how much she was willing to tell him.

He called ahead and told the grande dame that he needed to talk to her.

Regina met him at the door. "You have news about Lydia, or the bronzes?" she said.

"Not yet," he said. "I came because I need information."

Her shoulders sagged a small fraction, but she kept her head high and arched her brows at him.

"I've already told you what I know."

"I'm here about something else."

"Oh." There was more ice than curiosity in the word.

They hadn't moved from the foyer. Cubiak unzipped his jacket, and she took the hint.

"Please," she said, indicating an empty hook on the wall behind him.

She waited for him to brush the snow off his boots, and then she led the way through the living room to the fire.

A crystal decanter and two matching glasses stood on the table alongside her chair. One was half full of amber liquid and the other empty.

"May I offer you something to counter the chill?" she said once she was settled.

"I'm on duty."

She picked up the decanter and poured a careful measure into the empty glass. "Just a sip," she said, holding it out for him.

Then she lifted her drink. "*Nosdrovey*," she said, and gave him a quick smile. "You see, Sheriff, I know something of your ancestral language."

Cubiak raised his drink in turn. "*Slainte*."

Regina gave a nod and touched the rim of the glass to her lips. Then she set it down firmly. "Now, if your visit has nothing to do with Lydia's death or the Remingtons, what could possibly be important enough to bring you here at the end of the day with a new storm on its way across the bay?"

"Does the name Sarah Felton mean anything to you?"

The dowager stiffened slightly. "Should it?" She posed the query with a forced nonchalance.

"You're close in age and given that you were both born and raised here, it's not unreasonable to assume that you knew each other growing up. Perhaps you even went to school together."

She sighed. "We did—a million years ago. But that was a different lifetime. I haven't seen Sarah in decades. In fact, I'm not even sure she's still alive."

"Really? Not that long ago, you employed her daughter-in-law to clean for you, and now both of her grandchildren work for you, I wouldn't be surprised if your paths have continued to occasionally cross. Perhaps you've even maintained something of a friendship."

"Sarah and I haven't been friends for years." The elderly woman spoke abruptly and then reached for her glass as if suddenly remembering that it was there.

"Would that have anything to do with the land dispute between her father and your father-in-law?"

Mrs. Malcaster plunked the glass back down and skewered Cubiak with her gaze. "I was under the impression that you were investigating the death of my niece, that you had some concern about her being the victim of an internet scam, and that you were looking into the possible theft of valuable property that she owned. How this other matter could have any bearing on that—"

"It may not," Cubiak said, interrupting her. "But then again, it might. What I need and would appreciate is some history about what happened back then."

The matriarch turned toward the blaze and stared at the burning logs. The shadows from competing orange and blue flames danced across her face.

"There are two versions to the story, Sheriff," she said, talking into the fire and watching the tug of war being played out around the burning logs. "One is that my future father-in-law, along with Oscar Hanson, concocted an elaborate scheme to cheat Peter Felton out of his land. The other, that Felton was the author of his own doom."

She cleared her throat and went on. "Decades ago, there were three substantial tracts of property extending from the outskirts of Fish Creek across a good portion of the peninsula. Each man owned one segment."

"I've seen the maps," Cubiak said, interrupting her again.

"Ah, so you know what I'm talking about. And you understand how valuable it eventually became."

He nodded.

"The three men were shrewd businessmen, and as such each of them understood the potential. That's why they bought it. The parcels ran parallel to each other. Henry's father owned the northern segment and Hanson the southern one. Felton's was in the middle, and for their purposes was the most critical."

With her cane, she drew parallel lines on the rug.

"As Fish Creek grew, it would naturally extend into the interior and they could speak as one voice in demanding a higher price for the land if they sold it together—not all of it, of course, but the segments closest to the town. Although expansion was inevitable, no one could predict when it would occur. And, of course, no one could foresee the devastating financial turmoil that was unleashed upon the nation in the fall of 1929."

"October twenty-ninth."

"Precisely." Mrs. Malcaster thumped her cane as if to underscore the date. "The stock market crash, followed by the Great Depression, which segued into nearly a decade of suffering and deprivation."

She finished her drink and looked first at the decanter and then at Cubiak. He shook his head, and she put the crystal glass on the table.

"Rutherford Malcaster and Oscar Hanson were both financially equipped to weather the storm, but Felton was not. As a result, he was forced to sell his land. The other two men offered a fair price for the entire parcel, but their assets were not liquid enough to allow them to do so outright. Instead, they offered to buy the land on contract. The terms didn't suit Felton. Apparently, he was desperate for cash. He sold the property piece by piece and allowed himself to be swindled in the process. One poor business decision followed another, and Felton began to drink heavily. Eventually his continued lapse in judgment completely undermined his financial situation."

"You were a child at the time. How would you know all this?"

"I know the Feltons sold their house. I know that Sarah started coming to school in hand-me-downs and patched clothes. I know what I overheard the adults discuss among themselves, and I know what Henry told me when we were engaged."

"And the other version?"

Regina brushed at her knee. "As I said, it was some poppycock about Henry's father and Hanson swindling Felton."

"Did you ever try to find out if there was any merit to that version?"

"I had no reason to. Peter Felton's actions spoke for themselves. He sank as low as he could, dragged his family with him, and then took his own life, leaving them to get on as best they could. I never saw Sarah Felton again after the funeral."

"You went?"

"Of course, to represent the family. It was the least I could do. I was unacknowledged and ignored, but present." She raised her hooded eyes toward Cubiak. "I know what you're thinking, Sheriff, that I should have done more for her. In fact, that was impossible. Sarah Felton made it clear that she would rather starve than accept a helping hand from me or anyone else. Several years after the funeral, she sold the shack the family had been living in and then she vanished. She may have moved away or died. In any case, I never saw her again. Later, I heard that she had married and had a son. When his wife was looking for work as a housekeeper, I hired her. And after she died, I hired her daughter, Tracey. Look where that got me. Look where that got any of us."

The dowager went on. "You have a kind heart, Sheriff. It's written all over your face. But benevolence must be balanced with fact. No matter what you may think, my conscience is clear."

What about the biblical admonishments to do unto others and love thy neighbor? he wanted to ask, but he held his peace. He was there to garner information, not to lecture the old woman about the Christian duty she certainly knew and had justified ignoring on the basis of both logic and the merit of what her husband had told her.

It was also possible that her version was correct, the sheriff grudgingly admitted as he climbed into the icebox cab of the jeep. Peter Felton could have brought about his own doom and the sad legacy that he passed on to the family. Still . . .

Cubiak switched on the ignition and waited for the engine to thaw. Then he drove off in search of Sara Felton.

RECLUSE

21

Cubiak had barely left Regina Malcaster's house when the storm overtook him. The prediction called for an accumulation of one to three inches, nothing to be overly concerned about. Heading into the interior, he ignored the wind that howled at his back and the snow that fell like a wall in front of his headlights.

The sheriff was certain that the dowager knew the location of the remaining Felton plot. Had she ever searched for her one-time friend? Regina claimed that she didn't know if Sara was still alive, an unlikely statement coming from a woman who prided herself on her encyclopedic knowledge of the peninsula and its people. Perhaps the truth about Sara Felton was too painful to face and she chose to ignore it.

The GPS coordinates that Lisa had given Cubiak led the sheriff past acres of ghostly scrub oak drifted with snow. Twelve miles from Regina's estate, he came to a dead end at an isolated three-way stop. The transmitter's disembodied voice directed him to turn right. He did as told and started down a bumpy road that was flanked by thick pine forest. *Your destination is on the left.* The sheriff stopped and peered into the swirling maelstrom for a sign of habitation: a mailbox, a fire number, a driveway. Nothing but trees and snow. Déjà vu of his search for Bobby

Fells's trailer. He scrutinized the other side of the road as well. But there was nothing there either.

Bathard was right: Just because Sara Felton owned a speck of land in Door County didn't mean that she lived on the peninsula. Or that she was still alive.

Unable to turn around and unwilling to chance backing up in the blinding snow, Cubiak drove for another two miles or so until he reached the next junction. The interchange was piled with snow, but with the jeep's four-wheel drive, he managed a clumsy three-point turn and went back.

He crept down the lane from the opposite direction. After several minutes, he gave up and started to accelerate. He had made a mistake trying to search for Sara Felton's twenty acres at night during a snowstorm. He would have to return in the morning.

Suddenly, a large buck appeared on the side of the road. The deer froze in the headlights. Cubiak slammed on the brakes. As the jeep shuddered to a stop, the stag leapt across the road. For an instant, the sheriff thought the animal had jumped past him. Then he heard a thud, like the click of the deer's hoof against the bumper. He turned off the engine and stepped out into the heavy silence of the falling snow. The road was empty. There was no damage to the vehicle, and the stag was gone, presumably unhurt and swallowed by the storm.

Cubiak exhaled and glanced around. Deer normally sought shelter during snowstorms, but something had spooked this one. The buck had emerged between the trees on the same side of the road as the Felton land. Through the streaking snow, the sheriff spotted two thin ruts running perpendicular across the road. They looked like the tracks from a child's train set and were near the spot where the stag had appeared. He took a closer look. The tell-tale imprints had been made by a pair of cross-country skis. Whoever made them was in the woods.

The sheriff grabbed a flashlight from the glove box and clambered over the ridge of frozen snow along the road. He took two steps and stumbled to his knees. Pressing into the woods, he found the tracks, lost them, found them again. Clumps of snow dropped on his head and glasses. He pulled up his hood and wiped his lenses. Falling snow blurred his vision. He slipped and fell. Pushing up, he wondered how anyone could maneuver through the woods on skis. Then he smelled woodsmoke.

He was deep in the forest when the trees gave way to a small clearing. This time, instead of a red trailer, like the one registered to Bobby Fells, a log house stood in the middle of the opening.

Smoke whirled from the chimney and soft light filtered through the small frost-coated windows that flanked the solid plank door. A dog barked. Then the house went black and the barking ceased. With a jolt, Cubiak realized that the snowfall had eased, allowing a sliver of moonlight to slip between the clouds and illuminate the clearing.

The sheriff skirted fifty feet of perimeter in one direction and then back in the other. Certain that he was being watched, he took his time. There wasn't much to see. A hump of snow that might have covered a chair or a wheelbarrow. A snow-topped row of low bushes. A birdfeeder hanging from the porch. Low square towers that could be beehives or sculptures. Behind the cottage, a roofed woodpile and a neatly shoveled path that led to a doghouse. Another to a small shed and a third to a building that looked like a latrine.

The sheriff returned to where he had emerged from the woods and cleaned his glasses again. Then he walked toward the house. With each step the crunching snow heralded his approach, but the dog didn't react.

He mounted the porch and stomped his boots. He had his hand out to knock when the door creaked opened several inches.

A shadowy figure peered through the crack. The face was hidden behind a wide swath of scarf, the gender disguised by a heavy, dark barn coat. One gloved hand curled around the edge of the door and the other gripped the collar of a mangy German shepherd. The dog snarled and bared its sharp teeth. The hand that clutched the collar tugged the beast silent.

"Sara Felton?" Cubiak asked.

"Who are you?"

His question was answered with a question asked in a smoker's voice, gravelly but feminine.

He identified himself.

"Whad'ya want?" The scarf slipped and a leathery, wrinkled face jutted into the opening.

"I need to find Sara Felton."

"That's what you need, not what you want."

"Ma'am, I'm not here to play games. I'm here to ask you if you know where I can find your grandson."

The woman in the doorway looked out from under a tangle of gray hair and set her hooded eyes on him. "I don't have any grandkids," she said.

"That's not what the records show."

She snickered. "Oh yeah. And do the records show that I disowned my only son and therefore have no connection with his offspring?"

Cubiak let that pass. "Last week a fishing hut that belonged to your grandson exploded and burned near Sturgeon Bay."

She didn't blink. She knew.

"We found a body inside."

Again, no reaction. She knew it wasn't Bobby.

"It wasn't Bobby. But you understand that we have to ask him some questions about the victim. The problem is we can't find him. We can't find Tracey either." Cubiak shifted from one foot to the other. "Ma'am, do you mind if I come in?" he said.

"What do you want with her?"

She was testing him. Give the wrong answer and the door would slam shut.

"She hasn't been to her apartment for a few days. I'm worried for her safety."

"Are you now?" the old woman said. She scrutinized him again. "Why should I believe anything you say?"

"Because your grandkids' well-being may be in your hands. I've had several deputies trying to find Bobby before he freezes to death sleeping in his truck, if that's what's he's doing. As for Tracey, if she thinks someone meant to kill her brother, maybe she has reason to fear for her own life. Under stress, people don't always make wise decisions."

The old woman inched back, dragging the dog with her.

When the sheriff was in, she shoved the door closed. Then she stepped around him to the far end of the cramped entryway and watched as he unzipped his parka.

He held the front of the jacket open. "I'm not armed," he said.

She nodded. "You can put your coat there." A second nod indicated a hook on the wall.

"If you don't mind, I'll keep it on."

"Froze your moon off out there, didn't you? How'd you find me anyway?"

Cubiak glanced at the skis leaning in the corner next to a pair of snowshoes. "I knew the general vicinity of your homestead and followed your tracks in from the road."

"Ah," she said, and released her hold on the dog.

Cubiak waited for the beast to lunge at him, but the canine didn't move. Then the recluse opened the second door and snapped her fingers. At the signal, the dog trotted into the house. A moment later, there was a thump as it dropped to the floor.

"You may as well follow me again," the woman said.

She led him into a rustic room with a plank floor and rough-hewn walls. A candle chandelier made of deer antlers hung from the center beam of the pitched ceiling but the wicks were unlit.

"What do you want?" she said again.

"I'm trying to find Bobby. "

"Well, he ain't here. There's nobody here." She spun in a slow circle, and with a theatric sweep of her hand indicated the obvious absence of anyone else in the room.

"You think he killed that other guy?" she said when she faced him again.

"No. But he's gone missing and that's a concern."

"Hmph. What about Tracey?"

"I already told you. She's missing too."

"Maybe they went on vacation." She was playing him, but Cubiak went along with it.

"Maybe," he said as he slowly worked his hands out of his gloves. "Any idea where they'd go?"

A log popped in the woodstove. Sara Felton glanced toward the noise and then turned back toward him. "I wouldn't know, Sheriff. How could I, seeing as how I don't have anything to do with them?"

"It must get hard living out here on your own."

She grunted.

"Hard to turn your back on your family."

She pulled her jacket tight and glared.

"Tell me something," he said. "Your last name is Felton, but your grandkids go by Fells. Why's that?"

"Not that it's any business of yours, but I was a Fells too for more miserable years than I care to count. After my sorry excuse for a husband died, I went back to being a Felton." She tugged at her lapels again. "Anything else?"

Cubiak looked past her at the sagging sofa. "Would it be an imposition if I sat down just for a minute?" he said. "My hip has been giving me trouble and being out in the cold doesn't help any."

The old woman didn't reply, and he imagined her weighing his request against her own need to get rid of him. "If you must," she said at last.

She waited for him to settle on the lumpy couch and then retreated to the rocker, where she sat half hidden in shadow. There was no offer of tea or coffee, or of a shot of whiskey to take the chill off. He wouldn't have refused any of it. Even indoors he was cold. The stove was the sole heat source in the room, and just as the thin sliver of light that came through the glass door and the small circles that glowed around the two kerosene lamps weren't enough to illuminate the room, it wasn't enough to warm it.

Sara Felton lived a little more than ten miles from Regina Malcaster, but she may as well have been in an alternate universe. They were different women, and while personality dictated some of the choices in their lifestyles, it was clear that money played a substantial part as well. Sara may have been ornery by nature and cut from a distinct cloth, but her life was made from sackcloth while the queen's was fashioned from silk. According to the article that Bathard had discovered, the Feltons' wealth had disappeared more than seven decades ago. How long did resentment

last, how much could be preserved and handed down from one genera-
tion to the next?

"You were going to tell me why you disowned your son," Cubiak said.

"Was I?" She reached into the basket next to the rocker and pulled
out a crocheted throw. "You're new here, aren't you, Sheriff?" she said as
she draped the blanket across her lap.

He couldn't help but smile. "That's a relative term. I've lived in Door
County for nearly twenty years."

"That's new. New enough not to know about things that went on
in the old days, before the peninsula was transformed into a tourist
playground."

"You don't like tourists?" he said.

"They don't matter to me, one way or the other."

"What is it, then, that came between the two of you?"

"Our issue was a family matter, nothing of interest to anyone but us.
My son and I had a difference of opinion about how it should be handled. I kept doing what was right and he went his own way."

"Even turning your grandkids against you?" Cubiak said.

"Can't really blame them, can I? They can't help it that their father
got all religious and decided we'd all be better off embracing the gospel
of forgiveness. Love thy neighbor."

"Not your kind of creed, I take it," the sheriff said.

"Love thy neighbor goes both ways. I was never aware of an out-
pouring of love toward us. But you know the story, don't you? I assume
you've talked to Regina Malcaster, which means you've been fed the accepted explanation of what transpired."

"She told me that there were two versions."

"I'll bet she did. But I'm not naive enough to think that you didn't
believe her misrepresentation of the facts."

"I like to hear people's stories in their own words."

Sara Felton turned the handle on the stove door and yanked it open,
unleashing a flash of light and smoke into the room. In quick practiced
fashion, she lifted a log off the pile near her feet and tossed it through
the aperture. She stared into the flames a moment and then banged the
door shut.

"My father died a drunk, that's true. And the way folks here tell the story, it was his love of liquor that led to his downfall. The truth is, he was a cold sober man up until the time when he was betrayed by colleagues he trusted. It's true that he needed to sell parcels to get us through the rough time and that he offered them to Malcaster and Hanson. It was the plan they had agreed on initially when they first purchased the land.

"Each man offered to stand by the others. But when my father was down and needed them to step up, they strung him along until the situation was desperate. Then they said they were terribly sorry, but their assets weren't liquid, forcing my father to look elsewhere."

The old recluse grasped her hands and leaned forward. "What you may not realize, Sheriff, is that if they'd kept their word and bought the property from my father, then they'd have had to keep the other half of the agreement and sell it back to him when he was in a position to reacquire the land. But this way, they didn't have to do that. It was a case of greed triumphing over honor and friendship."

She sat back again. "Regina Malcaster and I attended high school together. After graduation she went to Sarah Lawrence College and then married Zack. His parents paid for their wedding and bought a house for the two of them with money that belonged to us. Do you know what I did? I dropped out of school halfway through junior year and went to work in a cheese factory outside of Algoma to help feed my family.

"And now Bobby and Tracey—my own flesh and blood—have the privilege of working for all those rich bitches. Oh, I could have kowtowed as well, but I refused. I wouldn't work for them. How could I? Not so my son's wife. That was the way life went for her and that's the way it's going to go from here on, for their children and their children's children. I never asked for a handout, Sheriff. All my father wanted was to get back what had been stolen, and that's all I ever wanted." She smirked. "Well, look around, and you can see how successful I've been."

"But have you given up trying?"

Her eyes flashed. "I'm an old woman now. The only thing I succeeded at was learning how to live so I didn't need anything from anyone. I'm self-sufficient, and there is satisfaction in knowing that."

"What about your grandchildren?"

"What they do with their lives—how they choose to exist on this wobbly planet—is their decision, not mine."

"You're not going to tell me where they are, are you?"

Sara Felton shook her head and reached into the folds of her clothing. Cubiak tensed. Was she armed? For a moment, he wished he hadn't left his weapon in the jeep. But instead of a handgun, she pulled out a long chain and held it toward the dim light. A gold pocket watch dangled from the end.

"This is the only thing I have left to remember my father by," she said as she swung the watch back and forth. "Time's up, Sheriff. Adios, amigo. I'd say shalom, but I don't intend to ever see you again."

THE STAKEOUT

22

When the sheriff stood to leave, Sara Felton remained seated. Her message was clear: this hadn't been a social visit; he came of his own volition, and he could see himself out. The dog stirred but quieted when she lifted her hand from the arm of the rocking chair. Though the old woman was half hidden in shadow, Cubiak felt her disdain follow him through the inside door and into the hall. He zipped his parka and then stepped out on the porch. As he pulled up his hood, he heard the clunk of the security bar dropping into place behind him.

During the half hour or so that he had spent with the old woman, the storm had blown out over the lake. The air was like ice. Cubiak scanned the yard. Light from the crescent moon and early evening stars rippled across the shadowy surface. Even with the fresh layer of snow, he made out the deep ruts of his footprints. Inhaling the frigid air, the sheriff tightened his collar. Then, with the flashlight still in his pocket, he stepped off the porch and followed his own trail across the yard to the woods.

He stopped at the edge of the forest and looked back. The log house was a black block silhouetted against the trees. The dark windows were meant to tell him that the old woman had extinguished the lamps and gone to bed. But the steady swirl of smoke from the chimney was a sure sign that she hadn't banked the fire for the night. Cubiak imagined her inside, moving about with catlike precision. She wouldn't need light. After years of inhabiting the sparse living quarters, she would be able to get around guided by instinct and memory. The entire time they had been together, he had the sense that she was taking his measure, anticipating his next steps and preparing to outmaneuver him. For all he knew, she was standing behind one of the frosted panes, watching him even as he studied the house. Or maybe she had slipped out the back and was circling the clearing, waiting to follow him through the woods.

Cubiak hadn't been surprised by anything Sara Felton said. As he expected, her account of the land dispute contradicted Regina Malcaster's version of history. And though she had denied having any contact with Bobby Fells, her pretended nonchalance about her grandson's fate confirmed the sheriff's suspicion that she was sheltering him. There was no place in the one-room cottage for him to hide, and the rear shed was too close to the house. Wherever he was, she would have made sure that he was safe and that she could reach him quickly if she had to.

The only revelation from the encounter with Peter Felton's heir was the extreme condition under which the woman chose to live, but this too was revealing. She was tough and wily and knew how to survive the elements. Maybe Bobby did as well.

From what Cubiak had seen, she didn't have a car or a snowmobile, just her skis and snowshoes. He was sure she would go to Bobby, and he had to act fast if he hoped to get back in time to have her lead him to the missing young man.

Following his own footprints, the sheriff plunged into the woods. As he moved between the trees, the steady huff of his labored breathing and the bite of the snow under foot broke the heavy silence. Distracted and worried that the noise would give him away, he rushed forward. Nearby, a branch snapped. He stopped and told himself that the noise was made by a limb breaking under the weight of heavy snow and not by Sara Felton. She wouldn't make a sound. Standing still, he looked around and realized that he was in fresh powder, nearly a yard from the trail. He had to get back to the path. The old recluse could have booby-trapped the forest to scare off interlopers like him. He may have made it safely through the woods and to the cabin on a fluke, but getting out was another thing. Backtracking was his only guarantee of reaching the road.

Cubiak latched onto an overhanging branch and tugged. When he was sure it would hold, he inhaled deeply, pulled on it again, and lunged forward. In one swift motion he planted one foot as close as he could to his original footprints and then brought the other down alongside it. He wobbled for a moment but quickly regained his balance and shifted onto the trail.

The rest of the way through the woods was a clumsy march between the trees.

When Cubiak reached the jeep, he crawled inside the cold cab and started the motor. After a couple of minutes, he gunned the engine. The snowpack would carry sound quickly and far, and he had to give Sara Felton the impression that he was done with her, at least for the time being. He drove off with a roar, pressing his stiff hands flat against the steering wheel to guide the vehicle. At the three-way junction, he radioed Rowe and gave him a quick rundown.

"Get up here as fast as you can and come prepared for a stakeout," Cubiak said as he flexed his fingers.

The sheriff was convinced that Bobby Fells was hiding on his grandmother's land and that she would go to warn him about his visit. He had to circle around and get back before she started off. With the heater set on high, he navigated a maze of county roads to the junction at the far end of the lane that bordered her property. From there, he drove back toward the house. He was about a quarter mile from the log cabin when he turned the engine off and coasted to a stop.

For the second time, he radioed Rowe.

"Where are you?"

"Just past Egg Harbor."

"Good. I'm in position and heading into the woods. Follow my tracks," he said.

The sheriff filled his lungs with warm air. Then he snatched his binoculars and handgun from the console and wormed the flashlight from his pocket.

The outside air felt colder than the zero on the jeep's temperature gauge. Cubiak pulled his insulated coveralls and extra gear from the cargo bin and suited up quickly. Rubbing his hands on his arms, he thanked Cate for the waterproof mittens she had given him at Christmas.

Orion's Belt hung low above the tree line. The three stars glittered like jewels in the black sky, and with the trio to guide him, the sheriff headed into the winter woods. This was the second time that night that he was venturing into an unfamiliar patch of forest. He had barely made headway when the ground began to slope up. The farther he went, the deeper the snow. Soon, the thick branches of the lofty pines blocked his view. He tented his hands over his mouth and cheeks, breathing warmth into his face. Sweat trickled down his back.

Though he was uncertain of his location, the sheriff trudged on. Another ten or fifteen minutes passed, and the ground leveled off. He was on top of a ridge, in a stand of young white birch. The trees grew straight and tall, positioned like silent sentries in the snow. Orion was directly ahead.

The sheriff leaned against a slender trunk and waited for his breath to slow. Then he started walking again. Going down the slope was easy. Too easy. He hurried and pitched forward onto all fours. As he pushed up, an owl gave a mocking hoot. Cubiak heeded the warning and slowed his pace. Eventually the ground flattened, and the faint outline of the cottage emerged through a break in the trees.

If he got too close, the dog might bark, so he kept his distance and skirted around the cabin, not stopping until he reached a cluster of cedars about thirty yards past the rear shed. Crouched behind the spreading boughs, he took out the binoculars and searched the clearing for fresh tracks leading from the house, but there were none. The cottage remained dark and the smoke from the chimney was reduced to a trickle. Either Sara Felton hadn't left yet, or he had been wrong and the old woman was nestled on her mattress while he sat out in the cold waiting.

"She'll come. She has to," the sheriff said, half aloud.

Sara Felton had boasted that she was self-sufficient, a claim supported by her austere, off-the-grid lifestyle, but the sheriff doubted that she was content with her lot. She had spoken bitterly about her father's downfall and had spent her life harboring resentment against the men she blamed for his financial disaster. When her son preached a gospel of forgiveness, she disowned him. But had Sara reconciled with her twin grandchildren? When Cubiak had told her that Tracey was missing, she had seemed genuinely concerned, but she was defensive and hard edged when he talked about Bobby. Still, her claim not to know where he was struck Cubiak as hollow.

For the twins' part, the bitter recluse was the only family they had left. They were just kids when their mother died and teenagers when Sara broke with their father. They may have grown up not knowing much of the family history or having heard only their father's charitable version. Later, left on their own at an impressionable age, they would have been susceptible to the old woman's influence. Sara Felton lacked both opportunity and means to get even with the descendants of the Malcaster and Hanson families, but the twins had both, with the added bonus that their scam would make the targets look like gullible fools.

Time passed, and the sheriff felt the cold seep into his bones. He lost feeling in his fingertips and rubbed them to keep the numbness from advancing further. He stepped in place to keep his knees and feet nimble. In a night sky unsullied by urban light, the stars spread above him like a blanket, but one that provided beauty, not warmth. Exhausted, he closed his eyes for a minute. He opened them just as a bright-green ribbon of light flashed above the horizon and then disappeared. It happened so quickly he wasn't sure if he had seen the aurora borealis or imagined it. He blew rings in the air with his breath. He checked his watch. Again.

Without warning, the cottage door sprang open, and Sara Felton stepped out. Cubiak watched for the dog, but the old woman was alone. She was cocooned in dark winter clothing and carried a small pack on her back. Her headlamp threw a pathway of light in the snow. Equipped with snowshoes and ski poles, she crossed the clearing and started into the woods. Behind and to her right, the sheriff struggled to keep up.

Moving between the trees was difficult. As they progressed, Sara Felton pulled ahead and he realized that she was following an established trail, perhaps an old logging road. No question she had the advantage. But as long as he kept her in sight, he wasn't worried.

A moment later, she disappeared.

Cubiak swore and quickened his pace. He was plodding uphill, and his lungs burned from the effort. Struggling to breathe, he finally topped the rise. A long field stretched out before him filled with rows of frozen vines hung on wooden trellises that cast spidery shadows on the snow. There was no sign of Sara Felton.

Then a light popped on. Not the bright, pinpoint beam from her headlamp but the warm, soft glow from a large domed tent at the far end of the field. Cubiak crept forward watching the two silhouettes inside, one towering above the other. When he was fifty feet from the tent, he knelt behind a large drift. The occupants were talking. The sheriff recognized Sara Felton's voice. The other was unfamiliar and anxious and sounded male and young. The sheriff lowered his hood and strained to listen to the conversation that ratcheted back and forth. The words were elusive, but the rise and fall of the dialogue sounded urgent and combative.

Cubiak checked the time. Where the hell was Rowe? The sheriff's knees ached. His fingers throbbed. In the distance, a coyote barked. It was either the real thing or a signal from his deputy.

Moments later, Rowe slipped into place beside Cubiak. The sheriff motioned for him to not talk. Rowe nodded. He slipped off his pack and reached for the zipper, but Cubiak stayed his hand and shook his head. Sound traveled over snow-covered ground like it did over water; they couldn't chance it.

As the lawmen waited, the chatter in the tent diminished to murmurs. Minutes passed and the outer flap unzipped.

Sara Felton emerged into the cold and closed the tent flap. She was as bundled as the two men crouched behind the pile of snow, but with perfect ease she hoisted her pack over her shoulders and clipped on her snowshoes. Without a backward glance, she floated across the snow away from the tent and back to her log house.

Inside the tent, the shadow moved in short jerky steps. They assumed it was Bobby Fells. First, he rolled up a sleeping bag. Then he crammed metal cookware into one bag and clothing into another. A moment later, the light went out.

By then a cloud layer had feathered the sky and blocked much of the starlight. Without the glow from the canvas dome, the clearing dimmed to a charcoal haze.

"We're on," the sheriff said, pushing up off the ground.

The man in the tent continued to mutter and shift from one spot to another as the two men advanced. They were standing ten feet away when he unzipped the flap, ducked his head, and stepped out, polluting the air with the stench of sweat and booze.

"Bobby Fells?" the sheriff said.

The man jerked up and froze. "Who the fuck are you?" he said, swiveling his gaze from Cubiak to Rowe.

Fells was tall and looked lean despite his bulky camo coverall. A black wool hat sat low on his forehead, the earflaps pulled in tight around his face. He had a pack on his back and several bundles in his arms. If he was carrying a weapon, it wasn't at the ready.

Cubiak held out his badge. "I'm looking for Bobby Fells, and I'm guessing that's you."

"What if it is?" the man said with a snigger.

"I'm sure that your grandmother Sara Felton has already told you, but in case she hasn't, five days ago, your fishing shack exploded and burned. We found the body of your friend Kyle Murphy inside, and we had to ask ourselves why he was in your shack. How did he die? I needed your help answering those questions, but you'd disappeared, a development that raised more questions. All I need now is for you to explain all this, you know, tell your side of the story."

Fells spat in the snow. "That's it? You came all the way out here in this fucking cold for that?"

There was much more, of course: the puzzle of how Lydia Malcaster ended up dead at the bottom of the stairs; the business about impersonating the dead James Dura; the scope of the internet scam that Bobby initiated; the role his sister, Tracey Fells, played in the venture; the question of who had stolen the Remington bronzes. But Bobby didn't know

173

that the sheriff was on to any of this, and Cubiak wasn't going to play the rest of his hand, not there. Not yet.

"It'll do to start," he said.

Bobby Fells was drunk and unsteady, and the hike back through the woods was slow. When the cottage came into view, Cubiak warned the young man to keep quiet. He responded by tossing his bundles in the snow.

"We should tell her," he said.

"She'll find out soon enough." The sheriff picked up the duffels and pressed them back on Fells. "Keep going."

When they reached the jeep, Cubiak served the warrant calling for the arrest of Bobby Fells on suspicion of manslaughter.

"You fucker." Fells lunged forward but Rowe nabbed him and held him as he yelled at the sheriff. "You got no proof of anything. This is harassment. You lured me here under false pretenses."

Thick clouds blanketed the sky by the time the two-car caravan left for the long drive down the peninsula. Cubiak led the way with a hand-cuffed Bobby Fells in the rear. Rowe followed close behind. Wisps of snow flashed through the headlights as they sped along the empty roads, past the dark farmhouses and the shuttered shops in the sleeping towns. In the back of the jeep, Fells sulked and then fell asleep, his chin on his chest. Cubiak was grateful for the quiet.

Near the Sister Bay marina, the suspect woke with a start.

"Hey, you, Sheriff, what the hell's going on? You gotta let me go. I ain't done nothing wrong," he said.

When the sheriff remained silent, Fells shifted his position until his gaze met Cubiak's in the rearview mirror. He had his grandmother's high cheekbones and hooded eyes.

"Where you taking me? I got a right to a phone call. This is police brutality." Fells kicked the back of the seat. "I'm telling you, I'm inno-cent. I'm the victim in all this, only everyone's too stupid to see that."

"Is that what your grandmother's been telling you all these years?" Cubiak said.

Fells sneered. "You want to know what she said? Ask her yourself."

"Actually, what I want to know right now is where I can find your sister. You haven't once asked about her. I find that odd. Don't you care about Tracey?"

Sweat glistened on Fells's face. "I'm fucking freezing back here," he said.

The sheriff cranked the heater up and turned the fan to high. "As you wish," he said.

For several miles, they rode in silence, and then Fells started up again. "Talk to me. What's going on?" he said.

Cubiak leaned into the steering wheel.

"What's going on? You want to know what's going on? Okay, I'll tell you. I've had half the department searching the peninsula for you for days. And I just spent half the night either tromping through the snow or sitting with my ass in it waiting for you to show your face. I'm tired and I'm cold and I want you to shut up."

RESPITE

23

It was nearly dawn on Friday when Cubiak left the justice center. Driving home, he straddled a thin line between the worlds of light and dark, good and evil. Ahead of him the bright spear of light that heralded the rising sun slashed the horizon. Behind, only a sprinkling of stars in the dark, western sky. He was going toward his family, toward the decency of his wife and the innocence of his still young son, and away from the moral stench of Bobby Fells.

The sheriff had been confined to the overheated jeep with the surly suspect for the long drive down the length of the peninsula. At the justice center, he had spent another hour and a half on paperwork with the thermostat in his office pushed to its upper limit. But he was still cold.

At home, he pulled off his damp wool socks and crawled into bed in his long underwear. Nestled against Cate, he pulled the quilt up over his shoulder, but he needed more. He piled another blanket on his side and curled into himself, hoping the cold would release its grip and let him sleep.

He woke at ten. Though stiff and sweaty, he felt refreshed and was startled by his reflection in the bathroom mirror. The face that stared back looked haggard and tired. That face had raw, splotched cheeks and weary, red-veined eyes.

A hot shower washed away the grit and eased the stiffness. He ran his fingers through his mop of damp graying hair, and the face in the mirror almost smiled.

In the kitchen, Cate waited with a fresh pot of coffee and a skillet of bacon and eggs. She put the food on a warm plate and set it on the counter, along with a short stack of buttered toast.

"I thought you might be hungry," she said.

He nodded and ate.

"I'm getting too old for this," he said when he finished.

Cate massaged his shoulders. "I've heard that before."

He reached up and clamped a hand over hers. "And you'll probably hear it again."

She kissed the top of his head.

"Come here," he said as he pulled her onto his lap. "I'm taking the rest of the morning off."

ALL'S FAIR

24

At a few minutes past one o'clock that afternoon, Cubiak stood out-side the interview room and studied Bobby Fells through the one-way window. The space was small and antiseptic, nothing distracting, noth-ing to look at and ponder. The sheriff liked to leave the suspects alone in the room for five or ten minutes before he arrived to start the question-ing. Most grew anxious; from where he stood in the hall, he would watch the shadows of concern play across their faces, see them tap their fingers on the table and furrow their brows with worry. Not Bobby Fells.

Bobby Fells was the picture of studied nonchalance. With his eyes half closed and his elbows draped over the back of the seat, he relaxed into the chair as if it was a banquette at an old-fashioned nightclub. His long legs jutted out under the table and crossed at the ankles in a perfect imitation of a lounge lizard from a black-and-white film.

Cubiak wondered how long the facade would hold. He waited a few more minutes and then he entered the room.

"Sleep well?" he said as he tossed his leather binder to the table. He made a show of waiting for a response, and when none came, he set down a cup of coffee. It was a cardamom latte, the kind of specialty drink he usually bought for Lisa. That afternoon he had ordered two, one for her and one for himself. Fells had a coffee, as well, but his was black and bitter and it came from the jail vending machine.

"A little more comfortable here than in that tent, isn't it?" Cubiak said as he hooked a foot around the leg of his chair and pulled it closer. Then he sat down. "You may as well sit up and pay attention because we're not leaving until I get what I need."

Fells scratched the back of his head.

"That's fine if that's how you want to play it. I've got nowhere else to go, and you're not going any place either." Cubiak took the lid off his drink. "Humph. They made a leaf in the foam. I always wondered how they did that. Do you have any idea?"

The suspect said nothing.

The sheriff snapped the lid back into place and took a swallow. "Pretty good," he said as he pulled a folder from the binder and flattened a crimped corner on the cover. He waited a minute and then started the recorder and went through the standard procedure, reciting the date and time and identifying those present. Fells had waived the right to an attorney, so it was just the two men in the room.

"Shall we get started?" The sheriff opened the folder and pulled out four photos. He often brought a packet of material to an interrogation. Even if the file didn't contain any useful information, it was often enough to put the suspect on edge. This time, the folder was loaded.

Cubiak arranged the photos on the table facing Fells. "I want you to take a look at these. These are pictures of your shack taken the morning of the fire."

Ignoring the photos, Fells inspected the nails on his right hand.

The sheriff slapped the table. "I said *look*."

Fells twitched and pulled up half an inch in the chair. "I don't need any damn pictures to tell me what happened. I was there," he said, pinning his eyes to the wall behind the sheriff.

"Where?"

"On the bridge with the rest of the curiosity seekers."

"My men were up there. They didn't see you."

"Go figure."

"You know what they found once the fire was out."

The suspect blinked but continued to avoid looking down at the photos. He worked his mouth.

"Did you kill Kyle Murphy?"

"No!"

"But you knew he was in there."

Fells's mouth hardened into a firm line.

"Or did you figure he'd sobered up and walked home, all the way to Algoma at night, in the cold?"

In the glare of the overhead lights, Fells's face was pasty white. He shifted on the chair. "Yeah, I knew he was there."

Cubiak leaned back. "Unless I hear something from you that makes me change my mind, I'll have no choice but to charge you with the death of your friend. The best you'll get is involuntary manslaughter. The worst, first-degree murder, which carries a life sentence in this state." He took off his watch and laid it in front of Fells. "You got three minutes to decide if you're going to come clean or not, and even that's more than you deserve."

Fells closed his eyes and went so still that he appeared to have stopped breathing. Just as Cubiak reached for the watch, the young man dropped his arms on the table and leaned forward, inclining his head in something like a nod.

"All right," the sheriff said. "Let's start then. Tell me what happened, beginning with the night before."

"Nothing happened. Me and him went drinking, that's all."

"Where?"

"The Old Gray Mare." He sniggered. "They sing the song at midnight, 'the Old Gray Mare, she ain't—' "

Cubiak cut him off. "You and Kyle. Was anyone else with you?"

Fells bit his lower lip. "Tracey was there. She came in later."

"Was your sister in the habit of hanging out with the two of you?"

"Sometimes. She and Kyle had a thing going for a while, but that was all over."

"What'd you talk about?"

"Stuff. Whatever. The bar was crowded and noisy, we were just shooting the shit."

"Can you be more specific?"

He shrugged. "I don't remember anything specific."

"Did you see anyone you knew?"

"Not really."

"What's that mean?"

"I recognized a couple of guys I'd seen before, but I didn't know who they were."

"Apparently you were pretty loud. Someone told you to quiet down."

"Yeah, some asshole."

"You didn't recognize him?"

"Naw. I wasn't paying attention. It was some dude who came out from one of the back rooms."

"What time was it when you left?"

Fells raised both hands and scratched his head. "I don't know. After midnight, probably around one or so. Tracey said she needed to get some sleep and I was ready to go home too, but Kyle wanted to keep drinking. He'd been out to the fishing shack before and knew that I kept a couple bottles of the good stuff there. It was his idea."

"You drove there in your truck?"

"Yeah." Fells rested his arms on the table again and played with his fingers. "I cranked the heater up and opened a fifth of vodka and we kept at it. Kyle had this notion about how he was gonna move to Florida to get away from the cold. He was yapping about how he was gonna get a job doing construction and spend his free time on the beach. He told me there's a town there called *Frostproof*. 'No ice in fucking Florida. I'm going fishing in the damn ocean,' he said." Fells's gaze shifted from the wall to the sheriff's shoulder. "How about that, huh? A town called Frostproof."

"What happened then?"

"He passed out and I went home."

"You left him there?"

"He was out cold, Sheriff. What the hell else was I supposed to do? Drag him over the ice to my truck? I shoved him onto the cot and covered him with an old blanket. It wasn't the first time. Next morning, I woke up, picked up a couple cups of coffee, and went back to get him. Time I got there, there were fire trucks and police cars all over the place and the bridge was full of people watching my shack burn. I got a real sick feeling in my stomach standing there, so I left."

"What do you think caused the explosion and fire?" Cubiak said.

Fells shook his head. "I don't know, some kind of crazy accident. Maybe Kyle woke up and did something stupid and then fell back asleep smoking. That would've done it. Me, I'm always real careful—no smoking inside. And I'm real careful with that heater. I check it out every year when I set up the shack and when I put it away. I turned it to low when I left, just like I'd done before. Hell, I must have slept in the shack dozens of times over the last two, three years and nothing ever happened." Fells's gaze drifted down to the images of the charred shack. "Nothing like this," he said.

"What if it wasn't an accident?"

The suspect twitched. "You think someone torched the place on purpose?"

"Don't you?"

Fells tugged at the corners of his mouth and made a noncommittal sound.

"What do you know about Kyle? Did he have any enemies?"

"Kyle? No way. He was one of the good guys."

"Maybe he owed money and couldn't pay up?"

"Naw. Nobody had any reason to kill him. Who the hell even knew he was there? No one."

"You did."

"I already told you, he was my friend. I didn't kill him."

"He didn't double-cross you on some deal the pair of you were in on? You weren't out for revenge? Or maybe he knew you were up to no good and threatened to talk. Could even be that he was angling to get back with your sister and you didn't want that."

Fells scoffed. "You're fishing."

"Am I?"

"You got nothing on me."

"So you think."

Fells sneered but Cubiak sensed a quiver of doubt in the young man's voice. "We can't find Tracey," he said.

"Whad'ya mean you can't find her?"

"I told you last night, but apparently you don't remember. She's not hiding out with your grandmother, like you were. She's not at her apartment. And she's not at your trailer. So, where is she?"

"Tracey knows how to take care of herself."

"Sure she does." Cubiak picked up his coffee and took a sip. "Or maybe you killed her too. Maybe she knew too much."

Fells was on his feet before the sheriff could put the cup down. "I didn't kill anyone. Tracey's my sister! My twin sister!"

"It's called fratricide. It's been done before. Sit down."

The young man bounced on the balls of his feet.

"Sit. Down."

Fells grimaced and dropped into the chair. "I didn't kill anyone," he said again.

"It's your shack, Kyle was in it, and he died. Maybe whoever did this thought you were inside. Maybe someone wanted you dead," the sheriff said.

The suspect swiped at the line of sweat on his upper lip. "Maybe."

"Any idea why or who that might be?"

Fells glared at Cubiak. "You're the sheriff, you figure it out. It's your job, ain't it?" He shoved the pictures across the table. "Why do you think I came in with you? When I saw you and that deputy waiting for me outside the tent, I said to myself, 'Bobby, if these dickheads could find you all the way up there in the woods, then maybe whoever killed Kyle—meaning to kill you instead—could find you too.' And I wasn't about to find out."

"You didn't seem any too pleased last night when you came out of the tent and found me and my deputy waiting," Cubiak said.

Fells grunted. "Yeah, well, I had too much to drink and was playing the role. But it's like this, Sheriff, I don't know what's gonna happen to me here in jail, but at least I know I'm not gonna die."

Cubiak gathered up the photos.

"Are we done yet?" Fells asked.

"For now." The sheriff slipped the pictures back into the folder. "Oh, one more thing," he said as he started to get up. "Where'd you buy the coffee that morning?"

At three, Cubiak reentered the interview room. Fells was already at the table. He had combed his hair and was sitting up almost straight in the chair. When he saw the sheriff, he arranged his face in a placid, almost friendly pose, as if they were meeting to continue a casual conversation. His story about the coffee checked out, as he knew it would. A week ago, when Cubiak was standing at the window of the yacht club waiting to deliver a talk on gun safety and the fishing shack exploded, the suspect was on the other side of town buying coffee at a gas station minimart.

Cubiak walked in carrying the leather binder and two bottles of water. He slid one bottle toward the suspect. Then he sat down, took a swallow from the other, and began recording the second half of the session.

"We found your center of operation," he said.

Fells's happy face disappeared. "Huh? Whad'ya mean, Sheriff?"

"Building B, Apartment 110, at the Oak Tree Arms." Cubiak removed a new set of photos from the file and set them down facing the suspect. These were the pictures Rowe had taken at Fells's studio.

"That's some pretty expensive equipment you've got for someone who makes a living shoveling snow and cutting grass."

Fells snorted. "I'm a gamer. The stuff is par for the course, and besides, it pays for itself."

"Really? You make money playing video games?"

"Yeah, sure, when I'm lucky."

"How lucky?" the sheriff asked. He took out the receipt from the Wisconsin Bank of Green Bay and set it next to the pictures.

Fells jolted. "How'd you find that?"

"Search warrant." Cubiak tapped the sheet. "Do gamers really earn that kind of money?"

The suspect slouched into himself. "Depends on what they're playing. E-sports are big business these days. This is chump change compared to what some of the pros earn."

"So I understand, but I'm more interested in learning where all this came from." Cubiak shoved the receipt closer to Fells. "Was it prize money? Or maybe you're a paid member of one of the competitive e-sport teams?"

Fells reached for his water bottle. "I dabble, that's all. But like I said, now and then I get lucky."

"What else do you dabble in?" the sheriff asked.

"Nothing. Why?"

"You haven't tried your hand at internet scams? The kinds that bilk innocent people out of money."

The suspect's hand faltered. Then he unscrewed the top of the bottle and took a hit. "People do that, I know. Hell, there are people out there pulling all sorts of scams. Survival of the fittest or maybe the smartest."

"Or the most dishonest."

Fells shrugged. "Life's a game, Sheriff, and we're all players, every one of us."

"Most people play by the rules," Cubiak said. He looked at Sara Felton's grandson. "Tell me, what do you think the rules are when it comes to romancing women?"

The young man blinked. He knotted his hands into a fist and then flipped them around and thrust them out over the table. "All's fair . . . you know how the saying goes."

"All's fair, unless it's illegal." Cubiak leaned back. "You said before, I should figure it out, and maybe I have. The money in your safe-deposit box isn't from gaming. You used the internet to fool gullible women into giving you money under false pretenses. It may have been a game to you, but in the eyes of the law, it's a crime. You didn't earn this money or win this money. You got it through deceit, or in this instance cyber fraud."

Fells laughed.

"You think this is funny."

"So, a couple of women gave me some money. What's wrong with that?"

"Under false pretenses. You conned them out of the funds."

"Come on, Sheriff. I didn't tell them anything they couldn't have checked out if they wanted to." Fells dropped forward, elbows on the table. "People can be really stupid. Women, especially. I learned that in high school."

"What do you mean?"

"I had this friend, who'd pick a different chick every month—it was always one of the ugly ones—and send her messages, none of that mean shit like these jerks say now, only nice things. He'd tell her how cute she was and how he wanted to date her, all anonymous of course. Then he says to me: you know what happens. And I'll be damned but the stupid chick would show up at school the next day with her hair fixed or wearing lipstick or a tight top, and then she'd sit in class or study hall and look around, kind of surreptitiously"—Fells bent down farther and shifted his gaze from one side to the other—"like she was looking for her beau. You know, trying to figure out which of us guys was her secret admirer. Even the brainy ones fell for it. My buddy messaged one of the smart girls and told her that he liked her in red. This girl, straight A's, National Honor Society, headed to college, wore a red sweater to school every day for a week."

"Then what happened?"

"He sent a message saying it was a joke: that she had a horseface and would never have a boyfriend. 'Laugh's on you, babe,' he wrote."

"You don't see the cruelty in that?"

"Hell, we were bored out of our minds. School sucked. That's what was cruel. Anyways, my friend dared me to try it, so I decided I would up the ante and beat him at his own game. I strung this girl along for weeks, telling her that my parents were real strict and that I wasn't allowed to have a girlfriend, but if I could it would be her. Finally, I said I couldn't stand it anymore. I said I needed to be alone with her for once and asked her to meet me after school the next day, behind the bleachers. She had to know what I meant, and she came. Stood out there in the pouring rain for an hour waiting for me."

"And you never showed."

Fells sniggered. " 'Course I didn't show. That was the whole idea."

"How do you know she kept the rendezvous?"

"Because I watched her from inside the gym. There was a place where you could see out the window, right to where she was."

"Did you ever ask any of these girls for money?"

"Naw. I should have, shouldn't I? It was more like an apprenticeship, a learning experience in how easy it was to get people to believe whatever you told them and to do what you asked. Once I graduated, I got into gaming and forgot all about that shit."

"So what brought you back to it?"

Fells shrugged. "I saw this story on the news about a woman who fell for some dude she'd met online and then sent him tens of thousands of dollars just because he said he needed it. Whoa, did he play her, I thought. That got the wheels spinning." He tapped his head and grinned. "I was broke and this seemed an easy way to fix the problem. What did I have to lose? Nothing."

"You figured if these other guys could do it, so could you."

"Something like that. I wasn't going international or anything, like some of these other dudes. I didn't need to. And I wasn't going to get real greedy, either, not like some of those guys you hear about who leave the targets destitute. Now that's a crime. I wasn't going to ask for any more than I figured they could afford to give. You know, like a charitable donation. And in the meantime, I'd add a little spark to their lives."

Cubiak reached into the folder for the list he had found at Fells's apartment. He laid the sheet down facing the young man.

"Tell me how you came to target these particular women."

The suspect barely glanced at the paper. "They met my criteria, that's all."

"Your criteria?"

"Yeah: old, rich, lonely—divorced, widowed, or spinster, it didn't matter."

"And how did things work out for you?"

Fells tapped Gladys Ingersoll's name. "No-go. She was one tough cookie. I knew not to come on too strong but she ignored every overture. Texts. Facebook friend requests. I even sent an email saying how much I admired the speech she gave at some stupid fundraiser."

"What about her?" Cubiak rested a finger on Helen Yaeger's name, the second on the list.

Fells grinned. "Now she was a real nice lady. I enjoyed talking to her online, pretending like I was the kind of sophisticated man she'd pay attention to, not the guy who shoveled her snow. It was actually kinda fun to switch from being one person to being the other. When I was out there clearing her driveway, she'd wave from the kitchen window and sometimes call me to the door and give me a bag of homemade cookies. 'A little bonus,' she called it. Shit, like a bunch of cookies were going to pay my bills, but I'd just smile and say thank you, ma'am, knowing the joke was on her."

"And the phony stock trade?"

"Yeah, that was pretty good, if I say so myself. It was something I read about and figured I'd try. I did my homework, Sheriff. I knew the old broad was educated—they all were—so I had to be credible. I went to the library and found ads for real companies in the *Wall Street Journal* and *Business Week*, picked up enough jargon to be convincing. The most important thing, though, was to gain her trust and that was easy enough, just like with the girls back in high school. Once you had that, you could say just about anything, and they'd believe it."

"Is that how you worked things with Lydia Malcaster?"

"Getting her trust, yeah, step number one, that's always the key. But with Lydia, I needed a different approach. She and the Yaeger woman were friends, and if Helen had said anything about her internet dating adventure, I was sunk. Actually I was hoping that she would be too embarrassed to tell anyone what had happened, but I couldn't count on that. I had to play it safe."

"How'd you come up with the idea of pretending to be James Dura?"

"He was in the school yearbooks. The library has shelves full of them. Lydia's late husband was a UW football star. I found a team picture and started googling the guys one by one until I had a list of those who were divorced or dead. I eliminated anyone who lived in the area and just kept going until I found Dura. He was ideal—dead and distant. And with Zack being a successful businessman, there was plenty of information out there on him, too. You just gotta know where to look."

"But you knew things about Zack that you couldn't learn from a yearbook or a business profile."

"Women talk a lot, Sheriff, especially when they're lonely. They blab about all kinds of stuff without even realizing it."

"That may be, but you had an inside track, too, didn't you? Your sister worked for Lydia. She could chat her up when she was there cleaning, get her talking about the old days. Could be the two of you were in on this together. Is that it?"

"Tracey had nothing to do with anything."

"How about your grandmother, then? She could fill you in on crucial details. She knew the family from way back."

"You're barking up the wrong tree with her, too."

"Am I?"

Cubiak laid down the note with the heart-shaped dot over the letter *i*. "Your sister's trademark. Go on, pick it up. It's a copy. I've got the original tucked away."

Fells pulled his hands into his lap and left the paper sitting on the table between them.

"As for your grandmother, she gave me her version of what happened to the family fortune. From her perspective, there's plenty of reason to want revenge against anyone connected to the Malcasters and Hansons."

"Yeah, well, she's got her issues, that's for sure."

"From the looks of things, she made them yours as well."

Fells scowled.

"What I'd like to know is how you got hold of the bronzes."

"The what?"

"The Remington statues that you stole from Lydia Malcaster's home."

Fells's hands flew into the air. "Whoa, stop right there, Sheriff. You got the wrong man on that one. I knew about the statues, sure. I even seen them a couple of times. But I never got my hands on any of them. I never wanted to."

"Why not? They're valuable enough."

"That may be, and I won't say that I didn't consider the possibility. But those statues are out of my league. I know how to get around the internet real good, and I can slide in and out of the dark web when I need to, but those bronze figurines? That's art, and I don't know shit about art. I'd be played for a fool if I tried to sell one of those." Fells leaned back, his hands behind his head. "Like I said, Sheriff, it's all a game, like poker. You gotta know when to hold 'em and when to fold 'em and when to get up and step away from the table."

"Is that right?" Cubiak said as he slipped the list into the file.

Fells nodded and then started to get up.

"Sit down."

The young man hesitated and then he slid back into the chair.

"Where were you a week ago Tuesday evening, between the hours of eight and midnight?" the sheriff asked.

"Hanging out with Tracey. Tuesday's our movie night."

"Where were you hanging out?"

"My place. We ordered pizza and watched a movie."

"What movie?"

"I don't remember. She picked it out. Some kind of girlie crap."

"Where'd you get the pizza?"

"The new place at the mall. Call 'em if you don't believe me."

"Oh, I will. But all they'll be able to tell me is that someone ordered a pizza using your credit card to be delivered to your address. It doesn't mean that you made the call or that you were there when the food arrived. Maybe Tracey did all that, and when she realized she was being set up as your alibi for the night Lydia Malcaster was pushed down the stairs, she got nervous. And then you got nervous and—"

Fells rested his forearms on the table and stared at the sheriff.

"You think you're pretty cool, don't you, Mr. Lawman," he said, interrupting him. The suspect's voice was steely, and he was breathing hard. "Trying to rile me up, trying to get me to say something stupid. Well, it ain't gonna happen. I didn't push Mrs. Malcaster down the stairs. And I'm not saying another word to you or anyone else until I get a lawyer."

Cubiak was smiling when he got back to his office. Fells didn't realize it but he'd given the sheriff exactly what he wanted.

While the suspect was being returned to his cell, Cubiak was on the phone with the Algoma police chief. The two men didn't know each other well but they had met.

"I'm looking for a suspect in a fraud investigation who's gone missing. She drives a gray compact, and I have reason to believe she's in your area." Cubiak told the chief that Tracey Fells, who was also a possible suspect in a murder case, had previously dated Kyle Murphy, an Algoma resident, now deceased.

"We heard about what happened to him. Talk about bad luck. You think he was involved in whatever you've got going on up there?"

"No. Like you said, it was just bad luck."

"But this woman, Tracey? You think she's holed up at his place?" the police chief asked.

"It's possible."

"I'll see what I can do," the police chief said.

Two hours later, the second Fells twin huddled in the back seat of Cubiak's jeep on her way to the Door County justice center.

THE POWER OF TWO

25

At nine o'clock the next morning, Cubiak walked up to the interview room where he had interrogated Bobby Fells the day before. This time Tracey Fells sat at the table, and this time the sheriff went in directly. He had met Tracey. He knew she was quick, nervous, and surly.

The leather binder was tucked under his arm. He carried a cup of coffee in each hand.

"Where's Bobby?" Tracey said as he approached the table.

Cubiak took the seat across from her. "He's here."

"Is he okay?"

The sheriff pushed the taller coffee cup toward her. "It's a vanilla latte. I get one for my assistant every morning and thought maybe you'd like one as well."

"Is my brother okay?"

"He's fine. Why do you ask?"

She reached for the latte. "No reason."

Cubiak pulled the lid off his cup and tossed it in the wastebasket. He was back to his usual: coffee, black.

"You haven't asked why he's here. For that matter, you haven't asked why you're here, but that's because you already know, isn't it?"

Tracey raised a deadpan face to the sheriff and glared at him with the same stone-cold gray eyes that Bobby had turned on him yesterday. Cubiak waited for her to challenge him. When she remained silent, he initiated the session.

"I'm going to start with the basics, Tracey. Over the past couple of months, you and your brother Bobby Fells operated an internet romance scam that targeted three local women and defrauded two of them out of seventy-five thousand dollars. Once the story comes out, other victims may come forward. Bobby has already confirmed many of the details—"

Tracey ran her tongue over her bottom lip and sank back in her chair. "Bobby ain't said nothing to you."

Cubiak took a sip of coffee. "As I said, Bobby has already confirmed many of the details, and as I understand things, it went something like this. Through your job as a house cleaner, you picked up details about the targets' lives, which you shared with him. Bobby connected with the women online and used the information that you fed him—much of it private and highly personal—to ingratiate himself with them and win their confidence and trust. Eventually this led to him finagling money from them through false pretenses. Bobby called it a game, but in fact what the two of you were doing constitutes a federal crime. The extent of your involvement will be up to a jury to decide."

"Why am I sitting here if you already know all this?"

"I want to ensure that you realize what you're up against in regard to the internet scam."

"Is that it?"

Cubiak hesitated. Was she that oblivious or was she putting on an act?

"You're also here to answer questions about the circumstances leading to the deaths of two people. We've already talked once about Lydia Malcaster's fatal fall. That was on the morning you discovered the body at the base of the stairs in her house. At the time, it was assumed that her death was an accident, but since then other factors have come to light."

"Meaning what?"

"Meaning it may not have been an accident."

Tracey's eyes narrowed.

"Then, two days after Mrs. Malcaster died, your brother's fishing shack exploded and burned, and the man inside died. The victim was Kyle Murphy, Bobby's friend and your former boyfriend. As with Lydia, his death was first thought to be an accident. But it wasn't. It was murder. That's two people killed. One a woman for whom you worked and the other a man whom you once dated."

"Kyle and me only went out a couple of times. And I don't know anything about either one dying."

"Why did you run away?"

Tracey twisted the ring on her little finger. "I don't have to say anything to you."

"That's true, but I'm trying to help you, and right now things aren't looking good for you. If you're lucky, you'll get off with supervised probation on the scam business, but if accessory to murder or manslaughter is added to the charges, well, you're smart enough to figure out what happens then."

She gripped the arms of the chair and stared at him. There were no shadows for her to hide in, but she could have been her grandmother sitting in the rocker. The resemblance between the women was uncanny. Sara Felton had kept her own counsel. Cubiak waited, unsure what Tracey would do.

After a moment, she let out a long breath. "Bobby called me the morning that the shack burned and told me what happened. I could tell he was worried and that scared me. He said he didn't know what was going on and that it might be best if we both laid low for a few days."

"Did you know he went to your grandmother's place?"

"He didn't say but I figured as much."

"Why didn't you join him?"

She grimaced. "I prefer indoor plumbing."

"Tell me about Kyle. Who might have had it in for him?"

"No one. He was a nice guy."

"What about your brother?"

She shrugged. "Bobby had his own ideas about things. We were close when we were young, but now he kept to himself mostly. When he wasn't working, he'd sit in front of his computers playing video games and stuff."

"Stuff? Seriously, Tracey."

She stiffened. "It was a game."

"Like high stakes poker? I don't buy that. In a game, the players know the rules. This was predatory behavior, theft, coercion. Shall I go on?"

Tracey shook her head.

"Say it for the recorder, please."

She bit the word off. "No."

"Who besides you and Bobby knew about your little enterprise?"

"No one."

"Not even your grandmother?"

Tracey started to shake her head again, then she stopped. "I never said anything to her."

"Did Bobby? Did your brother and grandmother cook this up together?"

"If they did, I don't know anything about it."

"What do you know about Sara Felton?"

"She's all right, I guess, but kind of crazy in her own way."

"You know that she doesn't care for the people you work for."

Tracey snickered. "That's putting it mildly. She hates them all. Look, Sheriff, I've heard the story about my great-grandfather and the land, but I'm not sure how much of it to believe."

"Does Bobby believe it?"

"You'd have to ask him what he thinks of it."

"I take that as a yes," the sheriff said. Before Tracey could protest, he went on. "That night before the explosion when the three of you were at the Old Gray Mare, did you see anyone you knew?"

"A couple of guys at the bar looked familiar but I don't know them by name. There was a big game that night and the place was crowded. Nobody paid any attention to us."

"Didn't someone ask your brother to quiet down?"

Tracey yawned. "Yeah, sure, that's right. Some old guy came out from one of the back rooms and said Bobby was too loud. They were having a meeting and couldn't hear themselves talk. Later on, somebody came out and slammed one of the doors."

"There were people from different organizations in the private rooms that night. Did you recognize any of them?"

"No, not really. I was sitting with my back to them. I didn't really see anyone." She blinked several times. "One man sounded kind of familiar, but I couldn't see who it was."

"He sounded like someone you know?"

She shrugged. "Maybe. I don't know. I listen to music and podcasts when I'm working, so I hear lots of different voices. It could have been from there. What difference does it make?"

"Probably none, but then again it could be important."

Cubiak let Tracey think about that while he drained his coffee and then opened the folder. Today's file was thinner than yesterday's, and it held a third set of photographs. He took one out and slid it across the table to Tracey.

"Do you recognize this?"

"Yeah, sure, it's one of Lydia's statues. The *bronzes*, she called them." The young woman lifted her chin and affected a phony accent.

"It's called *The Outlaw*. The real thing would be worth a million or more, but this one's a rip-off."

"It's fake?" She seemed genuinely surprised.

"That's not the terminology used but basically, yeah, it's a fake. Zack got the original from his uncle years ago, but somebody stole it and put this copy in its place."

"Hah! Oh man, that's really cool."

"Is it?"

"Sure, why not share the wealth? It's not like Lydia didn't have a house full of expensive stuff."

"You have a key to the house?"

"I did until you took it. I already told you that. I have keys to all the places I clean."

196

"How often were you alone in Lydia's house?"

The vein in Tracey's left temple pulsed. "Lots of times. Whenever I was there and she wasn't, I was alone in the house. I didn't keep track. Look, Sheriff, I dusted the damn statues, I didn't steal them."

"You didn't tell your brother about them? If he knew the dimensions and did some research, he would have been able to find duplicates that you could have switched for the real ones."

"I didn't tell him anything. I didn't have to. My grandmother did. That was part of the whole sad story of what happened years back. According to Sara, Zack's grandfather bought the statues after he and the Hanson guy cheated my great-grandfather out of the land. Sara always said that the statues belonged to us by rights."

"Your mother used to work for Lydia, didn't she?"

Tracey nodded.

"She knew that the bronzes had been passed down to Zack, and she might have said something to your father or your grandmother," Cubiak said.

"She might have told my father, but she didn't really talk to Sara. Anyway, lots of people knew about the statues."

"But not many of them had the kind of access to the house that you did."

"I didn't take the statues or push Lydia down the stairs. And Bobby didn't either."

"You knew that she planned to sell them, didn't you?"

"Yeah."

"When did you first hear this?"

"A couple of months ago, I guess. Regina Malcaster came for coffee, and I heard Lydia talking to her about it. Not long after that, she told John Overly that she needed to find someone who knew how to evaluate art. She might have meant the statues or some of the other stuff in the house. Later on, Lydia argued with both of them—Regina and John—but I figured it was about her romance with James Dura." Tracey smirked. "Neither one was pleased about that."

"Where were you that evening when Lydia died?"

"I was at Bobby's. We played a couple of video games and then ordered a pizza and watched a movie."

"From where?"

"The place across the street. It's not our favorite but we wanted it delivered and figured ordering from there meant it might at least be hot when it came."

"What movie did you watch?"

"I don't remember."

"What time did you leave?"

"I don't know, after midnight sometime."

"Was Bobby there when you left?"

"Of course, he was there. He was asleep on the mattress."

If that was true, Tracey was Bobby's alibi for the night Lydia died, and Bobby was hers. Cubiak doubted that would help either of them.

He switched off the recording device.

Tracey brightened. "That's it, we're done? Can I go home now? I need to water my plants."

ALCHEMY

26

By the following Monday, seven days after Vincent Yaync dropped the double bombshell about the fake Remington bronzes in Zack's collection and the nearly priceless bronze in Regina's Malcaster's house, Cubiak still hadn't heard back from him. Although the Madison art expert had held out little hope that he could unearth a paper trail for a transaction involving the missing statues, he said he would try. Cubiak knew that even if Yaync came up with anything, the information wouldn't necessarily lead to the thief. But it would be something, and the sheriff was anxious for any news.

"Most of the time searching for clues is like throwing seeds on a pile of rocks and hoping something grows." Cubiak was talking to his assistant, ruing the state of the investigation, when his computer dinged, announcing an email. It was from Yaync. *Call me*, the message read.

"*Call me*, as in good news? or *Call me* as in nada?" he said as he punched the phone number into his cell.

The appraiser answered with the same bombast he had greeted the sheriff the day they met.

"My hunch was right. *The Rattlesnake* was in that show in Houston. It took a lot of dancing around and I had to promise not to reveal the name of the new owner—unless, of course, it's positively and legally necessary—but I wrangled a copy of the purchase receipt. I'm sending it to you now. You there?"

"I'm here," Cubiak said as he stared at the monitor. "What about the seller? Did you get a name?"

"Robert J. Trop."

"Address?"

"None given. But there's a signature and a date," Yaync said. "It's the best I could do."

"We'll make it work." The sheriff thanked the appraiser and hung up. Then he looked at Lisa. "I'm forwarding the info to you. You know what to do."

While Lisa searched the internet for references to a Robert J. Trop, the sheriff headed out for his monthly lunch with Evelyn Bathard. It was Cubiak's turn to choose a restaurant, but that morning he had left a message suggesting they meet at the doctor's condo instead. He had something important to ask him. "I'll bring pizza and salad," he said.

The sheriff drove north under a cold bright sun that revealed Door County at its winter best, a land both pristine and strong that wore its snowy coat proudly. He should have been relaxed behind the wheel but instead he was tense and distracted. He was convinced that Lydia's death was connected to the explosion and fire that killed Kyle Murphy and the business with the fake bronzes. But how? No matter how he arranged the pieces he couldn't find a link.

Bathard met Cubiak at the door and nearly pulled him into the unit. "Please, tell me why the subterfuge? Are you ill? Is there anything wrong with Cate? Joey?"

"We're fine. Sorry, I didn't mean to worry you. It's just that I have to talk to you about the meeting at the Old Gray Mare and I'd rather do so in private."

"You want to know what a bunch of birdwatchers talked about at their monthly meeting?" Bathard looked amused.

"Not that. Other things. There was a lot of noise in the bar."

"Indeed." Bathard unfolded his napkin and laid it over his lap.

"Did you overhear anything that was said?"

"I was in the back of the room. All I heard was a blur of voices and some shouting, probably because of the game."

"A man got up to close the door. Who was that?"

"John, I think. Yes, I remember now. He was sitting a couple of feet from the door, but closer than anyone else."

"Can you tell me exactly what transpired?"

Bathard set his utensils on his plate and closed his eyes. "John walked over to the door and started to close it. Then he stopped. It was as if something outside the room had captured his attention. He stood there for several seconds, and then he slammed the door and turned around. His face was pale and rigid, like he was in shock, but it could have been the light."

The old doctor looked across the table. "It was all very strange. Up to that point, he was a commanding presence in the room, but once he closed the door, he was like a different person. He stumbled back to his chair and then sat just staring. I don't think he said another word the rest of the meeting. I tried to talk to him on the way home, but he was uncommunicative."

"Overly drove you to the meeting?"

"Yes, there and back. Going down was fine but coming home . . ." Bathard winced. "It was the worst ride of my life. I should have been driving. John was like a madman behind the wheel. He kept muttering to himself and was speeding the entire way. More than once, I had to ask him to slow down, not that it did much good. I tell you, Dave, I was greatly relieved to be out of the car."

Bathard folded his napkin and laid it on the table. "The funny thing is that after he dropped me off, he went back that way again."

"You're sure about that?"

"Positive. I have a clear view to the road from my living room window. He went down the driveway and then instead of turning north toward home, he turned south toward Sturgeon Bay. I wondered if he might have left something at the restaurant. But why go back for it that night? Why not wait until morning?" The old doctor paused. "What is going on? What does this mean?"

"I don't know—not yet," Cubiak said.

The sheriff was almost to the jeep when Lisa emailed her report on Robert Trop. Cubiak read the message and sat very still for a few minutes. Then he slapped his glove against the steering wheel and swore under his breath. Why hadn't he seen it sooner?

At John Overly's house, a chirping chorus drew Cubiak to the back field. Dozens of birds flitted across the landscape and swarmed the feeding stations. On the far side of the loop, Overly pushed a wheelbarrow down the path toward the sheriff.

"Nice day," he said as Cubiak approached. "The birds love it. Good weather brings out all the wildlife, damn squirrels included." He stopped alongside the feeder and shook his head. "This is the third time in a week that I've had to fill this station. But I guess they have to eat too." He slipped his coat off and tossed it over the handles of the wheelbarrow. "This winter's been hard on all the birds, especially the mourning doves. Look at that mess over there." Overly gestured along the path to a scattering of bones and feathers. "The juncos and doves are easy targets when they're feeding. It was probably hawks that got them."

Nervous chatter meant to keep him at bay, Cubiak thought. "How long before you're finished out here?"

The birdman secured the top of the feeder. "That's it for now. Why? What's going on?"

Earlier, when Bathard had asked the same question, Cubiak didn't have an answer. Lisa's email had changed that.

"There are a few things I need to go over with you," he said.

"About what?"

"Tying up loose ends."

"I've already told you everything I know and it's not much."

"This won't take long." He would combine fact with supposition and trust that the alchemy he had mastered over the years would lead to the truth.

The accountant brushed chaff and birdseed off his gloved hands. "Sure. Whatever you say."

The men crossed the yard to a symphony of birdsong. On the porch, they went through the ritual of stomping snow off their boots, and then moved inside, where classical music replaced the avian chorus.

Overly headed straight to the kitchen. "Coffee?"

"Only if it's ready," the sheriff said.

The birdman was already at the counter, scooping grounds into the filter. "It's no bother. Just grab a seat."

Overly took his time filling the carafe and readying the cups and arranging the sugar bowl and milk pitcher on the table.

When he couldn't delay any longer, he poured the coffee and sat down. "Now, what did you want to talk about?" he said.

Figuring that two could play the same game, Cubiak measured out one and a half teaspoons of sugar and slowly added milk to the coffee he normally drank black. After stirring the cup, he took a sip. "Let's start with the bronzes."

"The bronzes?" Overly frowned and rubbed the dark scruff on his jaw. "What the hell do they have to do with anything?" he asked, avoiding eye contact with the sheriff.

"Lydia was holding *The Bronco Buster* when she fell. Of the four statues in Zack's collection, it was the only authentic one. The other three were imitations, replacements that were worth far less than the ones he inherited."

"Regina gave me the rundown. From what I gather, no one is sure what the hell happened to them."

"Not true," Cubiak said.

Overly blanched. "Regina told me—"

"The appraiser said it wouldn't be easy to track them, but he did succeed in finding a paper trail for *The Rattlesnake*. The authentic cast, the one taken from Zack's office, was sold to a private investor by a man named Robert J. Trop. As it turns out, there are a dozen men named Robert Trop in the country. My assistant tracked down the likeliest suspects, but there was nothing to connect any of them to the transactions. It looked like a dead end, until I remembered the French cookbook at your house. I've forgotten most of what I learned in high school French, but a smattering of the vocabulary has stayed with me. Trop means *too much*, doesn't it? An excessive amount, something *over* what's needed. It turns out that two of the men named Robert Trop had the middle initial *J*. In one case it stood for *James* but in the other, it meant *John*."

Overly stirred his coffee. "So? What does that have to do with anything?"

"John Robert Overly. Robert John Trop. Not very creative, but then you're a bean counter so maybe you thought it very clever."

"I don't know what you're talking about."

Cubiak looked at his notebook. "No? I made the mistake of assuming that the three bronzes were stolen together recently, but when I asked about it, the appraiser said that wasn't necessarily the case. Each theft could have been carried out at a different point in time."

Overly toyed with the sugar spoon. "Meaning Zack took one each time he needed money."

"That would explain things, wouldn't it? Regina had the same theory, but I don't think that's what happened. I think you stole the bronzes, substituting some really good copies for the authentic ones in the collection."

The accountant reared back. "Me?" He banged the spoon on the table. "You better have proof before you go around spouting these slanderous theories."

"I need to do a little more digging, but I'd venture to guess that within a year or so of each sale of one of the authentic bronzes by Robert J. Trop, you purchased one of the rare bird prints that you keep tucked away in your private collection."

"That's no proof I took the bronzes. If anything, it's a coincidence."

Cubiak sat back. "I don't believe in coincidence. There's also the fact that two months before Lydia died, Regina advised her to have the statues appraised. She suggested that Lydia ask you to find an expert for the job, but you never did come up with anyone, did you? When I asked another local artist to step in, she found a qualified dealer within days."

Overly's features tightened. "I'm an accountant. I was busy preparing end-of-year statements for a dozen clients."

"Then there's this." Cubiak took a slip of paper from an envelope and laid it on the table. "The appraiser tracked down paperwork from the sale. This is a copy of a receipt signed by Robert J. Trop. And this"—he pulled out a second page and put it down alongside the first—"is a document with your signature. I picked it up from Regina Malcaster on my way over here. Even I can see the similarities in the signatures and I have no formal training in graphology. But just to be sure, I will submit copies to a forensic handwriting expert for review."

Overly crossed his arms over his chest and smirked. "That's it? That's your proof?"

"It's enough for now. Regina is handling Lydia's estate, and it will be her decision whether or not to press charges over the theft of the bronzes." Cubiak gathered the papers and put them back in the envelope. "She loved Lydia like a daughter, you know that. She's not going to look kindly on someone who stole from her, but she also has a great deal of respect for you, and knowing the full story might influence her decision."

Overly tried to laugh again, but the sound was more like the faint screech of one of the birds outside. "The full story. Does anyone ever really know the full story, does anyone care?"

"I do," Cubiak said. He got up and emptied the rest of the coffee into the mugs. Then he sat down again. "Are you going to tell me, or not?"

The birdman rubbed his temples. "I didn't steal anything from Lydia. I could never do that to her." He paused. "I took the bronzes from Zack."

"You stole them from him. Why?"

Overly trained his red-rimmed eyes on the sheriff. "You wouldn't understand. You strike me as one of those guys who had it made in life. Intelligent, good looking. Always got the girl."

Cubiak swallowed his retort. "This isn't about me," he said.

"I'm trying to answer your question. Why did I take the statues? Maybe because I was tired of living in Zack's shadow. Never smart enough, never cool enough, never anything enough. Do you know what his grandfather did? He was president of a railroad company. You know what my grandfather did? He made bricks. He didn't own the company that produced the bricks, he made the fucking things. And Zack's father? He was vice president of a paper company in Green Bay. My father—"

"I get it. But not everyone's born with a silver spoon—"

Overly went on as if the sheriff hadn't spoken. "Zachary Malcaster had everything. Not just money and pedigree, but personality and looks too. He was like a modern Adonis, and believe me, he knew it. He could have had any girl, but he married Lydia, the only woman I ever loved."

"You stole the statues to get even?"

"I waited for Lydia to get tired of him. I was sure that sooner or later she'd have enough of his bravado and philandering, but before I knew it, they were planning a party to celebrate their tenth anniversary. Ten years I'd sat on the sidelines and been a spectator to their happy life. Ten years of Zack having everything like always and me stuck with nothing. I had to do something. That's when I decided to take one of the bronzes. Zack didn't know anything about art. He didn't appreciate the statues. He just liked the idea of owning them. I don't think he ever paid any attention to them, and if he did, he wouldn't have been able to distinguish between what he had and a good imitation. There was a certain risk to it, but that was part of the thrill as well. The whole business went so well that I decided to do it again and take one statue for every ten-year anniversary."

"Thirty years and three statues," Cubiak said.

"That's how it played out. Zack kept the girl, and I got the satisfaction of pulling a fast one on him." Overly shook his head. "Pretty pathetic when you think about it."

"But lucrative. You got a substantial amount of money from each one you sold."

The birdman crinkled his eyes. "I admit that there was a bit of satisfaction in that as well. Zack was a man's man. He hunted grizzly and moose and belittled my interest in ornithology, but it was his money that bought the bird seed and the Audubon prints."

Cubiak drained his coffee. "You left *The Bronco Buster* for last. Why?"

The accountant shrugged. "I don't know. There seemed a certain vengeance in making the first last. But after Zack died, there didn't seem to be any reason to continue. Then I'd be stealing from Lydia, and I'd never do that."

"What about her?" Cubiak said.

Overly gave a sad, sweet smile. "I was biding my time, hoping that eventually I would have a chance with her. With Zack gone, I wanted to fall at her feet and tell her how I felt, but she was newly widowed and that seemed inappropriate. I told myself that I had to be a gentleman and forced myself to wait a decent interval. I didn't want to appear too hasty, as if I was dancing on his grave. And then James Dura waltzed into her life." He grimaced. "So much for propriety. Lydia was ready, and I was left out again."

"What do you know about Dura?

The accountant snorted. "There is no James Dura. Well, there was, but he's dead. I tried to tell Lydia, but she refused to believe me. I even showed her a copy of Dura's obituary, but she insisted I was wrong. It wasn't him, not *her* James, it was some other man with the same name."

"When I spoke to Dura's ex-wife, she said someone else had called asking about him. Was that you?" Cubiak asked.

Overly nodded.

"And you told Lydia?"

"I tried to, but she wouldn't listen. She was so innocent that she couldn't bear the thought of such deception. She couldn't fathom that the person she was in contact with wasn't Dura, that someone was pretending to be him. Then, that Tuesday, she called around seven and asked me to come over for a drink. She said she had something important to tell me. 'Just let yourself in,' she said."

"That was the evening she died," Cubiak said.

"Yes."

"You have a key?"

"I've had one for decades. I galloped over, thinking she'd seen the light about Dura. When I got there, she was in the living room with *The Bronco Buster*. Seeing it there on the coffee table, I had this crazy idea that she knew what I'd done. 'Come in, John,' she said when she saw me. I was in the doorway, still with my coat on. She poured a glass of sherry and held it out to me. I didn't know what else to do so I went in and took the glass from her. Then she patted the sofa and told me to sit down. 'Right here, next to me,' she said. She sounded giddy, maybe even a little tipsy. Lydia wasn't a big drinker, so it didn't take much to get her high. I put the sherry on the table, slipped off my coat, and sat down, like she'd told me to. I was so close I could see the yellow specks in her irises. We clinked glasses and drank, and then I asked her what was going on, why she'd taken the bronze from Zack's office. She said she wanted me to have it. Such a simple explanation. I nearly wept with relief."

The birdman hesitated. "I almost told her the truth then. And I would have, too, but she started talking about Dura again, and it really pissed me off. James was coming, she said, and after I'd met him I'd see that all my suspicions were for naught. I nearly spit up my drink. What do you mean? I asked her. She said that he'd sent a message that morning saying that he'd arranged for a long weekend off later this winter. He'd send her his itinerary as soon as he had the information. I told her it was a trick. James Dura wasn't real, and whoever was pretending to be him would make an excuse and cancel. We went back and forth about it. All those years Lydia and I had known knew each other, and that was the first time we'd argued about anything."

The sheriff took the plastic bag with the ring from his pocket and put it on the table.

"Did you give this to Lydia that evening?" he asked.

Overly braced his hands against the table edge and stared at the gold band. "In a way, I guess you could say I did." The wall clock ticked through several seconds. Then he stumbled to his feet and crossed to the rear window and stared out at his bird sanctuary.

"I went over there confident that she'd wised up about Dura. I went there intending to ask her to marry me. We were still arguing when I went down on one knee. Maybe it was the sherry that got to me or maybe I went a little crazy, but after all this time I was determined to tell her how I felt. She knew what was coming, she had to, because before I could say anything she put her hand on her heart and smiled. Not in the way you would smile if you were going to say *yes* to a proposal, but in the way you would if you were humoring a child who'd told a silly joke." The birdman turned from the darkness and looked at the sheriff again. "She was mocking me, just like Zack did."

"Is that why you pushed her down the stairs? You were angry because she humiliated you?"

"No!" Overly staggered back to the table. "I didn't push her. We were in the living room. She was still sitting on the sofa. I seized her by the arms and pulled her to her feet. 'Don't you understand,' I said. 'Dura isn't real. I'm real!'" He held up his hands and shook them, to pantomime his actions. "I told her I was in love with her, that I'd always loved her. I know it sounds ridiculous, but I had to say it to her face. I had to know that she heard me."

"What happened then?"

"Lydia shook her head and said, 'I know, John, I've always known, but I'm sorry. I can't.'" Overly choked and looked past the sheriff. "I laid the ring on the palm of her hand and pressed her fingers over it. 'Keep it,' I said. 'It's yours.' Then I turned around and walked away."

"You left her in the living room?"

He nodded. "Only she followed me to the foyer. 'John, please, try to understand,' she said. She kept pleading with me to turn around, but I refused to look at her. I couldn't. All I wanted to do was leave. I grabbed my coat and opened the door. I was halfway out when I broke down and glanced back and saw Lydia at the top of the stairs. That's when she fell. Oh my God, the sound of her scream and the soft thump over and over as she tumbled. Then nothing but silence. I don't even know how I got down there. All I remember is kneeling over her and calling her name, begging her to say something."

"You didn't phone for help?"

"Help?" Overly closed his eyes and cupped a hand over his mouth. Then he took a deep breath. "I was a volunteer EMT for ten years, Sheriff. I was the help. Lydia was dead."

The birdman rubbed his collarbone. "I stayed with her. I don't know for how long. An hour, maybe more. I couldn't think straight. Finally I got up and went upstairs."

"You washed and dried your glass and put it away?"

"Yeah, I guess. I must have."

"Which made it look like Lydia had been drinking alone."

"Yes."

"Why?"

"So I wouldn't be blamed? I don't know why, not really. It was like I was living a nightmare and was waiting to wake up and find out that everything was okay."

"And then?"

"Then I left."

"The same way you came in?"

"Yes, through the front door. I pulled it shut behind me like I always did."

"She fell on the statue," Cubiak said.

"I know. She must have been carrying it when she came into the foyer." Tears welled in Overly's eyes. "My compensation prize."

"What about the ring?"

"I didn't think of it until the next morning. I got up late and went back to look for it. I was downstairs when I thought I heard a noise out front, probably Bobby coming to clear the snow. I couldn't leave that way, so I went out the downstairs door and circled around to the road where I'd left my car."

Overly shook his head as if trying to get rid of a taunting memory. "What a fucking fool I've been."

From where he sat, the sheriff could see past him to the yard. The birds had flown off and the sun had disappeared behind a bank of gray clouds. Snow drifted from the sky. Against the backdrop of the tumbling flakes, the birdman's reflection shimmered like a misty veil in the panes of glass.

"But it's worse than that, isn't it?" Cubiak said. "A lot worse."

THE WRONG MAN

27

Cubiak waited for Overly to react, but the accountant remained mute. The uneasy silence in the kitchen was broken only by the persistent tick-tock of the wall clock. Oblivious to the drama playing out in the room, the second hand stuttered from one black dot to the next, measuring the passage of time. Ten seconds and then twenty elapsed, but Overly said nothing, did nothing.

Another minute passed before he moved. The hearty ruddiness that marked his cheeks when they came in from the yard had slowly drained, leaving his complexion pasty white. Splaying his hands on the table as he sat down, he glanced in the general direction of the sheriff. "What do you mean?" he said.

"Two weeks ago, you attended the birders meeting at the Old Gray Mare, didn't you?"

Overly brushed an invisible crumb from the table. "Probably. I'd have to check my calendar. I try to get to as many meetings as I can."

"The flyer was on your bulletin board." Cubiak pointed toward the hall. "I saw the notice the first time I was here."

Overly shrugged. "Okay, sure. I was there. I'm the president. What does that have to do with anything?"

"The place was crowded that evening, wasn't it?"

"I wouldn't know, Sheriff. We were in one of the private meeting rooms."

"The one closest to the bar?"

The accountant braided his fingers into a fist. "If you say so."

"According to the bartender, the three people—one woman and two men—sitting at the end were making quite a racket. The woman was Tracey Fells and the guy talking the loudest was her brother, Bobby Fells. You know Bobby, don't you?"

"I've heard of him."

"Oh, I think it goes further than that. Bobby worked for Lydia. He raked her leaves last fall and cleared the snow for her in the winter. As her bookkeeper, you wrote checks to him almost every month. In fact, a number of your clients who live in that area employed Bobby for the same kind of work, so it's reasonable to say you'd have heard him mentioned and might even have seen him working at one homestead or another."

Overly wet his lips and shifted in the chair.

"There's no question that you'd also seen Tracey. She cleaned and ran errands for Lydia and others as well."

"So what?" the birdman said.

"Some people get really quiet when they drink, but not Bobby. Liquor makes him loud and obnoxious, and he'd had plenty to drink that evening, which made him particularly odious. The bartender was busy, but he picked up bits of the conversation. Bobby was bragging about getting rich off a couple of old women. They thought they were so smart, but he was showing them. It was 'like taking candy from a baby,' he said."

Overly squirmed. "You seem to know an awful lot about what Bobby Fells said that night. How do I know you're not making this up?"

"I'm just telling you what the bartender told me. If he could hear what Bobby was saying, there's a chance that people in the private room could as well, especially someone who got up to close the door."

The sheriff continued. "The way I understand it, Bobby had to talk loud, so the other two could hear him over the noise from the televisions and the crowd watching the game. What I'd like to know is how much of this you heard."

"I was presiding over the meeting. All I heard was a lot of noise. I wasn't paying attention to a couple of drunks."

"What about when you went over to shut the door?"

It didn't seem possible that Overly could grow paler, but he did.

"Standing in the doorway, you heard enough to realize that Bobby was talking about Lydia. It must have seemed surreal. The man masquerading as James Dura was this good-for-nothing punk sitting on a bar stool less than three feet from where you stood. Lydia had fallen for him? The woman you loved had been conned by this buffoon? How was this even possible?"

Overly shrank back into the chair.

"By the time you closed the door and sat back down, you'd pretty much worked it all out and realized that Tracey was part of the scam too. That wouldn't have been so hard to figure out, would it? She had the inside track. She's the one who helped develop the James Dura charade.

"You were uncharacteristically quiet during the rest of the meeting. You must have been in shock. After the meeting, you drove one of the other members home, but then you came back. What were you going to do? Confront the two of them?"

The birdman opened his mouth and then snapped it shut.

"When the three of them left, you got up to follow them. As drunk as they were, they moved quickly through the crowd, not like you. By the time you got outside, the friend was nowhere in sight, so you assumed he'd already left. You didn't know he was slumped over on the front seat of Bobby's pickup. You watched Tracey get into her car and saw Bobby climb into the pickup. Which one should you follow? You didn't know what you were going to do, but you knew you had to do something, didn't you?"

Overly slumped over the table.

"In your mind both were guilty, but there'd be time to deal with Tracey later. That night Bobby's the one who stuck in your craw. It was Bobby you had to get to first. He was the focus of everything that had gone wrong with Lydia. You tailed him toward town, and when you saw him turn off on the trail that led to the bay, you knew exactly where he was going. The only things out there were the fishing shacks. You figured he owned one of the huts and was going there to sleep it off. People did that all the time, didn't they? They had heaters and stoves, things to keep the shacks warm, things that could blow up and burn. You watched Bobby open his shack and figured he was in for the night. When you left, you didn't know what you were going to do next but you knew you had to do something. Am I correct so far?"

"Pretty much."

"I can imagine what it was like for you, driving all that way in the middle of the night, alone and heartsick, humiliated and blaming Bobby for everything that had gone wrong. By pretending to be James Dura, he'd stolen Lydia from you. It was déjà vu all over again, wasn't it? First Zack, which was hard enough to take, but now this—beat out by a phantom lover. You'd knelt in front of Lydia and offered her your love, only to have her reject you in favor of the shadow man James Dura—a man that Bobby Fells had fabricated out of memory and thin air. That's enough to enrage anyone. You despised Bobby Fells. He'd scammed Lydia. He'd conned her out of her money and left her with a dream about a fantasy life. Caught up in this phony internet romance, she wouldn't listen to reason. She even ignored the facts of Dura's death when you showed them to her. Instead, she talked about downsizing and selling the bronzes, which didn't portend well for you, did it? It was because of Bobby, the make-believe James Dura, that Lydia wouldn't marry you and why you argued that fateful evening. All these pieces fell into place. Bobby was the source of the problems and angst that agitated Lydia and caused her to fall down the stairs and die."

Overly groaned.

"Have I got it wrong? If I do, tell me. Tell me the truth."

The birdman picked at his sleeve and stared at the floor.

"Did you sleep at all? Or did you pace back and forth, plotting your revenge? You knew that people warmed the fishing huts with wood-stoves and propane heaters. Anything could go wrong if someone was drunk enough, and plenty of people had seen Bobby getting skunked that night. Everyone would assume he'd been careless and done something stupid to cause the explosion and fire."

"I didn't care what anyone thought."

"By morning, you were set with everything you needed. You put on your coveralls, so to anyone who noticed, you were just another one of the fishermen out for the day. You took a chance that Bobby would still be there when you arrived and you were correct. There was someone asleep in the shanty but it wasn't Bobby Fells."

Cubiak opened the folder and laid a photo of the charred body across the table.

"I want you to take a look at this."

Overly pinched his eyes shut.

Cubiak slapped the table. "Look at what you did, John."

The birdman mumbled something, but the words were drowned out by the rush of warm air from the overhead heating vent.

"You'll have to speak up. I didn't hear that," Cubiak said.

Overly squared his shoulders and pulled himself to a full sitting position. Then he opened his eyes and stared at the far wall, careful to hold his gaze clear of the awful image on the table.

"I don't need to look at anything. I know what I wanted to do, and what I did. I went to the shack to destroy Bobby Fells." He thumped both fists on the table. "He didn't deserve to live, not after what he did to Lydia. I wanted to wipe him off the face of the Earth. You understand what I'm saying? I have no regrets about any of that."

"You killed an innocent man."

Overly gripped the edge of the table. "I'm sorry for that, Sheriff, sorrier than you can ever know. Nothing I do will make up for that mistake, but I'm even sorrier that I let the bastard live." Then he crumpled and looked at the picture. "That should be Bobby Fells," he said.

BLUE DAHLIAS

28

Regina Malcaster chose blue and white as the colors for her niece's funeral. Fourteen days after Lydia fell to her death, her body was clad in a dress of dazzling sapphire blue and laid in a special-order coffin made from the bleached wood of the white holly tree. The dowager special-ordered the day as well. Under a bright blue sky and against a backdrop of blinding white snow, a white hearse led the cortege to the church. Behind it were a white flower car overflowing with blue dahlias and the dowager's white Rolls. For the occasion, Regina donned a white wool suit, the color she had asked her friends to wear in celebration of Lydia's life. They rode to the church with her and walked with her behind the casket as the pallbearers escorted it into the sanctuary. Once inside, they sat alongside her in the first pew, each of them with a blue dahlia pinned to her shoulder.

Cubiak was seated across the aisle with Cate and Bathard. They were three rows behind the pallbearers.

"It's like a winter garden." Cate indicated the altar where massive bouquets of the vibrant blue flowers mingled with the red poinsettias and Christmas greenery.

On her left, Bathard seemed lost in thought. He nodded absently.

Cubiak nodded as well, but the truth was, he barely noticed the flowers. He was thinking of his daughter, who had been buried in a white coffin. Alexis was two months shy of her fifth birthday when she died, and for years, he punished himself over the hit-and-run accident that had killed her and Lauren. If he had been home, if he had kept his promise to come home, his wife and daughter would be alive. His failure to honor his word was a burden he would carry forever.

A noise from the back of the church interrupted Cubiak's reverie. He turned as a group of ten or twelve women crowded the trio of young ushers who distributed blue dahlias to the mourners, urging them to hurry. "Ladies, please," one said in a loud whisper. The women were middle aged and older. They were fierce and determined, each of them marked by a sad, knowing look. So many, he realized, glancing up and down pews.

Lydia claimed that she had led a sheltered life and had a limited circle of friends and acquaintances. These women probably had never met her, but something drew them to the service. Watching the influx of mourners, Cubiak understood.

After Lydia died, bits and pieces of her story began to circulate. Within days, five women called his office to relate similar experiences with internet romance scammers. When the host of a local radio program broadcast a segment on the issue and asked victims to call in with their experiences, the station's phone line was swamped with calls from Door County and beyond. The women in the Sister Bay church might not have known Lydia Malcaster, but he suspected that they were part of the same sisterhood and that they had come in a show of solidarity. Whether they had been tempted by phony romance schemers or ensnared like Lydia, they understood her plight because the same trap had been laid for them. Bobby Fells targeted women from the two families that had been involved in the land dispute with his grandfather, but there were other scam operators, an army of the unscrupulous who were eager and able, trained even, to prey on human vulnerability from a place that could not be seen or touched.

Cubiak squeezed Cate's hand. "Did you notice all the women?"

She glanced over her shoulder.

"So many!" Cate looked at him, puzzled. "You don't think . . .?"

"I wouldn't doubt it. Why else would they be here?"

The funeral ended with the Mass and final blessing. There would be no burial until spring when the ground thawed and a grave could be dug. Outside the church, most of the mourners dispersed quickly. Lydia's small circle, as well as people who knew her from her charitable work and whose organizations had benefited from her support, were invited to Regina's for a funeral luncheon.

At the house, Cate circulated among the guests, but Cubiak kept to the periphery of the great room. He was at the window when Regina cornered him.

"There's something I've been wanting to ask you since this started. Do you think this business with Bobby has something to do with the feud about the land?" she said, leaning on her silver-handled cane.

"Unfortunately, yes. That and greed," he said.

Regina shuddered. "Thirty years ago, my husband and I and the Hansons reached out to Sarah Felton. We offered to settle, to make amends as it were. It was never clear what had happened back then between her father and the other two gentlemen, and we felt guilty about how things had evolved. Sarah wasn't interested in anything we had to say. She mocked our offer of financial compensation and scoffed at the suggestion that we try mediation as a way to find some common ground. Rather than accept a compromise, she chose to bear a grudge. Then to prove whatever—maybe that she didn't need anything from us—she retreated to that shack in the woods. She even broke with her son over the issue. I can only imagine the poison she poured into those grandchildren over the years. And look what came of it, where it all ended. The twins under arrest and an innocent man subjected to the most horrendous death."

A woman from the catering staff approached, but before she could speak, Regina waved her off. "Yes, yes, please start serving," she said.

For a minute, the dowager and the sheriff watched as the crowd arranged itself into four lines and advanced toward the buffet tables that had been set up in the center of the great open room. Then Regina went on.

"I don't condone what Bobby did, but I can almost understand it. He didn't know us as people. He certainly didn't know Lydia. From his perspective, she was there for the pickings. For him, she represented easy money, and the scam was nothing more than lucrative entertainment, a spiteful game. He didn't care about the emotional pain it could cause. He had his fun and lined his pockets while getting the revenge he believed he was owed."

"What he did was criminal," Cubiak said.

"Oh, I realize that. But I can't help but think of him standing behind the green curtain and manipulating the levers to try and create his own version of reality, like Professor Marvel in the *Wizard of Oz*. Absurd, isn't it?"

"What he was doing, or what you thought of it?"

"Perhaps both," she said, patting his arm. "But Tracey? I know I disparaged her lack of interest in art but that was my own snobbishness. The truth is I liked her. I thought she had spunk."

Regina turned a sad smile on the sheriff. "I never connected the dots. All the times when she played the curious ingenue and plied me with questions or when I found her passing nearby when I was engaged in a private conversation. I thought she hadn't been brought up properly and always excused her behavior. Some judge of character, aren't I?" she said, pressing her hand to the glass.

"I wouldn't be too hard on myself if I were you. We've all been fooled at one time or other in our lives," Cubiak said.

"You're too kind, Sheriff." Regina pulled her hand off the window and swiped it against her wool trousers. "And then there's John. How am I to think of him? Is he poor John or evil John? The man I would have trusted with my life was running his own scam in full view of everyone. Oh, I'm sure he justified his actions one way or the other, but the truth is he was a thief. Worse than that, a murderer. And all the time fussing with his birds, protecting them from the elements and ensuring they were adequately fed while being so cold hearted about human life. What kind of a man is that?"

She turned to Cubiak. "And what else might he have been up to? He handled the books for Lydia, Gladys, me, and any number of my friends. He could have been embezzling from us for years. I was the first to hire him. I recommended him to the others."

"We'll investigate all possibilities, but I expect that any professional work he did for you was legitimate. As for the bronzes, it's up to you as Lydia's executor whether to press charges or not," Cubiak said.

"I realize that." She looked at the floor. "Life doesn't get any easier, does it?"

"No, but we all get smarter."

"Do we?"

"Hopefully," he said, and offered her his arm. "Let's get something to eat. I have something I want to discuss with you later."

Cubiak waited by the fire with Cate and Bathard as Regina saw the last of the guests to the door.

"Shouldn't we be going as well?" the old coroner said.

"Not yet. I need to talk to Regina, and I want both of you there."

"What is it?" Cate said.

"Something I started to think about when this all began."

The catering crew was clearing the tables when the grand dame advanced toward them. She took slow, deliberate steps and seemed to lean on her cane more than usual.

"Regina looks exhausted. I hope you won't keep her too long," Cate said.

Cubiak stood and offered the dowager his chair, but she shook her head. "Not here. Let's go where it's quiet."

They followed her down a short hallway and into a small sitting room. A tidy stack of logs burned in a ceramic fireplace, and another bank of windows opened to a sprawling mass of snow-topped bushes. Regina sank into a white leather chair and motioned them to the facing sofa and chair.

"Now, Dave, talk to me."

He cleared his throat. "This has been on my mind for several days. I'm sure you noticed the number of women who attended the funeral?"

"I did."

"I suspect that they came because they felt they had something in common with Lydia. If I'm right, your niece, Gladys Ingersoll, and Helen Yaeger weren't the only women on the peninsula who've been victimized by internet romance scams, and they won't be the last either. Bobby Fells ran an amateur local operation, but the real pros are out there in droves. Trying to curtail them is more than I can do as sheriff. Even the FBI can intervene only after the fact. But I believe there's more that can be done to help women protect themselves before they fall prey to these schemes."

"Go on, I'm listening."

"Lydia was an intelligent woman. When Bobby Fells first contacted her and pretended to be James Dura, she may have had her doubts about him, but she had nowhere to turn for guidance or advice, no one to talk to. She was too embarrassed to confide in you or her friends, and with him being so persuasive and credible, she found him hard to resist."

Cubiak leaned forward. "Imagine if there was a hotline she could have called anonymously, and someone had helped her understand how internet con artists operate. Even someone as convincing as the would-be James Dura. The hotline rep could have told her how to search for an obituary. Or how to verify the receipts he sent her for the so-called trip of a lifetime that he'd concocted. A single red flag might have been enough to give her pause and keep her from falling for the scam. The same for Helen Yaeger. Ultimately, she made the right calls, but only after she'd sent Bobby money for a phony stock deal."

"It is an admirable idea but you've already said your department could not take on such a project," Bathard said.

"That's true. We don't have either the money or the expertise and staff."

Regina thumped her cane on the floor. "But I have the money that can hire the staff and pay for the expertise, isn't that what you're getting at?"

The sheriff tried to hide his smile.

"You're a clever one, you know," Regina said with a teasing glance. Then she got serious. "I plan to sponsor a community garden in Lydia's name and perhaps I still shall, but why not do both? With the proceeds from the sale of *The Stampede*, there will be more than enough to fund such a program. It will take time and effort to establish, but it will be a fitting memorial."

The dowager glanced from one to the other. "I'll do it but only on one condition," she said.

"What is that?" Bathard asked.

Regina looked at Cate. "That you, my dear, agree to be the executive director, the woman in charge."

GOING HOME

29

After Lydia Malcaster's funeral and the arraignments of John Overly, Tracey Fells, and Bobby Fells, the days passed in a wintry haze. More quickly than Cubiak would have liked, they reached the last Saturday of the month. It was the day he had circled in red on his desk calendar. He had hoped a blizzard would close the highway, but the weak storm that started late the night before had fizzled in the early predawn hours. By midmorning the roads were clear. Cate was sifting through a stack of research material when her husband and son said good-bye and left.

"So, Mom's got this great new job. Do you think she's going to like it?" Joey said when they were on the highway headed to Chicago for the game.

"She seems to be enjoying it. Your mother's a very accomplished woman, you know. She can do a lot of things."

"Yeah, I know."

"You're a lot like her."

Joey flushed with adolescent embarrassment. "You think so?"

Cubiak glanced at his son. "I know so."

The boy squirmed and reached into his backpack for a chocolate bar.

"We're not going to be late, are we?" he asked as he unwrapped the candy.

"We'll be fine."

"Want some?" He held out a piece of the chocolate.

Cubiak shook his head.

"Did you bring the tickets?"

"Right here in my pocket."

"What about you?" the boy asked.

"What do you mean, what about me?"

"What are you going to do? I heard you and mom talking yesterday."

"Ah, that. Retirement, you mean," Cubiak said as he moved to the inside lane and accelerated past a milk truck. He switched on the wipers and waited for them to clear away the slush that had splattered the windshield. "It's something people start thinking about when they get to be my age."

"But you're the sheriff."

"Someone else can be sheriff."

"Like who?"

"Whoever gets elected. Maybe like Mike Rowe."

"He's too young," Joey said.

Cubiak chortled. "He's no younger than I was when I took the job."

"Huh," Joey said. "But what would you do?"

"I don't know. Maybe your mother would give me a job."

"Yeah, right."

They joked about the possibility for a moment. Then Joey got lost in the futuristic world of the internet and Cubiak drifted into the past. For twenty years, he resisted going back to Chicago. The one time he had returned was for Malcolm's retirement party. He owed his former partner that much. When Cubiak was at his lowest, when he had given up on life and himself, Malcolm had pulled him to his feet and demanded more of him. More than he thought he could give. Malcolm sent him north to Door County. Malcolm had saved him. At the party, when Cubiak hugged his friend, he had assured him that he was fine.

"You're sure about that?"

"Yes," he'd said. It wasn't completely true then, but it was true now. Cubiak patted Joey's knee. He wished Malcolm were still alive to hear it.

"I don't smoke."

Cubiak blinked. What was his son talking about?

"That night I came home from play practice, you asked if I'd been smoking. But I hadn't, and I don't."

"Good," Cubiak said. He glanced at his son. "Let's keep it that way."

They reached the stadium and were in their seats in time for the tip-off. They cheered their team. They ate hot dogs in steamed buns, buttery popcorn, and nachos dripping with melted cheese. They rued the Bucks loss but consoled themselves that it had been a close contest— three points would have tipped the scale in the other direction. They spent the night at a downtown hotel, where Joey swam in the enclosed rooftop pool. Then, after breakfast the next morning, they drove out of the Loop and away from the dark ridge of storm clouds forming along the lakefront.

"Where are we going?" Joey asked.

"To the neighborhood where I grew up," Cubiak said as he steered the jeep south on Halsted.

Near the new Sox park, he turned onto a narrow street lined with bungalows and two-flats. Cars and SUVs were parked bumper-to-bumper, leaving little more than a single lane for traffic heading in either direction. Within four blocks, they passed three churches. At the end of the street, he steered the jeep around a corner piled high with dirty snow and pulled to the curb alongside a row of squat, weather-beaten brick buildings.

Cubiak leaned into the windshield. "See the one near the corner with the green door? Second from the end."

Joey squinted out the window. Like the buildings, the doors were barely distinguishable from each other, the colors faded and peeling and tinged sad. He focused and found the slab covered in an ancient green. "That's where you lived?"

"We had an apartment on the third-floor rear." Cubiak rolled forward another fifty feet until he was even with the gangway. "Back there," he said, pointing down the tight walkway.

The boy's gaze followed the trajectory of his father's arm and then lifted to the roofline. "It looks kind of small."

"It was. People in this neighborhood didn't have much money. Most of my friends lived in apartments like that."

Cubiak showed his son the corner playground where he played baseball as a kid and the vacant lot where the parish school had stood. "It's gone now. Torn down. Lots of things are gone," the sheriff said.

They went past his old high school. "It's coed now, but used to be all boys," he said.

"What about where you worked, when you were a cop?"

"That's gone too. There's a new building there now."

When they were back on Lake Shore Drive, the boy pressed his nose to the window. He knew the sites and called them out as they drove past. "McCormick Place. Soldier Field. The Aquarium. Navy Pier. The Hancock."

At Belmont, Cubiak took the exit and headed west.

On block after block, storefronts blurred past. After a few minutes, Joey lost interest and pulled out his phone.

They drove several miles before Cubiak pulled to the curb. Joey was so absorbed, he didn't realize that the jeep wasn't moving until his father turned off the engine. The boy looked up, curious. They were on a quiet street lined with trees and neatly kept two-story houses. Christmas lights dangled from the eaves and bare branches, and wreaths hung on doors.

"Where are we now?"

Cubiak pointed to the yellow frame bungalow in the middle of the block. "That's the house I lived in before I came to Door County. It used to be white," he said, and opened the car door.

Joey set his phone on the seat and joined his father on the shoveled sidewalk in front of the yellow house. Unlit holiday lights hung from the gutter, and a lopsided snowman stood in the yard, next to a tall blue spruce.

"I planted the tree when Alexis was born," Cubiak said.

"Dad . . ."

"It's okay. I need to show you." He pulled up his hood. "This way," he said, and started walking.

When they reached the end of the second block, Cubiak stopped. "Back then, that was an ice cream shop," he said, motioning toward the small convenience store on the opposite corner. "They were going there." He stepped into the street. "The car came from there." His raised his left arm and held out his bare hand. He stood ankle deep in snow, but in the remembered heat of the day, his skin felt warm.

"Is this where she died?" Joey said.

"Yes."

"And your wife. Your first wife?"

"Both of them."

Joey stepped off the curb and took his father's bare hand between his. At thirteen he was just four inches shorter than Cubiak, tall enough to nearly look him in the eye.

"Do you still think about them?"

"Yes."

"Do you miss them?" the boy said.

"Yes."

"Do you still love them?"

Cubiak slipped his arm around his son's shoulder. "I'll always love them. You don't forget people or stop loving them because they're gone. They become a part of you and that never changes, no matter how old you get and whatever else happens to you in life."

Joey tensed. "And mom? What about her?" He hesitated. "What about me?"

Cubiak tightened his grip. "You were a part of me even before you were born. You have your own unique place here." He touched his heart. "It's your spot forever, no matter what. The same for your mom."

Looking down at the street, he could see the shadow of blood on the pavement beneath the ridges of snow. "After Lauren and Alexis died, I thought my life was over. But no matter how much I wanted to give up, I kept breathing. And no matter how tightly I closed my heart, it wouldn't stay shut. The heart is like that, I guess. It wants to be open, and it wants to love."

Cubiak pressed his fist to his chest. "In here there's always room for one more. First, your mother." He cupped his hand under Joey's chin. "And then, you."

Under the cold winter sun, father and son retraced their steps down the sidewalk. They walked silently and side by side. When they got to the jeep, Joey picked his phone up from the seat and slipped it into his pocket.

"What now?" he asked as he clicked his seat belt on.

Now?" Cubiak said. "Now we go home."

ACKNOWLEDGMENTS

To everything there is a season . . . and after nearly a decade and a marvelous run of seven books, the season of Dave Cubiak has come to a close. I approach the end of the series with a sense of melancholy because I will miss writing about Cubiak and Door County. At the same time, however, I will enjoy the satisfaction of having fulfilled a personal dream and garnering a couple of awards along the way.

Although I set out to write a collection of mysteries, I knew that the overriding story arc—the theme of the series—was Dave Cubiak's journey of personal redemption. When I introduced Cubiak to readers in *Death Stalks Door County,* he was a broken man. Burdened by grief and guilt, he had turned his back on the world and given up on life. Slowly and against steep odds, he regained his sense of purpose. Most surprising was the devotion he inspired. Readers embraced Cubiak and empathized with his struggles; many shared that his story of loss mirrored their own experiences. Rather than be disappointed that the series has ended, I hope that fans of Door County and fans of Cubiak will take heart in imaging him walking the beach with Cate and Joey and talking with his friend Evelyn Bathard over their monthly lunch.

Cubiak's story wraps up with *Death Casts a Shadow.* In writing this book, as with all the others, I depended on a network of people to help me progress from story concept to the completed manuscript. My heartfelt appreciation to my gallery of loyal and steadfast readers: Barbara Bolsen, B. E. Pinkham, Jeanne Mellet, and Esther Spodek. Sadly one name is absent from the list, that of my former boss and longtime friend Norm Rowland. I'll always treasure the fact that we were able to reconnect over the written word and work together again through the first six volumes of the series before illness claimed his life. Two other names are also missing but for joyful reasons. During the time I was writing and revising the book, my daughters Julia Padvoiskis and Carla Walkis were preparing to welcome my first grandsons into the family. Amazingly Julia produced another of her marvelous maps for the book, and for that I am grateful.

Details and facts matter, even in fiction. I am especially thankful to Laura Desmond, curator of the Frederic Remington Art Museum in Ogdensburg, New York, for shepherding me through the complicated world of the Remington bronzes. And to Tyler Mongerson, president of Mongerson Gallery in Chicago, who spent precious time explaining the subtlety involved in assessing the authenticity and value of the statues. For those interested in learning more about Remington's work, I recommend Michael D. Greenbaum's *Icons of the West: Frederic Remington's Sculptures*, a book I found immensely helpful. Thanks also to my friend and former neighbor Kathleen Lamb for her input on the work of John Audubon and to Rob Hults, executive director of the Open Door Bird Sanctuary in Jacksonport, Wisconsin, for educating me about the needs of Door County's winter birds.

In signing off, I extend my deep appreciation to my editor Dennis Lloyd, director of the University of Wisconsin Press, and his exceptional and dedicated staff: Sheila McMahon, senior project editor; Adam Mehring, managing editor; Alison Shay, publicity manager; Jennifer Conn, art director; Casey LaVela, sales and marketing manager; Julia Knecht, exhibits and data manager; and Terry Emmrich; production manager. Hats off to Sara DeHaan, whose covers have always delighted me and elicited high praise from readers. Many thanks as well to copyeditor Diana Cook, who, given her initials, was destined by fate to work on the series.

Finally, my gratitude extends to the literary community, a world composed of writers, publishers, editors, librarians, reviewers, book sellers, and readers. We are all in this together, all joined by our love of books. May our spirit remain strong.